Epic Peters
Pullman Porter

by Octavus Roy Cohen

Octavus Roy Cohen

James Montgomery Flagg

Epic Peters
Pullman Porter

by Octavus Roy Cohen

☙

Introduction by Alan Grubb and H. Roger Grant

Copyright 2012 by Clemson University
ISBN: 978-0-9835339-4-8

Published by Clemson University Press in Clemson, South Carolina

Editorial Assistants: Whitney Rauenhorst, David Rodatz and Dustin Pearson

Cover design by Myers Enlow

To order copies, please visit the Clemson University Press website: www.clemson.edu/press

Contents

ↄ℃

Introduction

I. Octavus Roy Cohen

by Alan Grubb

When Octavus Roy Cohen died in Los Angeles in January 1959, the *New York Times* noted that he had been an immensely popular and successful writer, a kind of "writer's writer," producing works in several genres from the early 1920s to the time of his death. While best known for his humorous stories about blacks in Birmingham, Alabama, the so-called "Darktown Stories" that appeared in *The Saturday Evening Post* in the 1920s and early 1930s, Cohen wrote 56 books, ranging from murder mysteries to detective stories to "race" or dialect stories, several novels set in the South, and, finally, "pulp" murder mysteries (more famous perhaps, and certainly more valuable to collectors today, for their sexy, provocative covers than his clever plots and hard-boiled prose). Along the way, he also wrote scripts for the *Amos and Andy* radio series, two plays, 30 movie scripts for Paramount Pictures, Columbia, Universal, and RKO-Pathe, including screen adaptations of some of his Birmingham stories, the latter noteworthy as some of the earliest films starring and about blacks and directed by blacks. Some of his stories were also adapted for television. In the early 1930s, Cohen reportedly made over $100,000 a year, largely from the stories he sold to popular magazines like *The Saturday Evening Post*, *Colliers*, and *Liberty*. Yet, despite his popularity as a writer, after his death Cohen was largely and quickly forgotten. The reason is not hard to fathom. For, since much (but not all) of his fame stemmed from his "humorous" dialect stories about Southern blacks, with the Civil Rights movement of the 1960s, his literary reputation became insupportable, a kind of embarrassment. Even his alma mater, Clemson University, has neglected him, along with his native state, although Alabama inducted him in 1925 into its Hall of Fame, along with Helen Keller, and he has often been cited, and praised, by groups interested in detective fiction and popular culture.

Octavus Roy Cohen (June 26, 1891–January 6, 1959) was born in Charleston, South Carolina, the son of Octavus Cohen, a lawyer and newspaper editor, and Rebecca Ottolengui. The Cohens were an old and distinguished Jewish family, very much a part of Charleston's literary society. Octavus graduated from Porter Military Academy in Charleston in 1908 and, so it is recorded in most of the standard biographies, from Clemson College in 1911. The latter claim may have been one of his early fictions or simply a mistake, for, in fact, he left college without a degree, which he only received in a special ceremony in 1937, after he had established his literary reputation. Kicked out of college, he worked as a civil engineer for the Tennessee Coal, Iron and Railroad Company in Birmingham (1909-1910), but his real interests were not in engineering, as he had already shown in his brief days as a student, but in writing. He soon turned to journalism, working during the next two years for the Birmingham (AL) *Ledger,* the Charleston (SC) *News and Courier,* the Bayonne (NJ) *Times,* and the Newark (NJ) *Morning Star.* In 1913, he returned to Charleston and read law in his father's office and was admitted to the South Carolina bar and briefly practiced law. On October 6, 1914, he married Inez Lopez of Bessemer, Alabama. She shared his literary interests, and he published a novel and a compilation of "humorous" malapropisms, compiled from black newspapers.

Cohen's real calling was obviously writing, not engineering or the law, and success came quickly. He sold his first story to the *Blue Book* for $25 in 1913, and soon his short story sales, as he later recalled, came with greater frequency than clients, and he was regularly publishing in the *Saturday Evening Post, Colliers, Argosy, Telling Stories, The All Stories Magazine, Black Cat, McCalls,* and *Munsey's.* His earliest efforts focused on mystery writing, with stories appearing in *Mystery Magazine, Illustrated Detective Magazine* and similar short story pulp magazines. Much of his book-length fiction grew out of these short stories, and one of his most interesting books is *Cameos* (1931), a collection of short, short stories. His first mystery novel was *The Other Woman* (1917), which he co-authored with another successful magazine writer, John Ulrich Giesey. Thereupon followed mystery novels each featuring, as was typical of the genre, a distinctive detective—the boyish David Carroll in *The Crimson Alibi* (1919), *Gray Dusk* (1920), *Six Seconds of Darkness* (1921), and *Midnight* (1922); the outrageously obese Jim Hanvey, whose size and self-deprecatory manner, along with his trademark gold toothpick, served as a foil for his detection skill and humanity in *Jim Hanvey, Detective* (1923), *The May Day Mystery* (1929), *The Backstage Mystery* (1932), *The Townsend Murder Mystery* (1933), and *Scrambled Yeggs* (1934); and later, in novels that capture well the period during and after World War II, down-to-earth police detectives Max Gold and Marty Walsh. These stories collectively show how adept Cohen was at incorporating into his plots exotic locales and activities, like nightclubs, gambling, sports and the world of popular entertainment of Broadway, radio, and motion pictures; they also reflect his Southern background, his travels, and the various places he lived.

Cohen's most successful literary creations and the cause of his celebrity and enormous popularity—Will Rogers himself praised his comic characters—were his "Darktown" or Birmingham stories, his series of "race" stories of the comical lives of Florian Slappey (the "Beau Brummel of Bummin'ham"), Lawyer Evans Chew, Sis Callie Flukers, and Epic Peters, the philosophical Pullman porter and Slappey's friend, and the denizens of the social club, "The Sons and Daughters of 'I Will Arise.'" These stories, besides being entertaining and detailing Cohen's perception of Birmingham's black community, were famous for their punning titles ("All's Well that Ends Swell," "The Survival of the Fattest," "Here Comes the Bribe," and "Hoodoo and Who Don't"). In writing these stories Cohen drew upon his Southern childhood and familiarity with Birmingham. Though early on some criticized him for his heavily dialect stories, Cohen drew his characters with affection and without bias, and, as his other novels set in the South suggest, in which poor and ignorant whites and their unscrupulous community leaders figure, he was in fact a man of progressive, moderate views on many issues confronting the South and the nation, at least by the standards of the day. More sympathetic (and perhaps more discriminating) reviewers praised him for his entertaining style, comic invention, meticulous handling of details and craftsmanship as a writer. Cohen was also an avid sportsman, which shows up in many of his stories. While he lived in various parts of the country, Cohen never lost touch with his Southern roots, as he showed by beginning one of his last novels, *Borrasca* (1953), in his native South Carolina during the Nevada silver mining days after the Civil War. He spent his last years in Los Angeles. Book titles such as *Polished Ebony* (1919), *Highly Colored* (1921), *Assorted Chocolates* (1922) and *Black to Nature* (1935), along with the stereotypical illustrations that appear in his books, may still seem off-putting, but his stories and his enormous popularity reveal much about the tastes, values, and cultural standards of America in the first half of the twentieth century.

In one of his later novels, Cohen has his main character, Jerry Franklin, a wounded ex-soldier returned from North Africa and soon to be detecting for a friend's father, remark: "A railroad trip is always exciting to me." Railroads figure prominently in most of Cohen's stories, nowhere more so than in *Epic Peters, Pullman Porter* (1930). It is time, I think, to reconsider, and to read, Octavus Roy Cohen.

II. The Pullman Porter

by H. Roger Grant

Octavus Roy Cohen understood the Pullman Company porter, making *Epic Peters, Pullman Porter* more than an entertaining series of eight short stories. He likely became acquainted with Epic Peters-types as a resident of Birmingham, Alabama, and as a frequent patron of those "hotels on wheels." Cohen effectively used his insights to capture the work-a-day life of the Pullman porter during the 1920s when long-distance rail travel reached its peak of popularity.

Until the twilight of private rail service in the 1960s, train-goers associated Pullman porters with luxury transportation much as they did with such speeding "name-trains" like the *Broadway Limited, City of New Orleans* and *Overland Lim-*

ited and the monumental railway terminals that served as gateways to America's urban centers. Most travelers expected porters, nearly always men of color, to assume the position of servant. As George Mortimer Pullman observed, whose Chicago-based company had gained a near monopoly on sleeping-car service by 1900, "by nature [blacks are] adapted faithfully to perform their duties under circumstances which necessitate unfailing good nature, solicitude, and faithfulness." Cohen supports that common white perception, but he adds much more, showing correctly that these railroaders could be smart, clever, and resourceful.

In the process of revealing the subtleties of Pullman porters, Cohen demonstrates the multitude of duties that these men performed and the constant challenges that they faced. Their chores might range from bringing passengers late-night hot toddies to polishing their shoes to a dazzling luster. In fact, the porter's routine was rigidly prescribed. The Pullman Company Book of Instructions, which was issued to porters after January 1, 1925, listed 217 matters for their attention, including the storage of bed linens, blankets and pillows, preparation of berths and car maintenance. The duties of the porter were mind boggling. It was a job that was a "cross between a concierge, bellhop, valet, housekeeper, mechanic, baby sitter, and security guard," as one study of Pullman travel has observed, "prepared at any moment day or night to be a good listener, answer questions, find lost articles, and handle emergencies." Every run, while different, included the stress of a demanding public, demeaning comments and sleep deprivation. And always there was the need to cultivate patrons for good tips. The public's generosity accounted for much of a Pullman porter's income. No wonder porters were renowned for their attentiveness and smiling faces.

In several instances, Cohen comments on the conductor-porter relationship, indicating how it replicated that of plantation overseers and slaves; white Pullman conductors were in charge and held sole authority. These sleeping car "masters" could make life pleasant or difficult for *their* porters, perhaps instigating better "runs" or possible dismissals. Concerns about matters of authority, compensations and other work-related issues explain the formation in the mid-1920s of the Brotherhood of Sleeping Car Porters, which rapidly became a prominent labor union and the first national labor organization led by blacks.

Cohen correctly points out that Pullman porters were regarded highly within their own segregated communities, even though their incomes were modest when measured in compensation for the time worked and perhaps their educational backgrounds. (Some black porters held college degrees.) These skilled and confident railroaders toiled in a clean, largely non-manual labor job (far superior to that of an agricultural worker), traveled widely and frequently, usually enjoyed steady employment (especially before and after the Great Depression of the 1930s), and developed an easily recognizable sense of confidence. Nattily attired when on duty, porters commonly kept up their appearances in their home communities, revealing their worldly good taste in clothing (and status) at church, fraternal, and other gatherings.

While *Epic Peters, Pullman Porter* covers well the black porter of the 1920s, Cohen conveys an intimate knowledge of passenger service on the busy main line of the Southern Railway between Birmingham, Atlanta, Charlotte, Washington and New York City. When he indicates the times for certain trains, contemporary timetables validate his statements, and his details of train and station operations are also historically correct. This adds more credibility to his writings and enhances their over-all historical significance.

The saga of Epic Peters is an excellent complement to such scholarly works as *Those Pullman Blues: An Oral History of the African American Railroad Attendant* by David Perata; *Miles of Smiles, Years of Struggle: Stories of Black Pullman Porters* by Jack Santino; and *Rising from the Rails: Pullman Porters and the Making of the Black Middle Class* by Larry Tye. Cohen's work is the next-best-thing to having an oral history of a Pullman porter during the hey-day of intercity train travel, a time when the Pullman Company was one of the largest employers of African-Americans. Epic Peters wonderfully encapsulates virtually everything that was once the life of a Pullman porter.

III. A Note on the Text and Acknowledgments

This new edition of *Epic Peters, Pullman Porter* constitutes a re-setting from the original printing, published in 1930 by D. Appleton and Company, New York and London. This book is long out of copyright and print. The following stories from the collections were printed first in *The Saturday Evening Post:* "The Berth of Hope" (12 Jan. 1924), "Ride 'Em and Weep" (23 Feb. 1924), "Traveling Suspenses" (22 March 1924), "The Epic Cure" (26 July 1924), "The Porter Missing Men" (20 Aug. 1927), "The Trained Flee" (17 Sept. 1927), "A Toot for a Toot" (19 May 1928), and "Bearly Possible" (11 Aug. 1928). One of Cohen's Epic Peter's stories, "The Berth of Hope," was included in a 1946 anthology of railroad stories edited by Frank P. Donovan and Robert Selph Henry entitled *Headlights and Markers*. *Epic Peters, Pullman Porter* (besides having one of the least offensive of titles of his collection of his Birmingham stories) has great historical value: of the life and work of a Pullman porter, of railroading in the early 20th century generally, of life in the segregated South, of the communities blacks themselves created within the larger white society, and of popular literature and what passed for humor.

IV. For Further Reading

Bates, Beth Tomkins. *Pullman Porters and the Rise of Protest Politics in Black America, 1925-1945.* Chapel Hill: University of North Carolina Press, 2001.

Brasch, Walter M. *Black English and the Mass Media.* Amherst: University of Massachusetts Press, 1981. Brasch is surprisingly sympathetic to Cohen as a writer and to his black dialect stories.

Breen, Jon L "A Note on Octavus Roy Cohen." <http://www.mysteryfile.com/cohen/Bren.html>. Online posting. 2004. A recent revaluation of Cohen as a writer, based largely on Cohen's mystery novels.

Grost, Michael E. "A Guide to Classic Mystery and Detection." <http://mikegrost.com/classics. htm>. Online posting. 1996-2011.

Harris, William H. *Keeping the Faith: A Philip Randolph, Milton P. Webster, and the Brotherhood of Sleeping Car Porters, 1925-37*. Urbana: University of Illinois Press, 1977.

Kornweibel, Theodore. *Railroads in the African American Experience*. Baltimore: The Johns Hopkins University Press, 2010.

Maurice, Alice. "Cinema and Its Sources: Synchronizing Race and Sound in Early Talkies." *Camera Obscura* 49, Volume 17, Number 1 (2002), 31-71. Maurice has interesting things to say about the early all-black films based on Cohen's Birmingham stories.

Perata, David. *Those Pullman Blues: An Oral History of the African American Railroad Attendant*. New York: Twayne, 1996.

Rzepka, Charles. "Race, Region, Rule: Genre and the Case of Charlie Chan." *PMLA*, Vol. 122, No. 5, October 2007: 1463-1481. Rzepka's article contains interesting references to Cohen as a "race" or Southern dialect writer.

Rubin, Louis. *My Father's People: A Family of Southern Jews*. Baton Rouge: Louisiana State University Press, 2002. The Rubins of Charleston were friends of the Cohen family.

Santino, Jack. *Miles of Smiles, Years of Struggle. Stories of Black Pullman Porters*. Urbana, University of Illinois Press, 1989.

Tye, Larry. *Rising from the Rails: Pullman Porters and the Making of the Black Middle Class*. New York: Henry Holt, 2004.

Windham, Ben. "Southern Lights: Old Bachelor's Intrigue Hides among Clutter." *Tuscaloosa News*, April 26, 2009. <http://tuscaloosanews.com/article/20090426/news/904269990>. A recent discussion of Cohen as a "forgotten author."

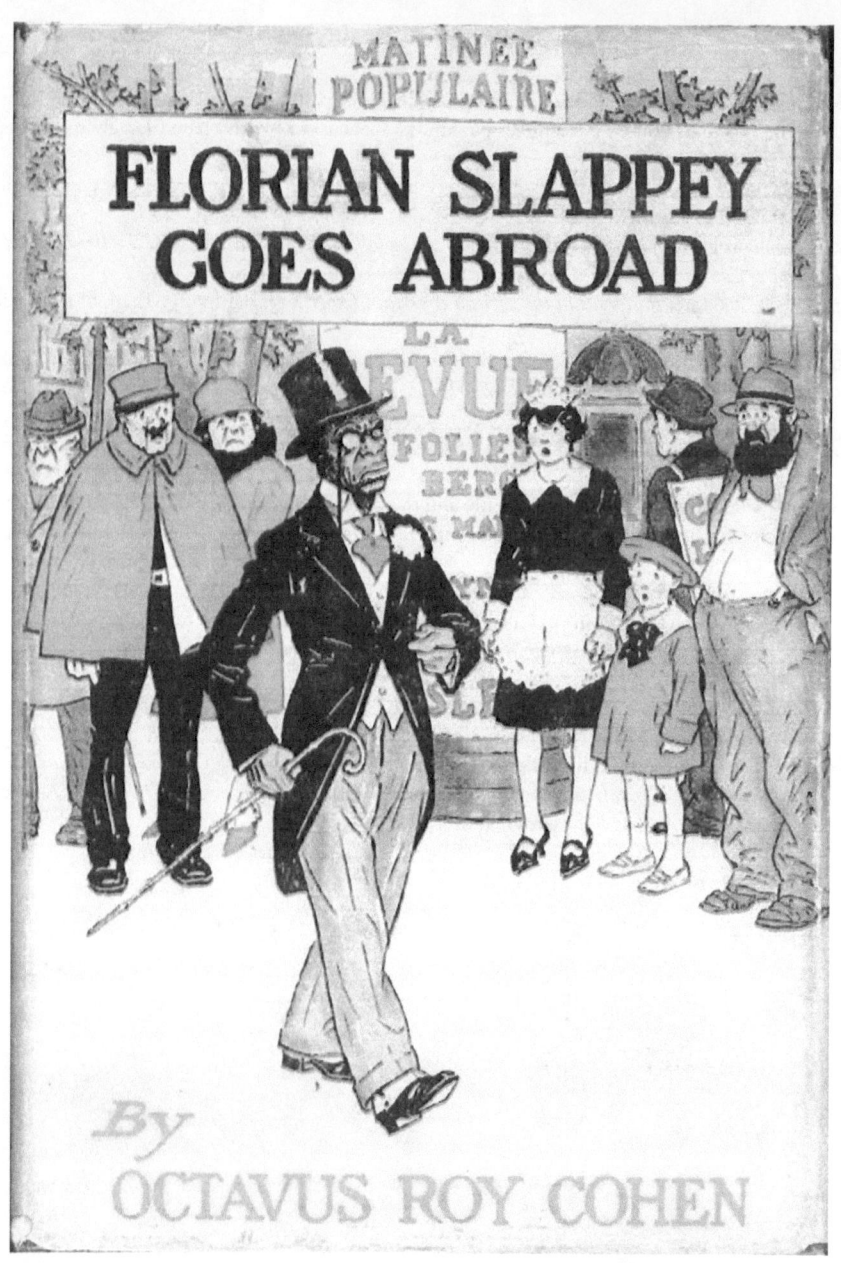

This is the cover of *Florian Slappey Goes Abroad*. Florian Slappey is probably Cohen's most famous black character and appears in one of the *Epic Peters* stories. These stories revolve around the crew-members of the black-owned Midnight Pictures Corporation in Birmingham, Alabama. Slappey, as their interpreter, takes them to Europe and Africa in search of background material for new silent films. The stories are quite funny in the manner of Mark Twain's *Innocents Abroad*.

FEBRUARY 3, 1924

SOUTHERN
RAILWAY
SYSTEM

THE SOUTHERN SERVES THE SOUTH

TIME TABLES OF PASSENGER TRAINS

Dust jacket for the first edition of 1930 published by D. Appleton and Company, New York and London.

The Berth of Hope

THE huge, cavernous shed of the Birmingham Terminal Station was no more dark and gloomy than Mr. Epic Peters. That gentleman deposited an elderly maiden lady in Section 9, plastered a professional smile upon his ebony countenance and shuffled unhappily down the aisle of the Pullman. In the geometric center of his tremendous palm lay something cold and round and hard. Once again on the platform, he opened his fingers and gazed with supreme and pessimistic disdain upon the financial offering of the spinster traveler.

"One dime!" commented Epic bitterly. "One single measly dawg-gone terrible thin dime! An' mebbe one mo' dime when she gits off. The porterin' business suttinly ain't what it used to be"

He flicked a speck of dust from the silver service stripe which decorated the sleeve of his blue jacket and meandered sadly down the platform to where sat the fat little porter in charge of the car for Atlanta passengers.

"How's tips, Joe?"

The pudgy face beamed.

"Pretty fair. One man give me a dollar. How they is with you?"

"Terrible! Folks ain't so loose with their change as they once was. Seems like when they goes to New Yawk they don't make no 'lowance a-tall fo' tips. I has got two dimes, one two-bit piece and one half dollar, an' leavin' time ain't so long off." Epic propped his elongated frame against the side of the Pullman. "Tell you the troof, Joe, Ise thinkin' of applicatin' myself into another distric'—Chicago or mebbe Los Angeles."

Joe sighed enviously. Seemed to him that successful men never were contented. Here was Epic Peters with one of the star through runs, and he was talking about transferring his efficient and engaging personality to other parts of the country. Two passengers appeared and Epic lurched slue-footedly away, leaving Joe staring raptly after him. Joe worshiped Mr. Peters. He knew that Epic was one of the star porters on the Southern system—a man with eight years of seniority behind him.

"Anyways," breathed Joe, "does porters like him get disallisfry, then mebbe some day I gits me a chance to remove myse'f off this pikin' li'l Bumminham-to-Atlanta run."

As Epic approached the two men who now stood gazing uncertainly at the silent Pullmans his eye lighted on the purple check which one of them held and a flash of interest crossed his features. Drawing-room, eh? Two men! The combination usually proved interesting financially. His face beamed as he approached them.

"What space you gemmun got?"

"Drawing-room to New York."

"Right this way, cap'ns; right this way. Gimme them grips."

They followed him down the aisle of the car. He flung open the drawing-room door and deposited their suitcases within.

Then he ostentatiously busied himself with rearranging the soap and towels in the lavatory and dusting the windows. One of the gentlemen appeared to comprehend that he was being hinted at. He thrust a dollar bill into the unreluctant hand of Mr. Peters. That colored gentleman bowed profusely.

"Thanky, cap'n. Does you gemmun want anythin', just press the button an' Ise with you soon as the echo comes. 'Tain't fo' nothin' they calls me Hop Sure."

The men glanced at each other and smiled. One of them was very tall and rather thin, but with a pair of cold gray eyes which contained little of softness. The other was short and stout; but, too, there was something about the set of his jaw and the hunch of his rather broad shoulders which informed Epic that neither he nor his companion was a traveling man.

Hop Sure returned to the platform. Somehow, with the crinkle of the dollar bill still tickling his palm, the train shed seemed less empty and gloomy. His lips expanded and he hummed a few lines of a little song that was always more or less in evidence when he was not unpleased with the world:

> I plays my cards against my chest,
>> I nusses all my chips;
> I never joke an' Ise never broke,
>> 'Cause Ise hell on gettin' tips.

A gentleman and his wife boarded the car and Hop Sure was enriched by another half dollar. The events of the past few moments had caused his spirits to soar considerably. No longer was he contemplating an immediate transfer to another Pullman district. That was Epic's way—he was an extremist, inevitably either thrilled to the zenith of beatitude or wallowing in the nethermost depths of dank despair.

After all, the portering profession had been rather unlucrative until recently, even on this choice run between Birmingham and New York. Travel had been light and parsimonious, and Epic's wages of sixty-six dollars a month were highly insufficient to his needs. Faithful and efficient on the road, he was yet considerable social pumpkins in Birmingham, and he required cash and plenty of it to maintain his position and dignity.

The huge engine which was to haul them on the first lap of their long journey backed under the shed and bumped gently against the waiting train. And just as it did so the two gentlemen of the drawing-room descended to the platform, lighted cigarettes and stood regarding Epic with an interest which was more than merely casual.

Returning their scrutiny, Epic Peters became more forcibly impressed with his original conclusion that they were a trifle different from the usual run of travelers. He felt an uncomfortable desire to shiver. Yet they were decidedly friendly in their manner to him and memory of the tip was still fresh in his mind. Too, he received the impression that they were discussing him. The tall, cold, gray gentleman flashed a fishy glance in his direction and nodded briefly; the smaller and stouter man bobbed his head in agreement; and then, as though prompted by the idlest sort of curiosity, they drifted into the vicinity of the porter and dropped into casual conversation.

"How long before we pull out?"

Epic consulted his watch.

"Eighteen minutes, cap'n. We leaves at 'leven-fifty."

They glanced at each other.

"Eighteen minutes? M'm!—where do we get breakfast?"

"Leavin' Atlanta, suh. We gits there at 6:15 Central Time an' leaves at nine o'clock Eastern."

"Do you make the run straight through to New York?"

"Yassuh. Ise the th'ooest-runnin' porter on the line."

"I see—I see." The taller of the two men closed his eyes slightly and Epic felt that he was being X-rayed. "What is your name?"

"Epic Peters, suh. They calls me Hop Sure."

"Hop Sure? On the job, eh?"

"Yassuh. You suttinly said it that time, cap'n."

Again with the searching scrutiny.

"Wonder if you could do us a little favor, Hop Sure?"

"Doin' favors fo' gemmun is the fondes'thing I is of."

The tall thin man cast a swift glance about the big shed. Then from an overcoat pocket he produced a package This he held tight against him, though to conceal it from the gaze of passers-by. But there was no mistaking the keen and proprietary interest with which it was regarded by the shorter man.

"This is a pretty valuable package," vouchsafed the spokesman. "Very valuable. We're afraid of leaving it laying around the drawing room. I wonder if you could take care of it for us until we get to New York."

Hop Sure eyed the packet. It was about twelve inches long, perhaps half that width and not more than an inch in thickness.

It was a very innocuous-appearing thing, wrapped in brown paper and tied with twine. At least it was not sufficiently bulky to contain liquor. Liquor was Epic's chiefest fear; there was entirely too much investigating going on along the road to suit him.

"I always aim to please…" he started uncertainly when the smaller man produced a wallet. From it he took a crisp new five-dollar bill, which he thrust into the not unwilling hand of the gangling porter.

"That's to pay for your trouble," he suggested softly.

Hop Sure's decision was instantaneous. Five-dollar tips were few and far between.

"Gimme," he commanded.

"Be careful," counseled the taller man. "It is quite valuable."

"Boss man, you don't have to warn Hop Sure none. This heah thing goes in my linen closet an' it don't come out until you-all gemmun gives the word. Takin' care of things like this is the bestest thing I does."

He climbed aboard the Pullman, packet in hand. The five dollars surcharged his soul with elation, although he was not unconscious of the appraising glance which bored into his back as he left them. He selected the key to the linen compartment, opened the door, made a nest for the package on the very top shelf and then carefully placed towels over it. Then, as he locked the door, he found himself face to face with the two owners.

"It's safe there?"

"'Tain't nothin' else."

"Good!" There appeared to be considerable relief on the faces of the two men. Then the taller one introduced himself. "I'm Mr. Carson," he said. "This"—designating his friend—"is Mr. Garrison."

"Yassuh," beamed Epic. "I know."

A startled glance flashed between them. "How do you know?"

Seen the names on yo' bags," explained the colored man. "Always likes to know my passengers pussonal."

They strolled into the drawing-room while Epic returned to the platform to await the inevitable late comers.

The Pullman conductor arrived; the big engine at the head of the train was puffing and snorting impatiently; and, less than five minutes later, the welcome "All abo-o-oard!" reverberated through the shed; the train quivered into action and nosed out into the chill night air. Epic closed the vestibule of his car and strolled inside. All twelve sections were made down and he gazed the length of green-curtained cañon, experiencing anew the thrill which had been his on occasion of his maiden run.

Epic was fond of portering; he had all the instincts of a railroad man; the thrum-thrumming of wheels on steel rails was sweet symphony to him, and even the insistent ringing of the porter's call bell was not at all times unwelcome.

Too, for the first time in his life Epic had opportunity to gratify the wander-lust. He was a traveled gentleman, was Epic, and a personage along Eighteenth Street in Birmingham, where he swelled about in a suit of screaming civilian clothes and spoke with well-studied casualness of "Well, when I was in New Yawk the other day I was walkin' down Fifth Avenue, an' —" They gave him rapt atten-tion when he spoke of New York, and he conversed with equal glibness of other towns along this prize run of his—of Atlanta and Spartanburg and Charlotte and Greensboro and Danville, not to mention Washington and Philadelphia.

He was well liked by the conductors with whom he worked. On more than a score of occasions he had received mention in the roll of honor published in the national publication which deals with the activities of Pullman porters, each of these honorable mentions having been earned by unsolicited letters written to the company by patrons who had cause to be unduly grateful for special services rendered by the somewhat slab-sided, but always genial, Hop Sure Peters.

Epic was prideful in his job, but he was thoroughly a business man. He gave perfect service to those who were frugal in tips; and if to those who tipped him generously the service rendered was superperfect, that was no business of anybody save Epic. Now his eyes were turned affectionately upon the door of Drawing-Room A, where slumbered the elongated and rather saturnine Mr. Carson and the pudgy and somewhat athletic Mr. Garrison. Six dollars was an unusual sum, even for a porter of Epic's experience, and he was determined that they should get value received in service.

As to that brown-paper parcel: Shuh! He was always glad to take care of things fo' the white folks. Wa'n't nothin' gwine happen to no package they tu'ned overto him; nos-suh.

"Fo' six dollars," he announced to himself, "I'd nuss a baby."

Three gentlemen occupied the smoking room until the train backed under the shed at Anniston two hours after leaving Birmingham, but between there and Atlanta the smoker was vacant and Epic curled up on the seat for a well-earned snooze. Outside he could see the silhouette of pine-studded hills against the face of a full moon; the train rocked and swayed as it pitched through the night on a roadbed which had been constructed in the days when railroad engineers believed it was cheaper to go around a hill than to grade through it. But Epic Peters was content; he never grew travel-weary. He hummed as he dozed off:

Ise a terrible care-free cullud boy,
    An' I lives all over the earth;
I takes my fun like a sonovagun,

Ise a houn' on fixin' a berth.
Ise got me a gal, a good-lookin' gal,
   A -waitin' fo' me to git back;
She's boun' to be true, I ordered her to,
   When I hit her that las' awful crack.
She listens at me—

And then Epic Peters dozed off to waken by instinct three hours later, splash cold water into his face and prepare for the arrival in Atlanta.

Outside, the first cold finger of November dawn was puncturing the chill of night. Epic shivered. He worked the stiffness from his joints and glanced at his watch, longingly counting the minutes against the time when he'd be under the shed in the Atlanta station and able to get his morning cup of coffee.

"Coffee! Yum! Tha's one thing which is sho'ly fond of me."

He busied himself making up the berths which had been unoccupied during the night. Then, marked by a faint curl of smoke here and there, and the gaunt, unimaginative outlines of occasional factories, the City of Atlanta appeared, in the background.

The nearly two hours in Atlanta were busy ones for Epic. There was first the all-important item of breakfast, then the tidying of his car and the switching back and forth in the yards, as the train was taken to pieces and made up anew for the journey northward. At a few minutes before eight o'clock someone stopped beside him on the station platform and he looked into the friendly yet forbidding eyes of the stout Mr. Garrison. Epic touched his cap.

"Mawnin', Cap'n Garrison."

"Good morning, porter." The man smiled a hard, dry smile. "You have a wonderful memory of name and faces."

"Yassuh, sho'ly has, cap'n. Tha's one of the mostest things I has got."

Mr. Garrison sighted the length of the train.

"Diner open yet?"

"Yassuh. 'Tain't nothin' else. Secon' car for'ard."

The white gentleman started off.

"See you later, Hop Sure."

"You suttinly ain't goin' to miss me, cap'n. Ise gwine stay in seein' distance all day."

The train pulled out of the terminal station. Epic, swapping blue blouse for white jacket bent himself with the job of awakening late sleepers. This included an insistent buzzing at the door of Drawing-Room A, with an eventual sleepy response from the attenuated Mr. Carson.

"Las' call fo' breakfast comin' th'oo, suh. Better git up right smart."

But evidently Mr. Carson did not get up right smart, for it was very considerably later that he emerged, in fresh linen and with a new close shave. He was without a hat, and Epic gazed with overt approval upon the single streak of gray which stood out in the very center of his black hair.

"A mos' distinction gemmun," commented Hop Sure to himself. "He's a houn' on han'someness."

Mr. Carson nodded briefly to Hop Sure as he moved toward the diner. That dignitary followed him down the aisle and almost collided with the bulky Mr. Garrison, who was just returning from his enjoyment of matutinal nourishment. Epic would have stepped aside, but Mr. Garrison stopped him, and he stopped him in a very peculiar and mysterious manner. He glanced first up and down the aisle of the car, then lowered his voice:

"Hop Sure?"

"Ise he."

"You remember that package we gave you last night?"

"Hot dam! Reckon I couldn't never forget that."

A still lower tone—"I want it."

"Now?"

"Yes. Bring it to me in the drawing-room right away."

Epic beamed.

"Yassuh, cap'n, suttinly will. You says it an' I does it."

Garrison moved on into the sanctuary of the drawing-room. Hop Sure ricocheted the length the car, opened the linen closet and unostentatiously removed the brown-paper parcel from the top shelf, tucked it in the voluminous pocket white jacket and journeyed back to the end of the Pullman, where he entered the drawing-room after a brief warning buzz.

"Got it?"

"I has."

The packet was extended. Immediately the Garrison hand disappeared in the Garrison pocket to show up a moment later with a bank note. Epic's eyes seemed about to pop from their sockets. Another tip—another bill. "These is the loosest gemmun with their money! I reckon I c'n be terrible useful with it."

Mr. Garrison accepted the packet, Hop Sure took the tip. Then a faint frown corrugated his Stygian brow.

"Boss man, if 'tain't too pussonal a request, would you min' changin' this two fo' two ones?"

Again that cold smile of impersonal amusement on the white man's face.

"Why? Two-dollar bill bad luck?"

"We-e-ell, not bad luck ezac'ly, but 'tain't good luck, neither—specially to cullud folks." The exchange was made and Epic escaped. Outside he paused to shake his head in worriment.

"Two-dollar bill—huh! That ain't the craziest thing I is about. Never did like no two-dollar bills."

The train slowed down. It came to a protesting halt at Peachtree, Atlanta's suburban station for through trains. Epic leaped to the platform and assisted with a considerable number of suitcases which had been wheeled down the platform on a truck. In order to be doubly efficient, he mounted the truck for a moment at the request of a prosperous-looking gentleman in a fur overcoat who gave promise of lavish tips. And from his perch on the truck Hop Sure was enabled to command a view of the interior of Drawing-Room A, his car. What he saw there impressed itself vividly on his subconscious mind. It was, matter of fact, nothing to excite particular comment. Nor was it so usual as to be without effect.

Mr. Garrison was standing in the middle of the drawing-room, his broad back toward the double windows. He was bending over and it was patent that he was working intensively. It took Epic just a small portion of a split second what his passenger was doing, and the very nature of the act aroused the porter's interest.

Mr. Garrison was engaged in the act of sliding the seat of the couch out from the wall. Peculiar! More peculiar still was the fact that, once having exposed the storage space beneath the seat couch, he proceeded to take from his coat pocket the brown-paper parcel which had been source of so many lavish tips and to conceal that parcel very carefully. Immediately thereafter Mr. Garrison replaced the mohair cushion, arranged overcoats with studied carelessness upon it and settled in a corner with his Atlanta *Constitution*.

Shortly after leaving Peachtree, Mr. Carson returned from the diner. Epic Peters was standing in the vestibule of his Pullman, staring out at the rolling North Georgia country and listening satisfiedly to the drumming of the wheels and the shrill blast of the locomotive whistle. Carson stopped, lighted a cigar and leaned against the steel wall opposite the porter.

"Nice morning," he commented.

"Yassuh. Suttinly is that."

Carson's thin lips compressed into a pinkish white line which was somehow quite hard.

"When is our next stop?"

He had a habit of clipping his words, making his manner of speech crisp, incisive, and not particularly soothing; it was as though he was not in the habit of having persons disagree with him.

"'Bout an hour fum now."

"Where?"

"Gainesville, suh."

"For how long?"

Once, many years before, Epic had been star witness in a big damage suit. The plaintiff's attorney had grilled him severely; and now, chatting thus idly with Mr. Carson, Hop Sure was reminded of that miserable hour on the stand.

"We ain't on'y s'posed to stop but fo' two-th'ee minutes, but we ginrally stays there about ten."

Carson's fingers quested slowly toward his pants pocket. Epic watched those fingers fascinatedly; they were long and slender and gave the impression of steely strength. But when they emerged the porter no longer found them of his interest. They held a five-dollar bill. Five! Epic's eyes opened wide under the severe stare which Carson bent upon him.

"See this, Hop Sure?"

"Does I? Boss man, I reckon I ain't never gwine be so blin' I couldn't see some-thin' like that. Or was I, I could tell it by the smell."

"Want it?"

"Aw, cap'n—"

"If you don't—"

"You talks foolishment with yo' mouf, cap'n—beggin' yo' pardon. Money is the mostest thing I always wants."

"H'm!" Mr. Carson puffed reflectively upon his cigar. "Remember that packet we gave you last night?"

Epic nodded. With himself he held puzzled communion—"Hot dawg! Some-thin' is sho' happenin' to me, but I don't know what it is."

"I want you to get that packet for me, Hop Sure."

It was on the tip of Epic's tongue to inform Mr. Carson that Mr. Garrison already had the package. But the five-dollar bill, waving slowly and insinuatingly before his nose, stayed his tongue. There came vividly to mind remembrance the scene which he had observed through the window at Peachtree Station—of the stocky Mr. Garrison meticulously hiding the packet under the lounge in the drawing-room. And, after all, the packet belonged to the pair of them, had been intrusted to him by both acting as one, and it was no business of his what they wanted with it or why this wealth was thus showered upon him.

"Can you get it for me while we're at Gainesville?"

Nothing could have better suited the plans of the long-legged porter.

"Yassuh, sho'ly can."

"I'll get my friend to walk up and down outside with me." Carson inspect-ed Epic very closely. "I want it handed to me personally. Understand what that means?"

"You yo'se'f alone?"

"Alone!"

"Boss, I has got so much understandin' my head aches."

The five-dollar bill changed hands and Carson disappeared into the car. He seemed so sure of himself—even sure of foot on the swaying floor. He walked without a lurch.

"Somehow," reflected Hop Sure sagely, "I wouldn't be awful happy was that gemmun to git real mad at me."

At Gainesville the two travelers strolled up down the platform. Epic, selecting his time with great care, boarded the train and flung into drawing-room. He was nervous, to say the least. This was something new to him. As a matter of fact, he was considerably at sea about the whole affair; but five dollars was five dollars, and if a man demanded his package that was no business of his.

The task of rescuing the parcel. from beneath the lounge took but a moment. Even less time that was required to conceal it in a capacious pocket. Five minutes after leaving Gainesville, Carson joined him in the vestibule.

Got it?" The packet was passed over. Carson's eyes narrowed. "Remember, this is between you and me."

"Us an' not nobody else a-tall."

"That's it. And be sure you don't forget."

"Boss, I never does nothin' that even soun's like forgettin'."

Travel was not heavy, nor were Epic's duties this trip unduly arduous. The particular *bêtes noires* of a porter's existence were conspicuously absent from his car—babies, invalids and normally healthy persons who are unable to withstand the quackings of railroad travel.

Epic dropped into Section 8, which was happily empty. He stretched his long, loose-jointed figure and stared out at the swelling Piedmont; the far-flung foothills merging into a background of blue mountains; the acres and acres of plowed fields which a few months since had been snowy with stalwart cotton and now were bare and brown, with here and there a touch of white where the staple had remained unpicked; long vistas of cornstalks, brittle and sapless and broken by the first ravages of genuinely cold weather; pine trees by the mile; little false-fronted towns flaunting themselves to travelers' stares; and everywhere dust-streaking flivvers catapulting along the more-or-less good sandy-clay roads.

Once in a while the buzzer would sound at the end of the car and Hop Sure would galvanize into action—a pillow here, a hat bag there. "Porter, are we on time?" "Yassum, we sho'ly is." At 11:30 he made his way into the diner, where, feeling wealthy, he ordered profusely and ate with gusto—soup and fish and fried eggplant and candied sweet potatoes and ice cream and cake. Even at the half rates allowed porters in the dining car, he was somewhat appalled by the size of his check, but paid it without a murmur and determined grimly that he would also commit the extravagance of eating a second meal when the dinner hour should come. The porter on the Atlanta-to-New York car the diner with him. The waiters were scurrying around straightening the dining car against the forthcoming invasion of white passengers. In the vestibule the two colored men conversed briefly.

"How's tricks, Hop Sure?"

"Tol'able, brother, tol'able."

"Prosp'rous trip?"

"Uh-huh. Kinda affluent."

The Atlanta porter grimaced.

"I got th'ee ten-cent passengers on my car. I hates a ten-center. Rather I gits me nothin' a-tall than ten cents."

Hop Sure shrugged sympathetically.

"I never fools with nothin' less'n two bits. Ten centses I th'ows out of the westibule. They ain't no good fo' slot machines."

The Atlanta porter drifted on. Hop Sure inspected his call board to make sure that there had been no summons for him, then once again he lounged in Section 8. The inner man had been placated and Epic Peters was at peace with the universe.

Georgia merged into South Carolina; the route gently northward and swung closer and closer to the alluring foothills of the Blue Ridge Mountains—the bewitching Sapphire Country. And then Mr. Epic Peters became uncomfortably conscious of the fact that a pair of eyes were boring into his head, that he was receiving a telegraphic command to come hither.

As he looked up and saw that it was the pudgy Mr. Garrison who was silently struggling to attract his attention from the passageway to the right of Drawing-Room A, a premonition smote Epic immediately beneath his belt buckle. Nor was that to be wondered at, for a thundercloudish look rested upon the countenance of the glassy-eyed Mr. Garrison, and it was immediately apparent that something had occurred which did not fill that gentleman with any wild surge of elation.

"Somethin' infohms me," postulated Hop Sure as he reluctantly hoisted himself to his feet, "that I is about to heah some more questions 'bout that package."

Immediately as Garrison saw that the porter was answering his summons, he turned on his heel and proceeded to the vestibule. As Epic joined him, he flung around with a few well-chosen words which were uttered in a manner entirely dissimilar to his erstwhile good-humored indifference.

"Porter, that package has gone!"

Epic disguised sudden and profound agitation with a disingenuous expression; his brain raced to the five-dollar transaction at Gainesville, which Mr. Carson had come into possession of the parcel.

"No!" he gasped with cleverly simulated amazement.

"It has!" rasped Mr. Garrison. "Gone!"

Instinct told Hop Sure that he had better hold peace. What, a few hours before, had appeared to be a logical and simple business transaction, now assumed an aspect which he neither understood nor liked. He rolled his head to one corner of his long neck and voiced a question.

"Where?"

"Where?" Garrison's eyes blazed. "How do I know?"

"That suttinly is right, cap'n. How does you know? Epic liked the sound of his own voice, it gave him a little more confidence. "Was you to know where yo' package was at you would go remove it away fum there an' put it somewheres else, an' then it wouldn't be gone no more; now would it, Mistuh Garrison?"

"I've got to find that package."

"Yassuh, you suttinly has. An' that ain't no lie. You sho'ly has got to recover that thing back. Does you reckon somebody abstracted it away fum where you put it at?"

"Yes"—grimly. "I reckon just exactly that."

"No! Cain't be!"

"It is. Now listen to me, porter! Recover that packet and there's ten dollars in it for you."

"Ten dol—"

"Yes, ten."

"Wigglin' tripe! Cap'n, you can consider that thing has done been got."

Garrison shook his head skeptically.

"I certainly hope so. Let me know the minute you think you know where it is."

"Ise gwine do that ve'y thing, boss."

Garrison moved slowly into the car, an obviously worried gentleman. Epic took stock of the situation.

"They's on'y two things I understan's about this heah mix-up," he ruminated, "an' I don't know what neither of them means."

The engine sirened hoarsely for a railroad crossing and a moment thereafter flashed by a big gaunt cotton mill; then another and another. Mechanically Hop Sure produced a rag from his hip pocket and dusted the vestibule rail.

"Greenville," he mumbled to himself. "Dawggone if we ain't got to this heah town in a terrible hurry."

They reached Greenville, the western gateway of the rich South Carolina Piedmont section. The station hummed with metropolitan activity; only one passenger at Greenville for Epic's car. The porter was amazed to find himself taking more than a cursory glance at the newcomer.

This passenger carried a New York ticket calling for Section 12 in its entirety, but that alone was not what attracted him to Epic's attention. It was rather that, in some subtle and entirely different way, he was remindful of Carson and Garrison, separate and collective owners of the package which already had brought to Epic much money and harassment.

There was no reason why the newcomer should have reminded Epic of either Carson or Garrison; he was as different from either as they were from each other. Yet there was a reminiscent confident set to his broad shoulders; the same inquisitive, distrustful, steely light in the eyes; an identical manner of studied disinterestedness.

But, whereas Carson and Garrison were immaculately tailored and exquisitely haberdashed, this man wore ill-fitting ready-made clothes, a cheap if stalwart shirt and a polka-dotted necktie. His shoes were unduly large and strikingly square-toed.

The stranger boarded the train. Epic deposited him and his bag in Section 12 and returned to the platform. Immediately something happened.

The figure of Mr. Carson detached itself from the shadows of a baggage truck which was piled high with suitcases and descended upon Hop Sure. Mr. Carson seemed more than a little excited, and his cameo face bore an expression of considerable annoyance. It was quite plain to the porter that his white gentleman friend was making vast efforts to control a surplus of emotion.

Carson's lengthy figure pressed close against the porter's side and into Hop Sure's hand was thrust a packet which long since had become strikingly familiar. Within Epic's heart there sounded a paean of triumph.

"Li'l package," he exulted to himself, "you has come home to papa."

Nor was that all. As he, scenting the need for caution, slipped the parcel in the pocket of his jacket, he heard Carson's voice, low and chill. He glanced at Carson's face and was amazed to see it guileless and expressionless. The man was talking without moving his lips.

"Put that thing back in your linen closet. Keep it hidden."

"Yas—"

"Shut your mouth! Just do as I tell you."

The slender fingers disappeared, then reappeared. "Here!"

It was a bill; a nice, new, crisp bill.

"Hot diggity dawg!" enthused Epic silently. "It never rains, but it gits wet."

Carson moved unostentatiously away. The all aboard was sounded; Epic hoisted himself to the platform. Arid then he stared popeyed at this latest crinkling bit of booty.

"Ten dollars! Great Gawdness Miss Agues! Fust it's a heap an' then it's twice as much."

Epic stood alone on the platform and tried to think. He had done entirely too much thinking during the day and the sustained and unnatural effort left him weak and headachy. Aside other gleanings, the two gentlemen in Drawing-Room A had netted him twenty-three dollars and he possessed a profound hunch that the end was not yet.

There was, for instance, the matter of the ten-dollar reward offered him by the portly Mr. Garrison for the return of the lost package. That package was now in Epic's pocket and the ten dollars was in the pants of Mr. Garrison. It was obviously a howling shame that the transfer should not be effected.

The ethics of the situation troubled Hop Sure not in the slightest degree. By their own mutual admission the package was the joint property of the two men; neither claimed sole ownership or disputed any claim which the other might make. Epic did not see his way clear to disobey the orders of either concerning it, and certainly, since that was the case, it would be the height of absurdity to do other than collect a maximum of profit.

They departed Greenville at precisely two minutes before one o'clock in the afternoon. Epic watched and saw Garrison and Carson disappear into the diner. Then, after a few additional moments of thought, he attained his own decision.

The train was approaching Spartanburg when they returned from their midday repast. Hop Sure, strategically stationed in the passageway, caught Garrison's eye and flashed him a signal wink. The rather-too-large head gave the briefest indication of a nod and less than five minutes later he joined the porter. Without a word, Epic shoved the packet into the huge pink paw of the white man. Garrison's eyes glowed eagerly as he shoved the package from view in his coat pocket.

"Where did you find it?"

Hop Sure's answer came in the nature of a comment.

"Seems like to me, cap'n, you must of dropped that thing behime the lounge in you-all's drawin'-room." Ten dollars was transferred to Epic. "I sho' ain't got nothin' but gratitude, cap'n."

"You've earned it."

"Jus' the same, Ise the gratitudinest man what is. I always has said that cash money is the fondest thing I is of."

They separated. Garrison was vastly contented with himself and with the situation. He 'strolled happily up the aisle of the Pullman, believing the world was a very comfortable place indeed. He favored his fellow travelers with benign glances of warm friendship, and then a sudden hot flush mounted to the very tips of ears and he unconsciously quickened his pace to disappear on the farthest platform. Once there he mopped a freely perspiring forehead with a lavender-bordered silk handkerchief.

"Phew!" he gasped. "That bird in Section 12! I wonder—"

Mr. Garrison felt weak and all gone inside. There had been a peculiar speculative quality in the stare of the heavy-set passenger in Section 12 which Mr. Garrison did not relish; it was as though the ill-clad gentleman knew a great many things and was intent upon adding to the sum of his knowledge. And then, whereas a moment before the brown-paper-wrapped parcel had suffused Mr. Garrison with a warm glow, it now scorched like molten metal and Mr. Garrison felt the urge to divorce himself from its possession until a more propitious moment.

He was nothing if not a man of action. Whistling with a fine, if nervous, insouciance he retraced his steps down the aisle of the car, rejoined Hop Sure on the back platform and slipped into the astonished hand of that bewildered colored gentleman the wandering package.

"Hide it!" he sibilated. "And keep it hidden until we get to New York!"

The hand dived into Mr. Garrison's pocket, and when the relieved white gentleman disappeared a half minute later Hop Sure was richer by an additional five dollars. He held it close to his eyes while a single horrid thought smote him—"cullud boy, you bad better pray that these heah moneys ain't counterfeit."

He arrayed his cash before him and compared minutely the Garrison-Carson money with bills which he knew had to be genuine. Then he sighed relievedly; obviously it was legitimate. So much then for that; the chiefest of Epic's worries was removed.

The afternoon dragged uneventfully. Messrs. Carson and Garrison remained in the seclusion drawing-room and the heavy-footed stranger sat stolidly in Section 12, earnestly perusing the pages of a magazine; only the thirty-eight dollars which Epic had collected from the mysterious travelers gave testimony to the fact that, whatever the situation might be, it was certainly unusual—and highly desirable.

At 4:05 in the afternoon they pulled into Charlotte, North Carolina, and ten minutes later departed. Between there and Salisbury, Hop Sure inhaled a noble meal which he ordered with reckless disregard for expense. It had been a red-letter day for Mr. Peters and he felt it only his due that the inner Epic be fortified against any further excitement. He even thrust a two-bit into the palm of an astonished waiter.

In prompt answer to the first general call for dinner, Garrison and Carson left their drawing room and proceeded to the diner. They studiously avoided the solemn and interested eye of man in Section 12, although it was plain to observant Hop Sure that they were far from indifferent to his presence. As they disappeared, the stranger beckoned to the porter.

"Call the conductor," he ordered peremptorily, and Hop Sure leaped to obey.

Somehow, the man's voice and manner impressed upon him the absolute necessity for un-questioning, efficient and prompt obedience. But even so, he couldn't help thinking that perhaps—

The conductor seemed to be expecting the summons, for he came wordlessly. Then for five minutes the blue-uniformed Pullman official and the man with the ill-fitting suit talked with low-toned earnestness. Hop Sure watched, feeling vaguely that he was not entirely an outsider. Nor did he have long to wait before learning that his instinct was correct. The two men arose, glanced quickly around the car and disappeared in Drawing-Room A. They closed the door behind them and Hop Sure could have sworn that he heard the click of the thumb latch. He sank heavily into a seat.

"Fo' eight yeahs," he reflected, "I has been porterin' on this road, but never befo'—nossuh, not even ever—did I see any seeh fumadiddles. 'Tain't nachel"— his fingers touched the crisp greenbacks which reposed in his pocket—"'tain't nachel—but it suttinly is highly financial."

Epic was aroused by the insistent sounding of his call-board buzzer. Drawing-Room A. Timidly he responded to the summons. The conductor and his flat-footed acquaintance turned to glare at the porter, who, in turn, stared with stern disapproval at the confusion into which the two men had thrown the drawing-room. Even to Epic's none-too-fast-moving mind it was immediately apparent that a search had been conducted and it was equally as apparent from their expressions that it had been bitterly unsuccessful.

The conductor's greeting was brief and to the point. He nodded toward the stranger.

"Do what this gentleman orders, Hop Sure."

"Yassuh, cap'n."

An order came crisply from the other man:

"Open that upper berth."

Hop Sure produced his key, inserted it in the berth and lowered it. Immediately the stranger swung himself into the berth. And then, article by article, each thing the berth contained was carefully opened, shaken out and thrown on the floor, where, under the conductor's orders, Epic refolded them.

Hop Sure labored silently. He had the disquieting hunch that the brown-paper parcel was object of this particular search. So far as he was concerned, he couldn't understand all the interest or excitement, and with the money in pocket he felt more like a participant in the drama than a mere spectator thereof.

The man lowered himself to the floor and bade Hop Sure set the room to rights—quickly. He turned to the conductor.

"Not here," he commented crisply.

The conductor answered with equal terseness, "Evidently not."

Then the stranger to the porter: "Not a word of this, understand?"

His hand extended a dollar bill. Hop Sure nodded eager agreement.

"I understan's absolute, suh."

"Good!"

The trio left the drawing-room. Fifteen minutes later the other pair returned from the dining car and secluded themselves. As they passed Section 12 Hop Sure fancied that he discerned glances of interest bestowed by them upon the heavy-set stranger, but that gentleman paid no heed.

At nine o'clock—halfway between Danville and Lynchburg—Hop Sure was summoned to the drawing-room and ordered to make down the berths. He was immensely relieved to note the complete absence of suspicion in the manner of his two benefactors. It was plain that they were unaware not only of the drawing-room having been searched, but also of the freedom with which Hop Sure had acted as clearing house.

His task completed, Hop Sure returned to the main car, where for the ensuing hour he was kept excruciatingly busy making down berths for tired travelers. By ten o'clock the car was composed for the night; but in Section 12 the stranger sat stolidly reading. Epic grew nervous; a task unfinished preyed upon his mind. He knew that sooner or later that section had to be made and he preferred to do it now. At length he approached the white gentleman and touched his cap.

"Shall I make up yo' berth, boss?"

The other man answered rather peculiarly—"You may bring me a table."

Wonderingly, Hop Sure obeyed. The man produced a deck of cards and plunged promptly into the absorbing intricacies of Canfield. Hop Sure hovered uncertainly in the aisle.

"Any time you craves to sleep," he suggested hopefully, "jes' press that button yonder."

The man answered without looking up, "I will."

Two men occupied the smoking compartment, the platform was chilly. Hop Sure perched himself upon his little stool at the lower end of the where he commanded a view of the drawing room door. He could see that at eleven o'clock the game of Canfield was still enthusiastically in progress. Less than five minutes later he saw something else.

The drawing-room door swung slowly back; the gray streak of hair which marked Mr. Carson appeared briefly in the aperture. It was evident that Mr. Carson saw the man in Section 12 and equally evident that he was not pleased thereby, for the door closed abruptly. A half hour later the performance was repeated. Hop Sure shook his head sadly.

"Ise dawg-goned if I understan's all I knows about this."

Shortly before midnight his buzzer sounded; the call-box indicated a summons from Drawing-Room A. Epic started down the car. As he reached Section 12 a steely hand fastened on his arm.

"Call from the drawing-room, porter?"

"Yassuh."

Two one-dollar bills passed from the man to the porter.

"You didn't hear it," suggested the other. "As a matter of fact, you are not going to hear any rings from the drawing-room to-night—understand?"

"B-b-but, cap'n—"

"No buts. The conductor told you to obey my orders. And in case that doesn't satisfy you—"

Heavy spatulate fingers flashed to the coat lapel and flung it back. Hop Sure found himself gazing horrifiedly at the glittering surface of a silver star.

"Oh, gosh!" he moaned, remembering vividly his participation in the comings and goings of the brown-paper parcel. "I might of knowed you was a detective!"

"Why?"

"'Cause wa'n't you tryin' to detect somethin' that drawin'-room a while back? Wa'n't you, cap'n ?"

"Perhaps."

"Cap'n"—Hope Sure lowered his voice—"them two gemmun ain't done nothin' wrong, has they?"

The detective frowned.

"Go back and disconnect the buzzer signal- and keep your mouth shut."

"Oh, gosh! Tha's the one thing I ain't gwine do nothin' else but."

Hop Sure staggered to the end of the car, disconnected the buzzer and sat depressedly on his stool. His mind groped heavily with the events the past twenty-four hours; the constant influx of money, the peregrinations of the brown-paper parcel, the presence of the detective—

Somehow, Epic Peters felt that he was an unwitting but dangerously incriminated participant in the evildoings which were coming to a head in this eventful journey. He didn't know what it was all about, but he did possess an overpowering hunch that he would not relish a general comparison of notes by the parties most vitally concerned.

He repressed without considerable difficulty an impulse to tell the detective what he knew concerning the package. The proposition seemed too fraught with the menace of the unknown. After all, the contents of that parcel were none of his affair; he had been asked to keep it in his linen closet until their arrival in New York, and he couldn't very well see why he should do anything else, particularly since it was liable to get him more deeply involved in a situation which already had creased his forehead with horizontal furrows of intensive worry.

And so through the long night, across the state of Virginia, during the long wait in Washington and on the trip northward from there over the Pennsylvania system, the peculiar vigil continued; the detective immersed in his game of Canfield, Hop Sure wide eyed and nervous on his stool at the end of the car, the occupants of the drawing-room occasionally poking their heads through a crack in the door.

The train reached and passed North Philadelphia. Hop Sure, weary of brain and foot, waked his passengers and busied himself half-heartedly with the task of putting the car shipshape. The detective's Canfield went incessantly on. Once Hop Sure approached the silver-star man.

"Shall I go make up the drawin'-room, boss? We is reproachin' New Yawk." The other answered without looking up.

"No!" he said.

At Elizabeth the drawing-room door was flung violently open. Mr. Carson, heavy of eye and haggard of face, boldly summoned Hop Sure by gesture. And as that dignitary started toward him, something else strange and unexpected occurred—the detective rose, smiled and edged his way into the drawing-room.

It was plain from the expression on the face of Carson that the visit was not relished. The door closed softly and Hop Sure stood swaying in the aisle. His brain was traveling like a race horse now. The journey was nearing its end; the brown-paper-parcel reposed in the linen compartment; it was obvious that Hop Sure would have no opportunity to return it to its owners—unless—

Hop Sure reached a difficult decision and drew a deep breath. Between his satanic majesty and blue depths of the sea there was apparently nothing for him to do but follow out the letter of instructions. He hunched that all was not well, and that it was shortly to become even less so; but more than he feared the results of wrong actions he dreaded the consequences of no action at all.

With heart pounding in his bosom, he opened his linen closet, took the brown-paper parcel from the top shelf, dropped it in the depths of his jacket pocket and made his way uncertainly toward the drawing-room. No matter what happened, the period of inaction was at an end; that much in itself was relieving. As to what the results would be—he dared not think. Sufficient unto the hour was the evil thereof. He was well content that the future held worries of its own.

He sounded the buzzer and immediately the door was flung back. Hop Sure met the level eyes of the detective. Behind the broad back of that official, Epic found himself staring at a graphic and expressive pantomime. Plainly as words, the gestures of the two gentlemen in the drawing-room carried the message to vamose. Hop Sure paid them absolutely no heed.

"What do you want?" It was the detective speaking.

"I has got somethin' belongin' to these gemmun," blurted Epic; "somethin' I was to give back to them when us arrove in New Yawk."

He plainly discerned the expressions of consternation which crossed their countenances; he fancied vaguely that they were regretting the lavish tips which they had thrust upon him. A big and dark hand came from his jacket pocket clutching the brown-paper parcel.

"Heah 'tis, gemmun," he announced with forced geniality. "I suttinly did take pretickeler care of it fo' you-all."

There was a general clashing of glances, a scrutinizing, speculative look in the eyes of the Both Carson and Garrison were visibly annoyed; the former indicating his perturbation by pallor, the latter by a display of beetlike redness.

"What I has done played," reflected Hop Sure, "is hell; but they ain't no backin' out now." He took one step forward and held out the packet toward the long, thin Mr. Carson. "Heah you is, cap'n."

And then Epic Peters received the ultimate of an amazing journey, for Mr. Carson stared at him gravely, shook his head with studied admirable calm and spoke in a cool, even voice:

"I never saw that package before."

"Good Gawdness—"

"And I've never seen it, either," interrupted Garrison.

Hop Sure stared amazedly from one to the other; a sensation of hot indignation suffused his bosom. This reeked strongly of a conspiracy to put him in a demoralizingly false light.

"Does you-all gemmun mean to stan' up there on yo' own two foots an' say you di'n't gimme this heah package to take care of fo' you ontil we arrove in New Yawk? Does you-all mean to say you di'n't tell me I was to keep it hid in the linen closet? Does you-all two inten' to stultifry that you di'n't infohm me—"

There was glacierlike chill in Carson's tones.

"I mean to say all of that and a great deal more. I mean to say that you are presumptuous and impertinent and I don't care to hear any more from you. We know nothing whatever about that packet; never saw it before and"—with sharp irony—"never expect to see it again."

Epic Peters collapsed limply on the lounge. He stared with helpless appeal into the amused face of the detective, who had been a silent but interested spectator.

"Will you listen at them gemmun, cap'n?" pleaded Hop Sure. "They gimme that packet in Bumminham with they ve'y own han's an' they said to me, they said, 'Po'ter, we craves you should take care of this—'"

The detective shook his head slowly.

"But they claim they never saw this package before."

"Oh, lawsy—"

"And you certainly wouldn't dispute the word 'of two gentlemen, would you, porter?"

"Nossuh! I wouldn't 'spute no gemmun no time nohow. An' I ain't claimin' that they is falsifryin', neither. But I does claim one thing, cap'n—I claims one thing an' I claims it passionate—I claims that these two gemmun is awful forgetful."

Gently the detective removed the package from Hop Sure's grasp. He faced the other white men.

"You are. quite sure this isn't yours?" he asked.

"Positive," came the chorused answer.

"You never saw it before?"

"Never!"

"You didn't intrust any package of any sort to this porter's keeping?"

"No!"

"Golly Moses, boss man, them gemmun ain't got no mem'ry a-tall!"

The detective smiled.

"Suppose we see what's in it," he observed, as though speaking to himself.

He produced a pocketknife with which he cut the string; he removed three layers of brown paper, disclosing to view a handsome leather case. With his eyes focused on those of the two other white men, he flipped the lid back.

"Oh-h-h!" came Hop Sure's hoarse voice. "Jools!"

They filled the room with glorious color; the collar of diamonds and emeralds glittered and sparkled and gleamed, fairly dazzling the popping eyes of Mr. Epic Peters, in whose charge this treasure had been for most of the journey from Birmingham. As from a great distance he heard the monotone of the detective, speaking as though to himself.

"Peculiar situation," the detective was saying. "Worth tens of thousands-and nobody to claim it. Funny thing too; they told me over long-distance in Greenville that this had been stolen in Birmingham the previous day and that it was supposed to be on this train. Police authorities in Alabama figured the men who took it wouldn't have had time to split up the loot and separate." He looked up friendlily at Carson and Garrison. "You're quite sure you never saw this before?"

"Positive," asserted Mr. Carson somewhat sickly.

"Never!" echoed Mr. Garrison.

"Then," smiled the detective, "there's nothing for me to do but turn this over to the proper authorities as valuable and unclaimed property."

It seemed to Hop Sure that Garrison and Carson were relieved—and then he noticed that the train was jerking to a stop.

"Manhattan Transfer!" he exclaimed, leaping for the door. "I has to git out an' do some porterin'."

Thirty minutes later they reached the Pennsylvania Station in New York City. Messrs. Garrison and Carson were the first two passengers out of Epic's car. The glares which they bestowed upon him were not unduly friendly, and Hop Sure was excessively pleased to note the celerity with which they ascended the exit stairway. Last out of the car was the detective. He seemed vastly contented. Hop Sure was positive that the grim-visaged man was smiling.

He halted at Epic's side and turned his bag over to a redcap.

"You were of quite some assistance, porter," he commented.

"Yassuh, cap'n, thanky, sir. They calls me Hop Sure an' Ise the servinest porter runnin' to nawth. Any time you craves my 'sistance—"

Still smiling, the detective produced a wallet. before the staring and amazed eyes of the porter, he counted off two gold-backed twenty-dollar bills and a pair of crisp fives.

"Fifty dollars," he announced. "That's for you, porter."

The detective walked swiftly off, leaving Epic staring in dumfounded amazement at this new and colossal accession of wealth. The events of the past thirty-six hours flashed kaleidoscopically through his brain. He shook his head in utter and happy bewilderment.

"Fifty dollars!" he murmured to himself ecstatically. "Fifty dollars cash money in hand!"

He withdrew from his pocket the thirty-eight dollars given him by Garrison and Carson. He gazed first at the fifty and then at the thirty-eight. The faintest semblance of a sneer appeared on his lips.

"Thutty-eight dollars!" he breathed disdainfully. "Shuh! What them two fellers don't know about tippin' is nothin'!"

RIDE 'EM AND WEEP

A MERE split second before the moment of impact the intoxicated young gentleman sidestepped and the yard engine rolled past. In acknowledgment of the stream of vituperation issuing from the lips of the engineer, the young gentleman doffed his velour hat in a courteous bow as he murmured an abject apology.

"'Smy fault, Mr. Engine. 'Sall my fault. Wouldn't put you to the trouble of killing me for anything. No sir, Mr. Engine. 'Scuse me. I 'pologize mos' humbly."

Having thus adjusted matters, the young gentleman· zigzagged across another track to the platform where the Pullmans which were destined to be attached to the midnight train were waiting silently.

He rolled unsteadily but happily toward the first of these Pullmans. There he was greeted by a long, gangly, slue-footed, dark individual the uniform of a Pullman porter. This colored person had horrifiedly witnessed the near-tragedy and his eyes were rolling wildly. There was a genuine solicitude in his voice and manner as he shot forward and imprisoned the arm of the inebriated young white man.

"Goodness goshness Miss Agnes, Mistuh Foster—I suttinly thought I was gwine see you become ain't."

Mr. Foster favored the porter with a pained expression.

"Hop Sure," he said thickly, "I'm s'prised at you. Absolutely s'prised. I knew all the time that engine was goin' to get out of my way. Tha's a very polite engine, Hop Sure; very polite."

"Hmm!" Hop Sure—christened Epic Peters—had his doubts. "I ain't so suttin 'bout how polite yahd injines is. How come you to cross those tracks anyway, Mistuh Foster, 'stid of comin' heah th'oo the subcutaneous passage?"

"Shortes' way," explained Mr. Foster airily. Shortes' way to your vishinity, Hop Sure." He paused; then lowered his voice to a confidential whisper. "Hop Sure," he announced dramatically, "I'm drunk!"

Epic considered that it was up to him to indicate surprise. "Does you say so?"

"I am. Gloriously drunk." Then, pridefully—"Never would have guessed it, would you?" Epic lied like a gentleman. "Nossuh. Not never."

"Well, I am. I have imbibed too freely. The groun' is moving but I am very steady. An', Hop Sure—I am in trouble. Terrible trouble, Hop Sure, an' I have come to you for 'sistance."

The face of the elongated colored man broke into a grin. "'Sisting you, Mis-tuh Foster, is the fondes' thing I is of."

"I knew it, Hop Sure: knew it. I cast my bread on the troubled waters, an' now it returns to me in the form of angel cake. Ain't it so, Hop Sure?"

"'Taint nothin' else, boss man. Anything Epic Peters is able to do fo' you can be considered as already did."

Mr. Foster waxed exceedingly enthusiastic. "Knew it. I certainly knew it. Of course I never did anything much for you, Hop Sure—"

The negro's eyes glowed with genuine affection. "Shuh! Cap'n—you talks foolishment with yo' mouf. I reckon you loant me money when I sick an' di'n't have no job—an' tha's the mostest thing a white gemmun can do fo' any cullud boy."

"'Smatter of 'pinion; jus' simply matter of 'pinion. The point is, Hop Sure, that you are willing to ' sist me, and I am most positively in need of 'sistance.'"

"Jus' you tell me—"

"I have to get to Atlanta, Hop Sure. Got to be there in the morning. Business. 'Portant business. Awful 'portant. An' I am in a very distressing position. I throw myself on your mercy, Hop Sure. I beg of you to get me to Atlanta."

The porter grinned broadly. "Git you to Atlanta? Mistuh Foster—tha's the one thing I ain't gwine do nothin' else but. Jus' you leave it to Hop Sure."

"Got to leave it to you—" The man's voice was rapidly becoming unintelli-gible. "'Snawful fix I'm in. Ought to be 'shamed of myself. But I ain't. Feelin' too good. Jus' you get me to Atlanta—'sterrible situation I'm in: too mush party...."

Hop Sure took his friend firmly by the arm and propelled him purposefully toward the New York Pullman. "Don't you go to worryin', Mistuh Foster. Cap'n Sandifer is conductin' this Pullman to-night an' I an' him is good frien's. He holps me out lots of times. Reckon Ise gwine put you to bed in the drawin'-room—"

Mr. Foster hung back. "Not the drawin' room, Hop Sure. 'Taint nessery...."

"Ise handlin' this, white folks. I seen the di'gram on'y a few minutes ago an' the drawin'Ride room ain't took out Bumminham. All I does is to make you com-futtable an' 'splain to Cap'n Sandifer that a white gemmun frien' of mine is slee-pin' there. It's gwine be all right, suh. Ev'thin' jus' as good as fixed. Ain't nobody gwine bother you. They don't call me Hop Sure fo' nothin'. Nossuh they don't."

Mr. Foster's eyes had taken on the peculiar glassy stare which immediately precedes the stage of intoxication which is technically known as "passing out." Supporting the man bodily Hop Sure hoisted him up the steps of the Pullman and thence into the drawing-room, where he laid him gently on the lounge, cov-ered him with a wool blanket and left him happily sleeping.

The lengthy porter then returned to the platform. The air was pungent with the odor of steam. The huge shed of the Birmingham Terminal Station was re-verberant with the cacophony of locomotive bells and steam exhausts. From the baggage platform came the crashing and banging of trunks. In the waiting room was a joyfully vociferous bridal party awaiting arrival of the southbound A. G. S. train from Chattanooga. Hop Sure consulted his watch ad noted that it was eleven o'clock. Fifty minutes later his train was scheduled to pull out on first leg of its long journey to New York.

Hop Sure was suffused with a warm glow. His eyes were still lighted affectionately at thought of this golden opportunity to do a favor for the physically and financially helpless gentleman in the drawing-room. Epic had many friends among the white folks, but no one for whom he entertained the same depth of affection that he bore toward Mr. Foster.

Mr. Foster had loaned him money once when money was the single vital need in Hop Sure's life. The inconsiderable loan had driven a ravening wolf away from the Peters' door, and Hop Sure was not one to forget a favor. It may have been true that the loan did not embarrass Mr. Foster to any appreciable extent, but the salient fact was that, without it, Epic would have found himself in the direst sort of distress.

And now Mr. Peters, eight-year service man in-the employ of the Pullman Company, found himself in a position to do a favor for his benefactor. Epic reveled in the opportunity. He promised himself that he would nurse Mr. Foster like a baby, make him comfortable for the trip and bring him to by the time they reached Atlanta.

It was fortunate indeed, reflected Epic, that Captain Sandifer was on the run that night. He thought a great deal of Sandifer, and Sandifer regarded Epic as one of the finest porters on the line. Times without number they had been of service to one another, and Hop Sure was certain that Captain Sandifer would readily accede his request for free Pullman accommodation (amd the attendant costless transportation) for the gentleman who was now snoring grandiosely in Drawing-Room A.

A free passenger was no new thing in the life Mr. Peters. His ebony countenance twisted into a smile of reminiscence at thought of the innumerable occasions when friends of Captain Sandifer had ridden without cost and thereupon extended the ultimate of service by the Hop Sure. It was little enough which veteran porter was to request: little enough indeed.

Clad in his blue uniform and wearing pridefully a gleaming silver service stripe on his left sleeve, Epic attended to the immediate wants of passengers as they boarded the train and turned in for the night. Nor was the task an easy one, for the car promised to be very nearly full.

"Suttinly is glad that drawin'-room wa'n't took—don't know where else I could of placed Mistuh Foster...." He strolled down the platform and addressed the dumpy little porter in charge of the Atlanta car. "Ain't seen Cap'n Sandifer has you, Joe?"

Joe shook his head in negation. "Ain't sawn him sence nine o'clock when us switched in."

Unquestionably the Pullman conductor was in the main waiting room taking tickets and checking off the list on his diagram. But even at that it was about time for him to come through. Already the engine which was to haul them had. backed under the shed and the train was ready.

And then, mounting the stairs leading to the train platform from the underground passageway, Hop Sure glimpsed the gold badge on the cap of the Pullman conductor. With a broad smile lighting his face he started impulsively forward to greet his friend and to appraise him of the presence of Mr. Foster in the drawing-room.

Suddenly he paused and the smile froze. For the conductor mounting the steps brought into Epic Peters' heart a premonition of disaster. Epic sideswiped himself, whirled suddenly, and wandered back toward his car.

"Sufferin' tripe!" he reflected. "Hahd luck ain't on'y pu'sued me: it has done cotched."

The Pullman conductor was waddling toward Epic. He was small and heavy-set where Captain Sandifer was tall and rangy, and whereas the latter had a genial personality, this man radiated grimness. "It's Cap'n Crosby," mourned Hop Sire "an' he's as hahd boiled as two eggs."

Crosby was the terror of Pullman porters. He was too confoundedly efficient and he demanded efficiency from the men who worked under him. He was, the porters declared unanimously, a man without a soul. No unfortunate, attempting to beat a ride, and presenting a tale of woe calculated to wring tears of blood from a block of granite, could hope to dent the adamantine emotional surface of Jim Crosby. Not only that, but Crosby was demented on the subject of non-paying passengers. He did not possess the easily adjustable conscience of the majority of his fellow-conductors....It was said of him, and said sneeringly, that he had never knocked down a dime or deadheaded a pal. Nor was that rigid probity regarded with acclaim: rather it was looked upon as sheer stupidity for, in running a friend through, the average conductor merely considers that he is reaping one of the perquisites of his arduous profession.

Crosby waddled by Epic's car and favored the terrified porter with a curt nod. There was no love lost between Epic and Crosby: at various in the hectic past there had been open friction between them, and Hop Sure possessed decided hunch that any dereliction on his part would result in immediate report to the authorities.

Crosby made his way down the platform. Epic, considerably puzzled and most decidedly ill at ease, beckoned surreptitiously to Joe and that pudgy individual—having been in the service too short a time to appreciate the ingrained meanness of Captain Crosby—sidled to Epic's vicinity.

Hop Sure spoke in a low, discreet voice.

"Joe," he asked bitterly—"Di'n't Cap'n Crosby stop an' make talk with you jus' then?"

"Uh-huh."

"What he said, Joe?"

The little man looked up into the eyes of the tall one. "He di'n't say nothin', Hop Sure, an' he said it frequent."

"I know...but he must of said somethin'." Hop Sure's hand rested pleadingly on the arm of his friend. "Joe—he di'n't say he was makin' this run to-night, did he?"

Joe smiled as he nodded horrid affirmation—"Tha's what he said, Epic."

"Oh Lawsy...Wha's the matter with Cap'n Sandifer?"

"Sick."

"What kind of sick?"

"Dunno...but fum the way Cap'n Crosby spoke he wa'n't neah as sick as some folks would like him to be."

Hop Sure turned miserably away. In a trice his enthusiasm for doing his friend a favor had vanished. Now he was confronted with the stark immediate problem of getting Mr. Foster off the car.

The prospect appalled Mr. Peters. Mr. Foster was three sheets in the wind; utterly and supremely helpless—but before passing out he had entrusted himself to the mercies of his Pullman porter friend. He had told him that it was necessary for him to be in Atlanta in the morning—very important business—he trusted Hop Sure to get him there.

Epic determined to brave the wrath of Cap'n Crosby—brave that and the possibility of discovery; until he reflected upon the consequences. It was then that he saw the impossibility of the thing. No question about it—Mr. Foster must put off the train until such time as he possessed sufficient money to properly pay his way.

But that decision, reluctantly arrived at, was not easily put into effect. It was a scant ten minutes before leaving time and Mr. Foster was being held in a stranglehold by Kid Morpheus. Epic struggled and tugged and pleaded—

"Git up out of heah, Mistuh Foster. Us is in a peck of trouble does you not wake up... an' it ain't gittin' no less ev'y minute. Cain't you heah me protestin' with you, Mistuh Foster—I begs you on my knees to git over bein' lit. Please suh... it's gwine be plumb sickly fo' us bofe does you remain where you is at."

The lips of the peacefully slumbering young man expanded into a beatific smile. He didn't move—nor was Hop Sure sufficiently strong to handle the inert figure.

From outside came the rattle of baggage trucks, the clanging of bells, the hiss of escaping steam—and, above all, the raucous call for "Po-o-orter" in the harsh voice of Captain Crosby. Mournfully dropping Mr. Foster back on the lounge, and closing the door carefully behind him, Epic sidled through the aisle and to the station platform where he met the irate glare of the Pullman conductor and a battery of peeved countenances on the persons of several late-arriving passengers.

"Where have you been, Epic?"

Hop Sure waved his hand vaguely in the direction of nowhere. "Jus' been, cap'n; jus' been."

"Where?"

"Inside yonder."

"Doing what?"

"Preparin'."

"Put these suitcases aboard. It's leaving time. And don't ever again let me find you loafing."

"Nossuh. You suttinly ain't gwine do that, cap'n. Whatever I does on this trip, I ain't gwine loaf—an' that ain't no lie, neither."

The new arrivals filled the car, excepting only a couple of upper berths. Epic barely had time get them comfortably arranged, when the "All aboard" echoed down the platform and he catapulted himself outside to grab his car step, mount the slowly moving train and close his vestibule. Then, rather sick at heart, he stood upon the platform and reflected bitterly upon the danger and misery of his lot.

It was too late now to change the situation. The train was moving toward Atlanta. He watched gloomily the dull lights of Birmingham as they passed slowly through the yards swung eastward after rumbling under the giant Avenue viaduct. He plunged questing fingers into his pocket and produced a paltry two and seventy-five cents. Nor was there any use requesting a loan from Joe, the porter in the next car. Joe was chronically broke…and notoriously averse to making a loan. So Epic's idea of paying for two tickets and then for his inebriated friend died a-bornin'.

Yet he knew that even with sufficient cash, the plan would, in all probability, not have been feasible. He visualized the ferocious glare of Captain Crosby's eyes and the acidity of his manner should he be told that a mere porter had usurped conductorial authority by accepting a passenger and assigning him berth space on the car. It would be rich, red meat for a stinging report to the Pullman Company. Epic shook his head sadly—"Of all the porters runnin' on the Southern, Ise the one Cap'n Crosby don't like the most."

Barring only a miracle, Epic knew that the presence of Mr. Foster would be discovered somewhere on the journey from Birmingham to Atlanta. In contemplation of the dire proceedings which would follow that discovery Epic shuddered. Captain Crosby would brutally demand railroad and Pullman tickets. Failing to receive them he would consult with the train conductor and they would pitch the helpless passenger from the train at the next station. That was a melancholy prospect indeed.... Hop Sure's lips compressed: come what might, he must use his best efforts to save his white gemmun friend. Mr. Foster had aided him when aid was most valuable...he knew now that he could not desert that gentleman in the hour of his extreme and hopeless trouble.

Of course there was the bare possibility that Mr. Foster might be safe in the drawing-room. Crosby was the only man it was necessary to contend with, as, this being a through run starting at midnight, the tickets were handled by the Pullman conductor only. Too, Epic had made run with Crosby on other occasions and knew that that stern official was not in the habit of sleeping. Crosby's attention to duty was simply shocking. Invariably he sat up in the rear car—failing that, in any car where sitting space was available, and he took good care to see that his porters did not avail themselves of opportunities for long, luscious naps.

If only Crosby could be kept out of the drawing-room. . . . Hop Sure suffered agonies as the man strolled through the car, then breathed a sigh of vast relief to notice that he was temporarily safe. The porter followed his chief on the platform where he stood staring out into the night.

The train was making fair time in the general direction of Atlanta. Beyond the windows, Epic could discern the silhouette of Alabama foothills and the oc-casional winking lights of small towns. The train was jerking and lurching on its way, rounding at good speed the countless curves on that particular 156-mile stretch of road.

Inside, the car was quiet as the grave. The latest of the passengers were com-posing themselves for the night and praying for rest. Epic stared gloomily down the cañon of green curtains toward the door of Drawing-Room A behind which lurked tragedy. Then, slowly, he lurched down the aisle of the car and his practiced eye noticed that all of the berths were occupied except Upper 10 and Upper 2. "Two mo' passengers," he mused, "an' the on'y place I could put Mistuh Foster—'ceptin' the drawin'-room—would be nowhere."

Epic seated himself at the lower end of the car where he commanded an excellent view of the drawing-room door. Thus far the affair had been running much too smoothly to satisfy him. This was entirely too good to be true . . . he prepared himself for a shock, but not quite for the shock he received when Crosby suddenly shoved by him, walked the length of the car and turned the knob of the drawing-room door.

Epic swallowed his heart as he stumbled to his feet and zigzagged down the car to join Crosby. That personage glowered upon him.

"Make up the drawing-room," he ordered briefly.

Hop Sure stared, his lower jaw drooping. His head bobbed slowly on the long, skinny neck.

"Drawin'-room?" he repeated.

"Yes—the drawing-room. It is engaged out of Anniston."

"Y-y-yassuh.... H-how them folkses want made up, cap'n?"

"Upper and lower. And be sure you do a good job. I'll come back and inspect."

"Cap'n—they ain't no need fa' you to trouble yo'se'f. What you ought to do, cap'n, is go back an' take a nap. You is lookin' pow'ful peeky, Cap'n Crosby; I ain't never seen you lookin' so bad."

"Nonsense. Don't talk like an idiot. I was never better in my life. Now—get busy."

"Y-yassuh—I shuah will. You don't know how busy I is rilly gwine git, either."

Hop Sure walked to his linen closet where for an inordinate length of time he pretended to assort the necessary linens. Crosby joined him.

"What's the matter? Why are you so slow?" Epic favored him with a pained expression— "I slow, cap'n?"

"You are." The conductor's eyes narrowed—"Are you drunk?"

"Me? Gosh goodness, no! B'lieve me or not, Cap'n Crosby—knowin' what I does 'bout the evils of licker, I wouldn't touch a drop even if there wa'n't nothin' else in the whole world."

"Hmph!" Crosby sniffed. "At any rate you better never let me catch you even fooling around where liquor is. Nossuh."

"Boss man, if I c'n he'p it, you suttinly ain't gwine catch me. Nossuh."

The conductor left the car. Hop Sure pussyfooted after him to the vestibule and made sure that he had departed completely. Then, with arms piled high with clean linen, he traversed the dimly-lighted green-walled corridor of the Pullman and let himself softly into the drawing-room.

Mr. Foster was yet asleep, but his slumber did not have the same lethal quality which it had appeared to possess an hour earlier. The young gentleman was stirring; faint mumblings came from his throat and occasionally his lips twisted into the ghost of a grin.

Epic stood over him and gazed down commiseratingly. "Mistuh Foster," he mused, "us is sho'ly in a hell of a fix."

He deposited the linens on one of the seats and set busily to work reviving Mr. Foster. The task was not without its difficulties. Mr. Foster was happier asleep and he voiced inarticulate protests against the none-too-gentle treatment the porter was passionately bestowing upon him.

Hop Sure rubbed the white gentleman's face and wrists—rubbed them raw. Then he filled sanitary drinking cup with ice water from the in the lavatory and pitched it full into face of the other man. That treatment proved sufficiently drastic. Mr. Foster scrambled unsteadily to his feet, hitting out wildly in frantic effort to ward off a hydraulic attack.

"'Swater!" announced the intoxicated gentleman. "'Man in the ocean—an' I can't swim—can't swim a lick ...."

Mr. Epic Peters had become a man of action. He sidestepped one of Mr. Foster's wild lunges and took his position behind the helpless gentleman. Then the porter's two stringily powerful arms slipped beneath the armpits of his Caucasian friend and he propelled that gentleman violently down the aisle of the car.

Until they pulled up short in the vicinity of Section 10, Mr. Foster was too entirely dazed to register a protest. He turned amazed, hurt eyes upon Hop Sure—

"Never thought it of you," he murmured reprovingly. "Thought you wash frien'....do' wanna go walkin'...wanna shleep."

"You is gwine sleep, boss; you suttinly is. You ain't gwine do nothin' else but it once I gits you in that upper berth. C'mon, be a good spoht an' climb up yonder—I ain't no derrick."

Mr. Foster surveyed the pitching, rolling precipice of green and shook his head helplessly. "Can't do it ... 'stoo high anyway ... might fall out."

"But," wailed Epic. "If you don't you is libel to git th'owed out."

"Never was no good climbin'. . . . Wanna shleep. . . . Wanna be rocked in the cradle of the deep. . . . You know, Hop Sure, rocked in the cradle. . . . Do' wanna go way up yonder. . . . 'stoo tall."

Hop Sure was up against it: "They is on'y two things I can do," he reflected miserably, "an' bofe of 'em is wrong." He stared uncertainly up and down the car ... and suddenly his face lighted as his eyes rested upon the pudgy, interested countenance of his fellow porter, Joe. He summoned that gentleman to his side.

"Hot dam, Joe-nothin' could look gooder'n you right now. C'mon he'p me h'ist this gemmun unto that upper berth."

Joe regarded the spectacle solemnly. "How come him cain't climb up hisownse'f?"

The answer came sibilantly: "Drunk!"

Joe smiled approvingly. "He do kind of remind me of a gin mill I useter know down in the Scratch Ankle distric'. Lo-o-oka yonder, Hop "Sure—he's done went to sleep."

"Dawg-gone if he ain't. Le's us lif' him."

Neither Hop Sure nor Joe was lacking in muscle, but they found the task almost too much for their straining bodies. At length, however, they managed to project a small portion of Mr. Foster over the edge of the upper and the rest a mere matter of shoving regardless of its upon the unfortunate's anatomy. Hop then ascended on the ladder which Joe braced and arranged his charge in what seemed to be a moderately comfortable posture.

For a minute or two the porter seriously debated undressing Mr. Foster: it seemed to him being in bed fully clothed savored somewhat indecency, but on second thought he shook his head.—"Nossuh, 'twould be mo' indecenter was he to git th'owed off the train 'thout no clothes on."

Joe was pledged to secrecy and sent back to his own car. Hop Sure, breathing more easily now that the menace of the moment had been taken care of, busied himself with the task of preparing the drawing-room for the passengers who were due to occupy it out of Anniston.

He worked efficiently and swiftly and just as he completed his task the train flashed by Anniston, then stopped and backed into the city, as is the way of all northbound trains on the Southern Railway.

At two o'clock in the morning they came to a pause under the shed of the Anniston station. The expected couple boarded the train, and much to Hop Sure's relief, no other through passengers came to his car: he had held a horrible dread that there would be someone at Anniston to claim the very much occupied Upper 10.

The whistle blew, the bell rang, the highball was wigwagged and the train pulled slowly out. Epic returned to his car and seated himself on a little stool outside the drawing-room door where he could command full view of Section 10. Once Captain Crosby came through and gazed with dark suspicion upon his porter.

"What you sitting there for?"

"Jus' restin', cap'n."

"Why aren't you in the smoking room? You're usually asleep in there when you're supposed to be on duty."

Hop Sure smiled in friendly fashion. "I has reformed, cap'n. Don't never sleep no mo' when Ise on a run."

"Pfft!" Crosby was skeptical. "I can't figure how you ever earned your reputation as a good porter. I've been watching you, Epic-watching you closely—"

"Listen heah, cap'n—they ain't no need of you watchin' me: honest there ain't. Tha's the mostest thing you ain't got no need to do. Jus' lemme be: I c'n han'le things fine."

"Be sure you do. I won't stand for any foolishness—"

"I knows it, boss man. I suttinly does. I has remembered that ever since us departed away Bummin'ham to-night."

Crosby moved on. Epic favored his back with a grimace of distaste—"That feller is suttinly ebarrassin'. Bet was he to 'scover' 'bout Mistuh Foster I would git kicked out of my job so hahd ancestors would starve to death."

They were yet more than four hours away Atlanta, and Epic was immensely worried. He loved his job for all of the fact that it guaranteed him only sixty-six dollars a month. But it was a job which carried with it worthwhile in the way of tips and social prominence at home. And Epic had been in the service sufficiently long to comprehend the enormity of the offense which he was in the process of committing: it was one of those things which is quite all right when it is all right, and decidedly heinous when it isn't.

Hop Sure was not particularly worried as to what would happen to Mr. Foster when they reached Atlanta. In the first place, there was every likelihood that he would have sobered up sufficiently to be able to navigate himself after a fashion, and the chances were that he would be sick enough to wish himself far away from a train. Besides, they were due in Atlanta at 6:15 and immediately after their arrival in the Terminal Station, Epic's car would be switched into the yards to await the making-up of the New York train of which it was to become a part and which was not due to leave until eight o'clock, Central Time.

Captain Crosby would not be in the yards with the car: Hop Sure would therefore have a free hand and more than an hour of spare time. "An' any man which c'n get a feller into a upper berth c'n sho'ly git him out. One—pull—one pushim' kerflump!"

Seated on his stool at the end of the car, listening to the monotonous thrumming of the wheels and the occasional shrill blast of the locomotive whistle, Mr. Epic Peters became drowsy. The car rocked and rolled as it skirted hills and careened around sharp curves; the clacketyclack-clatter was rhythmic and soothing.... Mr. Peters drifted off into a dreamful doze in which he saw himself attempting to conceal an inebriated Captain Crosby in the firebox of a furnace which somehow resembled an upper berth.

He was awakened from his delicious slumber by the insistent sounding of his buzzer and a strident howling for Hop Sure. There was no need for him to consult the buzzer box—he recognized the somewhat alcoholized voice of Mr. Foster and his first sensation was one of relief that gentleman in question was no longer entirely *hors de combat.*

He climbed the ladder and poked his head in Upper 10. "What you craves, Mistuh Foster?"

"Ice water."

"Yassuh—yassuh, I shuah fetches you a glassful."

"Glassful? I want a barrel."

"Cain't git no barrels, suh. Gits you all the glassfuls which makes up a barrel."

There seemed no limit to the amount of ice water which Mr. Foster could consume. After the sixth trip Hop Sure grew leg-weary, arm-tired and a little dispirited. Too, the gentleman in Lower 10 was becoming querulous.

"What's the matter there, porter?" he inquired.

"What's all the disturbance?"

"'Tain't no disturbance. Jus' a sick gemmun."

"Ain't sick," proclaimed Foster's voice irritably; "jush thirshty."

At length his surpassing thirst was quenched and Epic sank weakly on his stool. The night was dragging by on feet of lead, the progress of the train seemed interminably slow, Epic glanced at his watch every five minutes with all the eager hope of the weary traveler. For the first time in his eight years of service he was learning that there is a vast distance separating Birmingham and Atlanta . . . never before had he longed quite so keenly for a sight of the Georgia metropolis.

Of course Epic realized that there should be a vast deal of satisfaction in the knowledge of a noble deed being nobly done; but just at present that satisfaction was not with him. The moment was too fraught with danger—the immediate future too pregnant with horrid possibility. Hop Sure had a hunch that the end was not yet—or even almost yet. Mr. Foster was in a highly uncertain condition and the animosity of Captain Crosby was too disturbingly genuine. And so, as the train crawled eastward, Epic waited patiently for the inevitable outbreak—waited in the absolute certainty of its arrival. But when it did come, Epic almost pitched through the roof. . . .

Down the length of the car echoed a weird, high-pitched, staccato laugh. There was a brief pause then another peal of rib-tickling laughter. Epic came up standing—"

"Oh Gawd!" he muttered, "It's done turned into a laughin' jag. I was bawn unlucky an' Ise gittin' mo' so ev'y day."

The diagnosis was eminently correct. The full-throated laughter of Mr. Foster continued without intermission. Epic shook his head sadly he started toward the berth—"Laughin'…dawg-gone….Wonder what he thinks is so funny?"

There was certainly nothing funny in the situation that Mr. Epic Peters could discover. This was the ultimate unfortunate twist in a hopeless involement. Epic climbed to the side of the Mr. Foster was sitting bolt upright, braced on his hands, and he was laughing uncontrollably. Hop Sure's face was woefully serious—

"Mistuh Foster," he pleaded, "I begs you to cease that laughin'. They ain't nothin' funny happenin'—hones' they ain't.

Mr. Foster favored his dusky benefactor with a playful dig which almost upset that gentleman. "You haven't any shense of humor, Hop Sure. None wha'shoever. 'Sh very 'scrushiatingly funny. 'Sterribly laughable."

Epic was entirely unable to grasp that point of view, nor did he feel that his inability was due to lack of humorous perception.

"Mistuh Foster, you is shuah fixin' to th'ow us bofe in a hole full of trouble an' then pull the hole in after us. Please suh, leave off advertisin' how happy you is. Folks on the car is gittin' res'less. 'Tain't so easy to sleep on a train nohow an you ain't makin' it no easier."

"Can't bother 'bout other passengers, Hop Sure. Crowd of pesshimists—thash what they are. Need a li'l laughter in their lives…."

"Yassuh—they suttinly does. But they don't need *a lot*."

"'Stoo funny for words, Hop Sure. 'Stoo funny…'snawful peculiar situation…"

"Yassuh—it shuah is awful."

From the other end of the car came a deep bass voice, freighted with sleep and annoyance. "Porter!"

"Yassuh—comin', suh." Epic pitched from his ladder and hastened to answer the summons. "Is you cravin' anythin', suh?"

"Yes. Who is that damned fool that's laughing?"

"Dunno, suh. Jus' some humorous gemmun—tha's all. "

"Tell him to shut up. I can't sleep."

"Ain't it the truth, suh? I cain't either."

"If he don't shut up I'll complain to the conductor."

And from two adjacent berths came fervent echoes—"He's right, porter. Tell that laughing hyena to be quiet."

Epic passed the message to Mr. Foster. That person found in it food for additional mirth. It he explained, quite the funniest thing he had heard. Couldn't understand why folks to sleep anyway. No sense to it . . . guess he could laugh if he wanted to . . . and thereupon proceeded to prove it. His ribaldry rolled down the car corridor, exciting all within earshot to intense irascibility. Hop Sure, failing his efforts to stem the flood of mirth, retired hopelessly to the end of the car where he folded himself up on the tiny stool, his face transfigured with an expression of consuming discomfort.

And it was at this precise juncture that Captain Crosby, Epic's most acute *bête noire*, happened to stroll through the car.

For the two minutes preceding his unwelcome and unheralded arrival, Mr. Foster had been quiet. He was quiet when Crosby entered. But the stout gentleman in Lower 7 was not quiet. He was complaining loudly and bitterly that a decent person was being robbed of a decent night's rest owing to the cachinnations of some blankety-blanked-blank idiot, and if he once got his fingers on the gullet of that person. Crosby frowned as he quizzed Epic.

"What is he kicking about?"

"Don't hardly know, suh. Mebbe his dinner is disagreein' with him."

"Hmm ...anything gone wrong in this car?"

"No *suh*. Nothin' gone no way, let alone wrong."

A large bald head projected between the curtains and a pair of fiery eyes sighted the gold of Crosby's uniform cap.

"Conductor," he bawled. "Come here."

Crosby went. Three minutes later he was at Hop Sure's side again, grim-visaged and menacing. "The man in Lower 7 says someone has been creating a disturbance."

"No . . . he di'n't say that, did he, cap'n?"

"Yes—he did."

"Now ain't that the mos' peculiarest thing."

"Has there been any disorder here?"

"Nossuh. Not ary disorder. Ev'ybody in my car seems puff ec'ly happy. Some of them seems terrible happy."

Crosby frowned: he believed that Epic was evading the issue. "He complains that someone has been laughing loudly."

"Aw cap'n—what anybody would be laughin' at this time of night?"

"Who has been laughing?" Crosby's voice came in a deadly monotone, and Epic experienced a sinking sensation at the knowledge that showdown was imminent. He was all a-tremble for fear the miserable mirthful discord would burst forth. Then would come the discovery of Mr. Foster and the sudden exodus of that gentleman from the train, with its attendant misery and loss of position for Hop Sure. He conscripted an expression of intense innocence and plastered it on his dark countenance.

"Somebody been laughin'?"

"Yes. Who was it?"

Inspiration, born of necessity, came to Mr. Epic Peters.

Desperately he took the plunge.

"Why dawg-gone, Cap'n Crosby—ain't nobody been laughin' in this car'ceptin' me."

"You?" Crosby was frankly astounded."You?"

"Y-y-yassuh. Ise the one."

"*You* have been laughing? What at?"

"Somethin' funny, I reckon. Ise kind of 'flicted thataway, cap'n. I laughs terrible easy."

The Pullman conductor stared. He suspected that something was wrong, but he didn't know what that something was. "You've been laughing?" he repeated dazedly. "Laughing loud enough to wake the car?"

"Nossuh, cap'n; I di'n't wake no car. Mebbe I woke up a few of the gemmun, but I wa'n't meanin' no hahm."

Their eyes clashed: Epic presented a pitiful sight as he made this heroic sacrifice on the altar of his gratitude to Mr. Foster. He knew quite well that in the face of the natural antagonism of Captain Crosby, he was jeopardizing his position with the Pullman Company by thus assuming the responsibility for Mr. Foster's hilarity . . . but he shivered at the prospect of what would happen to that gentleman should he be unceremoniously dumped on some station platform.

Captain Crosby was amazed. He was fairly well convinced that Hop Sure was sober, and despite his dislike of Mr. Peters he respected Epic's record. That an honor-roll porter should be rousing his car with uncalled-for and senseless laughter. . . .

"I don't know what ails you to-night, Epic," the conductor announced grimly, "but whatever is, it promises to get you into trouble."

"Boss man, it does mo' than promise."

"I'm going back to my seat in the next car. One more complaint and I shall make an official report."

"Shuh! Cap'n—I reckon they ain't nobody gwine make no mo' complaints—nossuh. Does anybody crave to complain, I reckon I does my ownse'f."

Crosby disappeared. Hop Sure sank lugubriously upon his seat. His head was aching with pangs of worry. He gazed reproachfully upon the now quiet Upper 10 and reflected that had done his duty nobly. But the role of martyr did not sit well upon the Hopsurean brow...it did seem to him that the whole miserable affair could have been avoided by a display of a trifle more consideration on the part of Mr. Foster.

Five minutes passed—ten—fifteen. No additional evidence of enjoyment came from Upper 10. In the sad heart of the porter was born the hope that Mr. Foster had once again succumbed to sleep. Eventually he strolled out to the platform,where he stood gazing through the glass door upon the dark vista beyond.

And as he looked, the first finger of dawn pierced the velvet mantle and Epic's soul expanded hopefully. A glance at his watch indicated the hour of five. One hour and fifteen minutes more . . . if only Mr. Foster would continue to slumber. . . .

It had been a hectic night, but the moment was approaching when Hop Sure would glory in the knowledge that he had discharged an obligation: in what agony of soul nobody—least of all Mr. Foster—would ever know.

They passed Austell and commenced the last lap of the journey into Atlanta. At length the serried skyline of the city showed in the distance. Never before had Hop Sure been so glad to see the capital of Georgia. Usually, in his capacity of through-run porter, it meant to him only a spot at which one could get passably good coffee. Now it represented surcease from worry.

The houses were closer together-they passed two street cars, city bound, and filled with workmen whose jobs called them to early labor. Then puffing ponderously, the big locomotive pulled through the heart of the city and halted under the big shed of the Terminal Station.

There was the usual exodus of anxious passengers, then the interminable switching back and forth, the congestion in the men's washroom. . .and finally, with Captain Crosby safely out of picture, Epic decided that this was his golden moment to rid the car of Mr. Foster.

He found that gentleman sleeping peacefully, a cherubic smile upon his lips. "All night long you enjoys a good time," reflected Hop Sure, "While I cotches thunder fo' what you does. . . ."

He waked Mr. Foster. That gentleman voiced an ardent craving to be let alone. "But is in Atlanta, boss man. Heah is where you gits off at."

The other struggled to a sitting posture. His twitched with pain and he clasped both to throbbing temples. "Ow!" he commented, "my head aches."

"Yassah. . . .I reckon it do. You is pow'ful lucky nothin' else aches also."

Fortunately Mr. Foster was already dressed. Protesting violently, he clambered down from the berth and sagged up the aisle of the car in of the wake of the anxious Hop Sure. He was sufficiently sober to be conscious of his headache and sufficiently intoxicated to be not entirely miserable.

As they attained the station platform, Hop Sure experienced the first moment of genuine peace which had been his since the departure from Birmingham. The job was done...and the sensation of relief which came to Epic was accompanied by the first twitching of relief that it was perhaps worth a small portion of the travail he had suffered.

Mr. Foster paused. "Where are you taking me, Hop Sure?"

"Ain't takin' you nowheres, Mistuh Foster. Ise done took you all the way heah. We is in Atlanta."

"Atlanta! Oh yes...." Then his face brightened under the impact of a thought. "Atlanta! I've got friends here—out on Peachtree Circle. Think I better go there and drink some coffee. Lots of coffee."

"Yassuh. *Jus'* coffee."

Mr. Foster bent reproachful eyes upon his colored friend. "Don't say it that way, Hop Sure. Don't you know that I'm on the wagon now?"

"Now! Mistuh Foster, you suttinly should of clumb on it yestiddy."

They reached the long flight of steps leading from the station platform to the waiting rooms. There Mr. Foster shook himself loose from the firm grip of the porter and commenced fumbling around in his pockets. Hop Sure watched interestedly.

And then the eyes of Mr. Epic Peters widened with amazement as a slow smile creased the lips of his late charge. The hand of Mr. Foster emerged from Mr. Foster's pocket. In that was an envelope bearing the official stamp of the Southern Railway.

"You know, Hop Sure," commented Mr. Foster, "'Snawful funny thing about last night."

Eyes focused upon the envelope, heart filled bitter misgiving, Hop Sure voiced a question—

"What—what strikes you as bein' so terribly funny, Mistuh Foster?"

"Just this—" Mr. Foster was chuckling—"That darned fool conductor never even asked me for my tickets!"

Traveling Suspenses

EPIC PETERS, eight-year service man, gazed into the startled eyes of the student porter and said, "Hot dam!" Then gently but firmly he placed his hands on the shoulders of the other colored gentleman and caused him to turn slowly. Mr. Peters' survey was meticulously conducted and Mr. Peters' countenance was wreathed in a smile of ineffable bliss, as though he was not yet entirely certain that luck so superb as this should have come to him.

"Dawg-gone!" said he at length. "It suttinly is you, ain't it?"

"Mr. Kenneth Sprigg, of New York, did not appear to share in any measure the delight of his blue-uniformed instructor. In fact, Mr. Sprigg's high-yellow countenance betrayed unmitigated perturbation, and for a few brief moments he contemplated immediate and complete flight. This second meeting with Epic was not at all to the liking of the New York negro, and he would fain have called it a day.

"Mistuh Peters," he vouchsafed respectfully, "I surely has got regretments for what happened night."

"Boy! You says words, but my hearin' ain't keen. You suttinly ain't got no need to do no pologizin' now. All which needs to be did I does betwen heah an' Bumminham."

And in the dissonant vastness of the Pennsylvania Terminal the two negroes stared at each other and knew that they were alone with their feud. To Mr. Peters that knowledge was unutterably delicious, but to Mr. Sprigg it brought a premonition of disaster with himself cast in the disasteree, and only his long-cherished ambition to become a regular Pullman porter deterred himself from immediately divorcing himself from Mr. Peters' proximity.

They stood side by side on the train platform near the vestibule of the Birmingham Pullman of the Piedmont Limited. Above the tintinnabulation from the tremendous underground yards the cacophony of New York traffic—shrieking taxicabs, clanging street cars, roaring subway trains. All about them was the welter of activity which is continual in the great terminal—monster electric engines; clanking cars; long lines of waiting Pullmans; trains halting slowly and disgorging their regiments of eager, tired passengers; currying redcaps; porters; conductors; baggage trucks. From another section came the clatter and clangor of the Long Island Railroad. It was ten o'clock of a New York night and the through sleepers of many southern and western roads were awaiting the arrival of those passengers who desired to count the Morphean embrace in advance of the regular starting hour.

For the first time in his eight years of faithful and eventful service, Epic Peters, of Birmingham, Alabama, was finding that New York is a very good city indeed. Ordinarily Mr. Peters experienced in the great metropolis the uncomfortable sensations commonly attributed to a fish which has been suddenly and unceremoniously removed from its native wetness. Mere crossing of the Mason-Dixon line habitually afflicted Mr. Peters with a sense of futility; it robbed him instantly of his characteristic insouciance and reduced him to a modestly inquisitive condition. In the several years of through running, with New York as the eastern terminus, he had never lost—even in part—his awe of the great city. New York impressed him with the feeling of personal unimportance.

But to-night a miracle had happened. It occurred at a moment when Epic was dog-tired and heavy-eyed and not at all certain that railroading was the vocation for which he had been predestined. At 9:15 that morning he had completed his northbound run on the Limited. There been a restless day at the porters' hotel, where sleep eluded his most passionate courtship, and the prospect of an additional thirty-six hours of arduous duty was entirely lacking in appeal.

Then, to add to his worries, he had been informed that he was to carry with him on the long strenuous return trip a student porter—a dusky individual who had completed his preliminary education in the New York yards under tutelage of a retired veteran and was now the first time to practice berth making and errand running above the thrumming of wheels. That meant additional responsibility and labor. Epic had made certain pertinent inquiries, and was peeved to learn that the student in question was a native of Birmingham who, despite a New York rearing, had selected Birmingham as his station. Much influence had been used in negotiating this delicate task of employment through the New York office with immediate transfer to Birmingham and the southbound run of the Piedmont had been selected as the first step in the final training course.

Wherefore Epic had come on duty with mournful face and heavy heart. But now there stood before him the gentleman who was to take this advanced course in practical portering, and Mr. Peters gazed upon him and knew that the fates were kind indeed and that the ensuing thirty-six hours would be fraught with opportunity for rare and delectable revenge.

"It's Mistuh Kenneth Sprigg," he repeated happily, placing a rather insulting emphasis upon the Mistuh. "Ise a boll weevil if it's anybody else."

Mr. Sprigg gazed into the unrelenting eyes of his tormentor. He knew nothing to say and he said it.

"Mistuh Kenneth Sprigg, of Bumminham an' New Yawk—an' he's learnin' porterin'. Now who would of thought that? I asts you—who would of thought it?"

"Y-y-yassuh." It was Mr. Sprigg's idea that concurrence in any thought of Mr. Peters' was the most advisable policy.

"Yassuh which?"

"Yassuh it is."

"Well, hush my mouf! Ain't you the mos' respectfulest cullud man I ever met up with? An' you is goin' to Bumminham with me?"

"Yassuh."

"On my car?"

"Yassuh."

"With me to learn you how to porter?"

"Uh-huh."

Once again Mr. Peters grinned. And once again his lips uttered the words, "Hot dam!"

Something in the general demeanor of Mr. Peters informed Mr. Sprigg that the journey confronting him was not to be fraught with any degree of happiness—at least so as the party of the second part was concerned. Epic was entirely too ecstatic to suit Kenneth, and Mr. Sprigg had reason to know that there was no love wasted upon him by Epic.

The episode which engendered the enmity between them had occurred about two months previously in The Twinkling Star Restaurant and Cabaret, on One Hundred and Thirty-fifth Street, New York.

There Epic Peters had wandered, resplendent in his best Birmingham regalia, sartorially the peer of any blasé Gothamite.

Circumstances had conspired to give Epic a night's leave in New York and this venture into jazzy heart of the black belt was a dream held. Mr. Peters, lean and tall and gangling, found himself strangely ill at ease; it was not that the patrons were any more well dressed or socially at ease than this adequate representative of Birmingham's colored society, but they did carry with them an air of smug complacency and blatant self-sufficiency which impressed Mr. Peters vastly even while it irked him.

He took a corner table and gazed with keen interest upon the immodestly dressed young damsels who cavorted over the polished surface of the floor to the urge of strident jazz music; and then he learned from an intolerant and amused waiter that the dapper young man two tables removed was originally from Birmingham.

That sounded like home sweet home to Mr. Peters. The person in question was short and slender, and with him were three highly attractive young colored girls and another man. Epic crossed to the table, secure in the knowledge of his own social importance in the metropolis of Alabama. He introduced himself and learned that the name of the ex-Alabaman was Kenneth Sprigg. Epic's face lighted.

"Sprigg! Kenneth Sprigg! Why, dawggone if I don't know yo' brother Eleazer. He lives in Fifth Alley."

And there, quite innocently, was where Mr. Peters slipped. Proclamation of Mr. Sprigg's brother's residence in an alley caused a burst of merriment from Mr. Sprigg's fair companions; they announced that it was quite the snake's hips, the cat's meow and the doggie's wigwag. It was irresistibly amusing—the thought that Kenneth's nearest relative should occupy a dingy cottage in a Birmingham alley. Whereupon Kenneth took diabolical revenge. He invited Epic to join the party and then proceeded—with Machiavellian cleverness—to make life miserable for that ordinarily self-possessed and dignified gentleman.

Within an hour Epic found himself the butt of the others' ribaldry. Despite his most heroic efforts it appeared that everything he did or said was wrong, and each thing funnier than the last. He struggled against it, but his very struggles made him more ridiculous, and the climax came when the check was presented and Kenneth out-fumbled him. Twenty-one dollars and ten cents was the amount of that check; it left Epic with subway fare to the porters' hotel—with just one nickel and a deep and abiding hatred of New York colored society and particularly of the insufferable Kenneth Sprigg whose brother lived in an alley.

Never had Epic been able to understand his intense discomfiture on that night. The insouciance and the pretense of his fellow revelers did not blind him to actualities, and he knew that was just as polished and just as debonair as they.

It was rather that he squirmed under the certainty that they considered themselves better than him; it was their self-esteem which humbled him. Besides, they were in their element and Mr. Peters was not. When he finally parted from them it was with bitter invective on his lips and in his heart a vow that if ever, by any miracle, opportunity presented itself he would make each and every one of them suffer as he himself had been tortured through that long and hectic evening.

And now his opportunity had come. The shoe was most decidedly on the other foot. For this time Mr. Sprigg was face to face with the unknown, and Mr. Peters was where he belonged; a very certain and impressive figure in his dark blue uniform, his silver-touched cap and a service stripe on his left sleeve. Here he represented authority and power and efficiency. He gazed long and earnestly at Kenneth.

"Boy," he announced, "you sho is welcome!"

"'Bout that other night," hazarded Kenneth—"us was just havin' a li'l innocent fun."

"Uh-huh. You sho'ly was. An' what I aims to have with you is mo' of the same. Ise one of the most funnin' men you ever met up with, Mistuh Sprigg. I just craves to show you how much fun I can enjoy."

A young couple, bearing three suitcases, appeared. Mr. Peters inquired as to their reservations and turned to conduct them into the car. The suitcases he relegated to Mr. Sprigg."Tote them luggage, cullud boy," he ordered gruffly. "Show a little service."

The suitcases were heavy, unbelievably heavy. Kenneth struggled manfully with them. Epic chided him upon his awkwardness and explained sweetly to his passengers that they must excuse any dereliction on Kenneth's part. "He's just tryin' out," explained Epic. "He's awful dumb an' seems like he gits dumber all the time; so anything he does wrong you just tell me an' I splains to him."

They thanked Epic and gave him a half dollar. To Kenneth they donated a quarter. Once again on the platform Epic extended his hand.

"Gimme!" he ordered briefly. "Give you which?"

"Them two bits."

"Huh?"

"Gimme them two bits which they give you."

"H-h-how come?"

"Listen at me, Wuthless. When you is stujentin', all the tips I gits is mine an' all you gits belongs to Epic Peters. Now han' it over."

The transfer was made and thereby a status was established. Kenneth Sprigg, inspecting Epic out of the corner of his eye, marveled that he had ever succeeded in destroying the massive assurance of this dignitary. The night at The Twinkling Star was a vague memory which reeked of impossibility. But Mr. Sprigg knew that his immediate task was to placate Mr. Peters—no matter at what cost to pride or dignity.

Other passengers arrived. There was an old lady who required great care and promised to be somewhat of a nuisance with her constant and querulous demands. There was a young mother with lusty-lunged twins. This young matron brought with her two bottles of certified milk, which she demanded be put on ice. There was a gentleman somewhat the worse for a last evening of revelry in New York.

And finally, at a trifle after midnight, the tall and shapely figure of Captain Sandifer, Pullman conductor in charge of the sleepers between New York and Atlanta, descended the stairway and paused to speak with Mr. Peters.

"Hello, Hop Sure," he greeted. "How's tricks?"

"Fine, cap'n—thanky, sir. How you is?"

"Oh, pretty fair—nothing extra. Pretty full car to-night."

"Yassuh. Suttinly ain't nothin' else. By the way, cap'n, I reckon you know us is carryin' a student this trip."

The conductor turned slowly to stare at the wide-open and frightened eyes of Kenneth Sprigg. It was plain that Captain Sandifer did not think very much of him, a fact which did not serve to alleviate the depression which Kenneth was experiencing.

"H'm! What's your name, boy?"

"Sprigg, sir. Kenneth Sprigg."

"Where from?"

"New York."

The faintest suggestion of a smile creased the of the Pullman conductor.

"New York, eh? Well, I reckon Hop Sure can take care of you pretty well."

Epic grinned a golden grin. "Tha's the one. I ain't gwine do nothin' else but. I aims learn him a heap."

Captain Sandifer extended toward Hop Sure a new black leather suitcase. It was a small affair but there was no mistaking its handsomeness.

"Look after this for me until we reach Atlanta,"he requested. "It's a wedding anniversary present for Mrs. Sandifer."

"Yassuh. I sho' will, cap'n."

Sandifer moved down the platform. Hop handed the suitcase to Kenneth. "Look after this heah thing," he ordered.

Kenneth appeared surprised.

"Me?"

"Yes—you. Who you reckon I was talkin' to?"

"But, Mistuh Peters—"

"Don't gimme no back talk. I aims to learn you somethin' on this trip, an' the on'y way you can learn good is by doin' ev'ything that has to be did. Now git busy an' put this heah suitcase in the linen closet."

Kenneth took Epic's keys and disappeared into the car. A few minutes later he was back.

"I put it in," he announced.

"Yeh—an' you took a heap too long 'bout doin' it. Does you crave to be a porter you has to snap into it."

A brief silence fell between them; a silence broken at length by Mr. Sprigg, who was distinctly worried about something.

"What kind of a man is Cap'n Sandifer?" he queried.

"Him? Well, I an' he is awful good frien's, but when it comes to cullud fellers fum New Yawk he's pizen mean."

"How come?"

"He 'lows they is uppity. They ain't nothin' which pleases him better than to 'sterminate one befo' breakfas' ev'y mawnin'. Was I you, I wouldn't go foolin' roun' much where he is at."

Kenneth resolved that he would adopt that particular bit of advice. The portering business appeared to assume new twists with the passing of each moment. Kenneth was already doubtful.

During the half hour immediately prior to their departure from New York, Epic saw to it that Mr. Sprigg was kept continually busy and unrelievedly unhappy. As for himself, he was having a most noble time. All the work which was to be done Kenneth was doing, and when that gave out Epic invented new tasks. Nor did Kenneth contemplate balking; Mr. Peters was a most impressive personage and Kenneth was afraid to incur his wrath. And finally the air was given its final test, the A -a-a-all aboard! was called, and the big train pulled out. For want of something else, Epic set Mr. Sprigg to work cleaning up the vestibule, and then busied him with the task of polishing the nickelware in the room. Through it all Epic hovered nearby, maintaining a running fire of comment on the rigors of a porter's life and Kenneth's inefficiency.

At Manhattan Transfer they dropped the huge electric engine which hauled them from York and took on the mogul which was to them on to Washington. They roared through Newark and settled to the run. Epic and Kenneth seated themselves in the gleaming smoking room.

"Well," announced Hop Sure, "we has started."

Kenneth sighed. "Golly! I shuah am tired."

"Tired? Boy! You ain't stahted to git tired yet. Time you gits to Bumminham you is gwine to be mos' daid."

Mr. Sprigg shivered. He believed Epic.

"Well," he inquired at length—"what next?"

"Nothin'—that is, 'cept keepin' watch."

"Says which?"

"Keepin' watch. You looks out fo' the passengers while I sleeps."

It was on the tip of Mr. Sprigg's tongue to protest, but he permitted the words to die unspoken. Perhaps, after all, he would be better off with his inquisitor asleep; at least Epic asleep could not invent further tortures. And so he sat bolt upright in his seat while Hop Sure quite deliberately made himself comfortable for the night.

At North Philadelphia and West Philadelphia the train paused briefly, and then at Wilmington and Baltimore. Between stations, however, Mr. Peters snored with vast enthusiasm while the student porter stared uncertainly into the night.

Mr. Sprigg felt as though he had embarked upon an enterprise which was fraught with danger and uncertainty. His sensations were not dissimilar to those of the house fly which finds itself enmeshed in the silky strands of a spider's home. All in all, Mr. Sprigg was obsessed by two keen regrets: The first was that he had ever allowed ambition to snare him into the portering profession; the second, that he had attempted to discomfit Mr. Peters on that gala night some two months since, when the porter, sans uniform, had strayed into a certain dusky cabaret on One Hundred and Thirty-fifth Street.

The cold gray finger of dawn punctured the horizon beyond the eastern shore of Maryland as they left Baltimore and roared into the home stretch of their Washington journey. Mr. Sprigg ached in every joint and he yearned for their arrival at the nation's capital, that he might quaff long and steaming drafts of coffee.

For two hours he had contemplated that coffee, until the very word had become a shibboleth to him. But when they did reach Washington he found that he had figured without his host.

The car was switched into the yards; passengers, taking advantage of a four-hour layover, streamed from the car and disappeared into the vast recesses of the Union Station. Hop Sure summoned Mr. Sprigg into the car and directed that he make up the berths.

"B-but, Mistuh Peters," protested the student porter, "I ain't had no breakfast."

"Breakfast?" Epic arched his eyebrows in cleverly simulated surprise. "Why shuah! If you aims to 'commodate yo'se'f to the porterin' business you has got to learn quick how to git along 'thout no breakfas', an' also lunch an' dinner. Sometimes you makes a whole thutty-six hour run' thout ever gittin' no eatments a-tall!"

He moved off. Kenneth gazed sadly after him.

"Where you goin,' Mistuh Peters?"

"Me?" answered the veteran porter. "Ise gwine into the lunch room an' eat me fo' eggs, a big ham steak, some hot cakes an' country sausage, a half a orange an' about th'ee cups of coffee. An' when I comes back I aims to inspec' yo' work. Now git busy—an' don't forget all I has told you."

Kenneth groaned as he groped his way into the car. That ham steak had been the final touch; he felt weak and depressed and unutterably hungry. He moved mournfully into the car and stared in horror at the disheveled interior—berths in various stages of disarray, open suitcases, scraps of paper, magazines, orange peelings, bits of candy boxes. The twins were filling the car with amazingly strident outcries, and at the parent's request Kenneth tended one of them while the young mother looked after the other.

And scarcely had he rid himself of the nursing job and turned his attention to the nearest berth when Captain Sandifer came through. He frowned with dark disapproval upon the disorder.

"What's the matter here, Sprigg? Why isn't this car made up?"

Kenneth was frightened. "Dunno, sir. I ain't hahdly gotten to it yet."

Sandifer snorted.

"Haven't gotten to it? Hop Sure would have finished before this."

"Y-yassuh, but I was—"

"Never mind excuses. Get busy."

Kenneth got. He labored as he had never labored before, but with the ache for coffee and ham steak still the paramount sensation of his body, his fingers were all thumbs and they loaned themselves with ill grace to the unaccustomed tasks; nor did the student porter dare makeshift methods; he was well aware that the inspection of the well-fed Epic Peters would be rigid and merciless; wherefore each separate berth was given scrupulous attention, and when all but two had been finished Mr. Peters strolled into the car and stood in the aisle critically surveying the clumsy but earnest work of the light-complexioned young person who had so confounded him one night a few months back.

The work became increasingly difficult under the severe eye of the veteran porter. Nor did Epic's low-toned soliloquy put Kenneth any more at ease. Mr. Peters stood in the aisle, arms akimbo, and spoke to no one in particular.

"Dunno what's happenin' to me a-tall. Useter be that bacon an' eggs fo' break-fas' was the fondes'thing I was of, but seems like lately that cook has been broilin' the ham steaks so good I cain't hahdly git the bacon habit no mo'. Reckon that ain't unnachel, though; a big slice of sizzlin' ham steak with lots of gravy is kind of appetizin', 'specially does you git the eggs an' the ham steak bofe. An' them biscuits, an' coffee—mm-mmm! An' hot cakes an' country sausage don't never hurt no breakfas' none neither. Looka heah, boy! What you starin' at me fo'? Git you about yo' job."

Kenneth at length completed his berth work and shuffled sadly into the smoking room, where he recoiled from the disorder which greeted his tired eyes—water on the floor, towels, bits of soap, newspapers, cigars and cigarettes—more than slightly used; discarded razor blades. It was with difficulty that Mr. Sprigg conscripted sufficient energy to undertake the colossal task of putting the room to rights.

But at length he was finished. Praying now that he would be permitted to forage for food, he staggered into the body of the car, and there an additional horror smote him hip and thigh. At the far end of the car stood the lean and lanky figure of Epic Peters and between him and Mr. Sprigg was stern and silent reproof in the form of a half dozen sections, recently made up by Kenneth, which had been flung open by the inspecting porter.

Epic swung down the car and informed Mr. Sprigg what he thought of him. "Why, dawg gone yo' hide, cullud boy, you ain't even got the beginnin's of the learnin' of how to make up a car! Lookit them berths the way you done 'em; just look! They ain't ary single one of 'em right. Now fix 'em up as they should ought to be fixed."

"But, Mistuh Peters—"

"Don't but me. Git busy." And then, as an afterthought, "Ain't you cravin' to learn the porterin' business?"

Weary in body and well-nigh broke in spirit, Mr. Kenneth Sprigg bent to his task, and as he worked he marveled again over the night on One Hundred and Thirty-fifth Street when he had made merry at the expense of Mr. Epic Peters. It was inconceivable in the light of the present situation. Mr. Sprigg could not believe that the awkward, embarrassed visitor to The Twinkling Star was the same man who now was master of all he surveyed—all, at the moment, being Mr. Kenneth Sprigg.

At 9:30 Hop Sure conducted his final inspection and pronounced the work adequate. "Of course it's rotten," he amended, "but I reckon it's 'bout all I could espect fum you."

Mr. Sprigg then went in search of food. He found it, and partook without stint. As the second cup of coffee steamed from the outside world into Mr. Sprigg's interior the cosmos brightened and Mr. Sprigg began to believe that, after all, life wasn't so very terrible. When all was said and done he had wrought havoc with Epic's dignity that night in the cabaret; and, too, the portering profession was worth a struggle. He fairly swaggered back to the Pullman, almost convinced once again that he with his New York upbringing was infinitely superior to any Birmingham negro.

Epic saw him coming and Epic knew the signs. The eyes of the star porter narrowed slightly and Mr. Peters grimly determined that his job would be better done before the day reached its end.

"Nawth of Washin'ton," reflected Hop Sure, "is where Kenneth Sprigg belongs at. But ten minutes after us leaves this town we gits to Virginia—an' Virginia is South." A sardonic grin played briefly about the lips of Mr. Peters. The South was his home; it knew him and he knew it. And memory of his first meeting with Mr. Sprigg still rankled.

Precisely at eleven o'clock they pulled out of the Washington Union Station, rolled smoothly along the banks of the Potomac and then crossed into Alexandria. In that brief seventeen minutes of time the entire aspect of the country had altered; perhaps the most abrupt scenery change in all the United States. Seventeen minutes before, they had been in the heart of a hustling, bustling northern city; now they were in a town which was of the Old South—red-brick residences built flush with the sidewalks, quiet streets, gently swaying trees, and then the rolling Virginia countryside, as different from the fields of Maryland as wine is different from water.

The twins demanded attention and Kenneth was pressed into service. He helped unwillingly and when the job was ended Hop Sure took him to task.

"That was rotten," anathematized Epic. "Don't you even know what tact is?" Kenneth shook his head uncertainly. "Nossuh, Mistuh Peters—what is it?"

"Tact," explained Epic, "is something that when you ain't got it, ev'ybody knows you ain't; an' when you has got it, nobody notices."

Mr. Sprigg nodded. "Y-yassuh," he agreed. "I reckon I must ain't."

The big train settled down for its run through the Virginia valley. The cars clanked and rattled as they sped along; the passengers reconciled themselves to a long and tedious day. Mr. Peters and Mr. Sprigg seated themselves side by side in Section 9, which was temporarily vacant. Mr. Peters was not at all satisfied; he had hazed Mr. Sprigg with every device known to the profession; work had been done and redone by the student porter; all tips collected had gone into the capacious pockets of Epic's pants; Mr. Sprigg had been caused to suffer agony of spirit and emptiness of tummy; but Kenneth was still entirely too unbroken to suit the delicate fancy of Hop Sure.

Epic Peters possessed other enemies. In Mr. Peters they found a worthy and generous opponent. But whether they had triumphed over Hop Sure or whether his standard had been borne to victory over them, no one of them had ever robbed him of his priceless dignity. It was that unforgivable sin which Kenneth Sprigg had committed; done it without rime or reason, actuated by unadulterated cussedness.

Wherefore Mr. Peters operated with malice prepense; it was his purpose so to crush and break the spirit of Mr. Sprigg as to render that gentleman's tongue entirely hors de combat before reaching Birmingham, lest the story of The Twinkling Star should leak out and make Epic ridiculous in the eyes of the Eighteenth Street élite.

Thus far Epic had not been signally successful. He had seen Kenneth suffer and squirm, but he well knew that the active flame of enmity still smoldered, awaiting its opportunity to flare openly. Hop Sure's lips compressed into a straight line; the battle with Mr. Sprigg had not been of his own seeking, but since Kenneth had started something, Mr. Peters was quite determined to see that something through to a conclusive finish.

He racked his brain to devise new methods of torture. Kenneth bore each insult and indignity a placid fortitude which enraged Epic. And finally he bethought himself of the handsome black leather suitcase which Captain Sandifer had intrusted to him; the suitcase which was to be taken to Mrs. Sandifer as an anniversary present.

At half-past two in the afternoon the train rolled out from under the long train shed at Charlottesville, Virginia. Epic, his plan matured, dispatched Kenneth to the dining car for a packet of cigarettes. And immediately after Mr. Sprigg disappeared Epic got busy. He hurried to the linen closet and took therefrom Captain Sandifer's black suitcase. This he carried to Section 7. Under one of the seats of that section was a suitcase, and Epic placed Captain Sandifer's under the other. When Kenneth returned to the car with the cigarettes Epic was lolling back comfortably, gazing innocently from the window, and from his expression of contentment Mr. Sprigg gathered no hint of the misery in store.

It was a trifle more than a half hour later, as they were hurtling disdainfully by Rockfish, that Epic turned casually toward the man at his side.

"Well," he asked, "how does the porterin' business like you?"

Kenneth was willing to be agreeable. "Pretty good."

"Ain't findin' it hahder than you espected?"

"Nossuh. I reckon nothin' wuth while don't come easy."

Epic was visibly annoyed. So Kenneth had expected all this, had he?

"This ain't such a hahd trip anyway," volunteered the eight-year service man. "Sometimes it's awful. But us has got a mean conductor along this time. Honest, I'd ruther have a job nussin' a dozen pythoons in a circus than runnin' with Cap'n Sandifer, once he gits peeved."

"Yassuh—reckon so. But he ain't seemed so awful peeved."

"Not yet. But if'n he ever did git—Oh, sweet sufferin' tripe! An' if there's one thing which is don't-liked by that man, it's a cullud boy fum the Nawth. He's so mean when he gits goin' with Nawthern cullud boys that if he happened to have enough appetite he'd eat one each mawnin' fo' breakfas' 'thout salt n'r neither pepper. Yassuh, Mistuh Sprigg, was I you I suttinly would go out of my way to keep Cap'n Sandifer fum gittin' peeved at me. That is, less'n you craves to cash in on yo' life benefrits."

Kenneth was ill at ease. He knew instinctively that he was not popular with the pullman conductor, and Epic's assurances did not cheer him overmuch.

"I ain't doin' nuthin to git him mad, is I?"

"Nothin' 'cept bein' wuthless." Epic paused, and then, in a matter-of-fact voice, "You is keepin' yo' eye on that suitcase of hisn, ain't you?"

"Which suitcase?"

"Which suitcase? Well, will you listen at that? I reckon you has plumb forgot the suitcase he brung with him to the train las' night an' said was for his weddin's anniversary present. I reckon you is so dumb you don't remember that, huh?"

Kenneth nodded slowly.

"Yeah—I does kind of recall. But I has been so busy. It's in the linen chist all right."

"Yeh? Is you shuah?"

"Suttinly. How could it git to be elsewhere?"

"Is you askin' me somethin'? How does anything come to git to be elsewheres? Pussonally I ain't got no int'rust in that suitcase. But I does say this—las' time I sent you to the linen closet you forgot to lock it; an' I ain't promisin' nothin' to nobody 'bout nothin' which was there."

Kenneth was not at all worried, but he decided to make assurance trebly sure. Wherefore he rose and sauntered down the aisle of the car, bearing in his hand the bunch of keys which Epic loaned him. Mr. Peters pretended to gaze from the window, but from the corner of his eye he closely watched the tableau.

It was worth watching. Mr. Sprigg blithely opened the door of the tiny compartment. Then he became rigid, his eyes seemed about to pop from his head, and his jaw dropped slowly. With a visible effort he pulled himself together and extended a probing hand. Then his head followed, and all that was visible to Mr. Peters' sardonic stare was the nethermost portion of his anatomy.

A few seconds later Mr. Sprigg's physiognomy reappeared. His face was the color of ashes, and his lip was quivering. He locked the door, braced himself against the partition and staggered in the general direction of Mr. Peters.

Limply Kenneth flopped into the seat beside Epic. The keys clanked onto the seat from nerveless fingers. Mr. Sprigg was breathing audibly. Epic distinguished the horrified words "Oh! Lawsy!"

He turned a mildly inquiring head. "Says which?"

Silence, broken only by the drumming of the cars and a triple blast from the brazen throat of the locomotive as the train rounded a curve. Mr. Peters gazed camly upon the locomotive, regarding with approval the manner in which the steam feathered from the whistle. Then came the voice of Mr. Sprigg, freighted with terror.

"It's gone!"

"Huh?"

"It has."

"Which has what?"

"The suitcase."

Epic frowned. "You says words, Kenneth, but they don't mean nothin'. 'Splain yo'se'f, boy."

"'Tain't my fault," moaned Kenneth.

Epic favored him with a disapproving stare.

"It is," he insisted. "Ev'ythin' which happens on this trip is yo' fault."

Mr. Sprigg laid his hand on Epic's arm as though seeking protection.

"I put it right in the linen closet an' I don't know how come it ain't there, but—"

Epic turned. His eyes opened wide.

"Words what you utters! Is you sayin' that you has went an' lost Cap'n Sandifer's suitcase?"

"N-n-not exactly, Mistuh Peters. It went an' lost itself."

"Great swimmin' gol'fish! Boy! I would suttinly hate to be as close to the grave as what you is."

"Me?"

"Yeh—you. All you lacks is one lily. You don't even need no disease. Cap'n Sandifer is a gun-totin', trigger-itchin' fool, an' stujent porters don't mean nothin' mo' to him than pa'tridges. He shoots 'em on the wing, tha's what he does."

"You is foolin'."

"Oh! I is, is I ? Well, just you wait an' see is it so. Minute he learns you has los' his anniversary wife's present he gits out his six-shooter an' oils it up fo' six-shootin' you fum heah to where the Angel Gabriel toots his trumpet. Golly Moses! Mistuh Sprigg—if you jus' nachelly had to git careless, why did you pick on Cap'n Sandifer?"

Mr. Peters had sought the utter moral rout of his *bête noire*, and now glorious success blessed his efforts. Mr. Sprigg had degenerated into a wide-eyed quivering mass of apprehension.

"Wouldn't really shoot me, would he?"

"He wouldn't do nothin' else."

"But folks don't shoot one another nowadays, Mistuh Peters."

"Tha's what you says. Trouble with you, Useless, is that you ain't never lived in the South. Up Nawth it's diff'ent, which is how come you di'n't die real sudden that night in the cabaret. Does somethin' happen to a gemmun in the South, all he does is to telephone the undertaker fo' latest prices on caskets an' pay up his back dues in the buryin' sassiety. Tha's all. After that he ain't got nothin' to do but wait. Pretty soon he furnishes a home fo' some wanderin' bullet."

Kenneth Sprigg gave thought to the horrible fate in store for him. He was convinced that the portering business was no profession for him, and he knew also that despite certain obvious disadvantages, New York was the city in which he most desired to live. But he was far from New York—and getting farther every minute. In fact, his situation was even more than embarrassing; here he was, imprisoned on a swiftly moving train with the death-dealing conductor and a merciless porter. Cold beads of perspiration stood out on the yellow forehead and Mr. Sprigg was quite certain that the thumping of his heart was drowning out the roar of the wheels.

How long he sat there he never knew; he had settled into a state of horrified coma, from which he was aroused by the voice of Epic Peters.

"Ain't no use of yo' dyin' yet, Mistuh Sprigg. Us is just arrivin' at Monroe an' they is sev'al folks gittin' off heah. Go he'p 'em with their baggage."

Kenneth Sprigg staggered to his feet. Mechanically he consulted his list. The young mother and the twins were getting off at Monroe, and so was the traveling man in Section 1 and the gentleman in Section 7. Kenneth swayed down the aisle of the car and collected the baggage of the departing passengers.

Nor did he notice that among the suitcases which he gathered was the handsome new one belonging to Captain Sandifer which Epic had hidden under one of the seats in Section 7.

Fortunately, too, for Mr. Peters' peace of mind, that personage had forgotten that the man in Section 7 was alighting at Monroe; and he did not bother to inspect the bags which were piled in the vestibule.

At five minutes after four o'clock the train stopped at Monroe; the three adult passengers and the twins departed. Epic remained in the car, letting Kenneth Sprigg attend to the platform duties. On the platform also was Captain Sandifer, and once, as Epic glanced through a car window he saw Kenneth regarding the Pullman conductor with anxious eyes.

At 4:10 the "All aboard!" was shouted; the bell rang, steam hissed and the big train swung slowly ahead. Epic glanced casually from the window—and saw something.

That something which he saw caused a cold hand of fear to tighten about his heart, for there was the handsome suitcase of Captain Sandifer perched on the station platform in solitary grandeur. And the train was moving.

Hop Sure emitted a howl. This was carrying' a joke entirely too far. It was all very well to terrify Kenneth Sprigg with the belief that Sandifer's anniversary present was lost; but actually to lose it was a gray horse of another color.

Epic leaped down the aisle like a wild man, wherefore he missed another little incident which had a very important bearing on the situation. This incident had to do with Captain Sandifer. For a half minute before starting time Sandifer had been eying that suspiciously new suitcase which departing passengers had left behind. It seemed very familiar, and when eventually the train started to move and the suitcase had not been claimed, Captain Sandifer knew that the thing was his.

A great and abiding indignation welled up in his conductorial bosom. From the hour of their departure from New York he had been cognizant of the hazing to which Kenneth Sprigg was being subjected, and thus far he had not interfered; that was a matter for the two porters to settle between themselves. But when that hazing attained the point where he—Captain Sandifer himself—was the unwitting victim, it was entirely too much.

Sandifer thought quickly. He knew porters, and was instantly and grimly determined to punish Hop Sure for his laxness in permitting such condition as this to arise. Sandifer seized the suitcase and swung aboard the train with it. Kenneth Sprigg saw him and dodged into his car. Epic Peters was, at the moment, leaping down the aisle in the vain hope of rescuing the grip and catching the train again. Meanwhile Sandifer dropped the suitcase in the adjoining vestibule and when Epic appeared, wild-eyed, on the platform, the Pullman conductor blocked his passage.

Sandifer was smiling genially, but there was great anger in his heart. His eye transfixed the frightened Mr. Peters and he voiced a question.

"What's your hurry, Hop Sure? Where are you going?"

Epic cast one glance at the flitting scenery and knew he was too late. He shrugged hopelessly.

"Ain't in no hurry, cap'n, 'cause I ain't goin' nowhere."

Sadly he turned away. This indeed was more he had contemplated. No longer was Kenneth Sprigg the solitary victim. He, Epic Peters, had committed an act which boomeranged, and he knew well enough that Sandifer would hold him to a strict accountability. And so, quite reasonably, his rancor turned against the student porter. Logically it was all Kenneth's fault; if he had not ambitioned to become a Pullman porter the incident would not have occurred. Besides, it was Kenneth himself who had put the suitcase from the train.

Epic found Mr. Sprigg seated in the car and plumped down beside him.

"Good-by," he said grimly.

"Huh!" Kenneth was surprised. "Where are you goin'?"

"I ain't goin' nowheres." "But you is."

"Where?"

"That depen's," retorted Hop Sure, "on what kin' of a life you has led."

The grim nuance of Mr. Peters' voice informed Kenneth Sprigg that this was no light and airy persiflage. He inquired for information—and received it.

"An' so," finished Epic, "I has got a hunch that the minute Cap'n Sandifer learns how you went an' lost his anniversary wife's present you is suddenly gwine to become ain't."

Mr. Sprigg's eyes were distended, his slender frame was trembling like a leaf. Too late he remembered the new and shiny suitcase he had put from the train and which, at last glimpse, was unclaimed by departing passengers. He shook his head dazedly.

"B-b-but how come that thing to git under the seat in Section 7?"

"I dunno. Reckon it must of growed legs an' walked there. On'y thing I do know is that you put it off the train with yo' own hands; an' Cap'n Sandifer ain't killed no cullud folks this afternoon yet."

Epic gazed upon his handiwork. Kenneth was a quivering mass of apprehension. But Epic's triumph was tinged with bitterness. The involvement was entirely too thorough to suit him. Captain Sandifer was his friend, but there was no questioning the fact that Sandifer would be stern and relentless when the loss of the suitcase should be discovered.

And just at that moment the Pullman conductor appeared at the lower end of the car. He glimpsed the two porters sitting together, and beckoned to Hop Sure. Mr. Peters struggled to Sandifer's vicinity.

"About that suitcase I bought my wife for a wedding present," said Sandifer; "I suppose you're taking good care of it?"

His gray eyes never wavered from Hop Sure's terrified orbs. Mr. Peters used diplomacy, deferring to the ultimate moment an inevitable show-down.

"Yassuh—I sho'ly ain't doin' nothin' else." Then, laying the predicate for a future shifting of blame—"I an' Kenneth Sprigg bofe."

"That's good. I certainly would hate to have it lost. It would just about ruin me."

"Ruin you? Aw, cap'n—you is foolin'."

"Fooling?" The conductor's eyes snapped; he was deriving some measure of satisfaction from the torture to which he was subjecting Mr. Peters. "I was never more serious in my life. Why, Hop Sure, what do you suppose is in that suitcase?"

"N-nossuh," replied the porter. "What is it?" The conductor lowered his voice to a whisper. "Jewels!"

"Jools?"

"Yes. Three thousand dollars' worth of diamonds and sapphires." "Th'ee thousan'—Oh, my goshness! Cap'n, you ain't meanin' that!"

"I do. I bought them for my wife's anniversary present. We've been married ten years. And if that thing ever got lost—"

He turned away. Alone again, he gave vent to a prolonged chuckle. His work had been well done and Epic had absorbed his fiction about the jewelry without question. As for Mr. Peters, that gentleman kerflumped alongside Mr. Sprigg and groaned.

"Now look what you went an' done, Mistuh Sprigg. Just look!"

"What?" gloomed the frightened porter.

"You not on'y has lost Cap'n Sandifer's anniversary weddin' suitcase but also you has lost th'ee thousan' di'monds which he had in there. He's ruint." He paused a moment. "But he ain't near so ruint as the man is gwine be which put that suitcase offen the train."

At first Kenneth did not believe, fancying that this was a figment of Epic's imagination, an added touch to make his misery more embracing. But Epic spoke too feelingly for Kenneth to entertain his doubts very long. Epic knew that the suitcase was gone; he knew that it contained three thousand dollars' worth of gems—and he made Kenneth believe.

"Wh-what you reckon Cap'n Sandifer is gwine do?" quavered Mr. Sprigg.

"Well—they's two or th'ee ways which he prefers to extinct cullud boys which come from New Yawk an' lose things fo' him. One of them is by carvin', and one is by th'owin' 'em offen the train while us is crossin' a high bridge, but the way he's fondes' of is jus' plain shootin', 'Tain't so awful messy does he plop you right in the heart."

They formed a happy pair as they sat gazing out upon the colorful Virginia landscape. Epic suffered mental agony and Kenneth wallowed in the depths of dank despair. The call buzzer sounded, and Kenneth started to rise, but Epic held him back.

"I'll go," he announced "Mos' likely you'd th'ow some mo' jools offen the train an' git us bofe kilt instead of jus' you."

Epic answered the call. Kenneth stared after him, but Kenneth was entirely too frightened to retain any of his active hatred for the veteran porter. Mr. Peters' own fear of Captain Sandifer was so genuine that it had been communicated to Kenneth Sprigg; but whereas Epic knew precisely what form the conductor's anger would assume, Kenneth, in his unhappy ignorance accepted Epic's postulation of a sudden and complete demise.

Nor was Kenneth anxious to die. He thought enviously of New York and of his many friends; already he had decided unanimously that he was against the South, despite the fact that Birmingham was his birthplace. He was disgusted with the portering business; it was all very well for adventurous persons who relished the spice of continual danger, but for a peaceful, law-abiding jazz-loving colored boy it was no kind of a profession. The train flashed by a station bearing the name of Winesap. Consultation of the Southern Railway folder informed Mr. Sprigg that they were very close to Lynchburg. He shuddered at the ominous name. Why couldn't it have been Pleasantville or Happy Valley?

Meanwhile Mr. Peters had completed the errand demanded by the passenger who summoned him. He passed into the car and by the drawing-room. The shade of the corridor window was up, affording a clear view of the interior. There he glimpsed Captain Sandifer at work upon his reports.

The captain was seated before a little table on which his official bag rested. Papers were spread before him and he was busily engaged entering figures on a report sheet. All of that Epic saw; and he saw something else. He had seen that something many times before; but now, despite the fact that he had been tormenting Kenneth Sprigg, the vision brought no surge of happiness. For there, right beside the Pullman conductor, lay a large and shiny revolver. It was the most prominent thing on the table. Epic closed his eyes and shuddered. Of course Captain Sandifer would never commit homicide, but Epic didn't like the looks of that gun. He knew that the conductor always carried it in his bag—all conductors did—but just at the moment his conscience attributed to all revolvers a nauseating significance.

He lurched down the aisle of the car. Kenneth Sprigg, craving human companionship, joined him. They paused in the vestibule, and just at that moment the buzzer sounded again. Hop Sure poked his head through the door. The arrow below the drawing-room letter had turned.

A summons from Captain Sandifer. A summons into the presence of that revolver. Without hesitation Epic addressed the student porter. "Mistuh Sprigg," he said earnestly, "that call is fum the drawin'-room, an' it's fo' you!"

Kenneth dragged leaden feet toward the drawing-room. He sounded the door buzzer and entered. But he did not see Captain Sandifer; he did not see the report sheets. His eye lighted upon the revolver, the gaping muzzle. And Mr. Kenneth Sprigg did not hesitate. With a polite, "Howdy, cap'n!" he turned, made his exit, and closed the door quite thoroughly. Only one thing did Mr. Sprigg know, and that was that he wasn't going to remain in any room with Captain Sandifer and a revolver.

"Mistuh Peters," he announced firmly, "that call was fo' you!"

Five minutes later Epic returned. "Cap'n Sandifer wanted to know was you crazy, an' I told him yes."

"Well," answered the other man, "you didn't tell so much of a lie, at that."

"He's lookin' fo' you," continued Epic. "I think he wants to find out somethin' 'bout his suitcase."

Kenneth ducked. He gazed from the window and saw that they were swinging through the outskirts of Lynchburg. He wasn't particularly impressed, but he did know that anything was preferable to a train which contained Captain Sandifer and his artillery.

Kenneth Sprigg disappeared. He vanished through the vestibule, headed in the general direction of the day coaches. A hopeful grin decorated Epic's features. The train was slowing down; Epic piled in the vestibule the suitcases of two men due to alight at Lynchburg. They rolled toward the Kemper Street Station, and then, at a crossing, the train paused briefly.

And in that instant Epic Peters was rewarded by a spectacle which filled his heart with thanksgiving. A white-coated figure leaped from the train. It belonged to Mr. Kenneth Sprigg, late Pullman porter, and it was traveling at top speed. Straight toward the open country moved Mr. Sprigg, cleaving the afternoon at a ten-second gait. Epic stared, open-mouthed.

"Golly Moses! Ain't he the runnin'est man!"

Until the train rounded a curve Epic viewed the flight of his late enemy. It was speedy and purposeful; an obvious effort to place a maximum of space between himself and Captain Sandifer in an irreducible minimum of time. And when the train finally did halt at Kemper Street, Mr. Peters was smiling. True, he yet faced the wrath of Captain Sandifer, but that was nothing when weighed against the perfection of his vengeance. Three thousand dollars—that was a mere bagatelle as against this heart balm. Epic even whistled as he trod the platform; he was grinning as he swung aboard the train, and only the faintest tremor of fear smote him as he was again summoned to the drawing-room by the buzzer.

Captain Sandifer was closing up his little grip. Even as Hop Sure entered the room he saw the revolver disappear, the cover come down and the catches snap together. And then Captain Sandifer did something very impressive. Holding Epic's eye with his own he reached under the seat. He produced the missing suitcase—the suitcase which Epic had last seen on the station platform at Monroe.

Sandifer's eyes never left Epic's face. And that face was a study.

Hop Sure's jaw dropped slowly, his eyes popped, his knees sagged. His long narrow head craned forward on a skinny neck, the shoulders hunched and the body bent at the waist. Epic gazed upon the lost treasure as one who has been mesmerized. Amazement, wonder and delirious joy struggled for supremacy.

But Epic was not a person to probe too deeply for causes; physical facts were sufficient for him. His arm shot forward and long slender fingers wrapped around the handle of the suitcase in an affectionate grip.

"Hot dawg!" he breathed fervently. "Jus' look what I has found!"

Sandifer's face went blank. This was not at all as he had planned.

"Found?" he echoed.

"Yassuh." Epic was laughing aloud. He was intoxicated with relief. "I has found yo' suitcase!"

"What do you mean—found it?"

"'Tain't nothin' else, boss man. Of course"—lightly—"you di'n't know it was lost, but I did. Y'see, it was thisaway." Epic, still holding the suitcase, seated himself on the lounge. "I turned this heah thing over to that wuthless, good-fo' nothin' stujent porter, Kenneth Sprigg, an' he went an' lost it. Fust off, he lost it at Monroe, an' I hopped right offen the train an' mos' killed myse'f gittin' it back. Then he went an' lost it again. On'y fa' me, Cap'n Sandifer, you wouldn't have no suitcase to take to yo' anniversary wife a-tall."

The Pullman conductor was staring in amazement. Then the sheer humor of the situation struck him and he grinned. Epic's explanation was irresistibly amusing.

"So you've been taking care of this, eh?"

"Yassuh, I ain't been doin' nothin' else. An' believe me, it was some job! That Kenneth Sprigg is the losin'est man. Gosh! He's the wust I ever did see. He went an' lost yo' suitcase twice, an' the last I seen of him he was busy losin' hisse'f."

"What do you mean—losing himself?"

"Cap'n, I means this: Kenneth Sprigg has gone, went an' depahted. Lemme show you somethin'."

Together they walked the length of the car. Epic unlocked the door of the linen closet and threw it open. He pointed to a coat and a hat hanging disconsolately on a hook.

"See that coat an' hat, cap'n?"

"Yes."

"Them belongs to Kenneth Sprigg," explained Mr. Epic Peters. "They is his resignation."

THE EPIC CURE

EPIC PETERS, Pullman porter superb, sat beside his car and mourned. Up and down the long platform he could see passengers; all manner and shape of passengers—long ones and short ones, genial and grouchy ones, young ones and old ones—but none of them approached the car over which Mr. Peters presided.

The cacophony of the huge Pennsylvania Terminal was relieved by the fairy tinkle of silver coins. A short and pudgy, uncompromisingly black individual answering to the name of Georgie, and who portered the Atlanta car which adjoined that of Mr. Peters, scurried hither and yon with a broad grin on his ebony countenance. The Atlanta car was filling with passengers, and according to the enthusiastic Georgie they were a pleasant and tipful lot.

"One of 'em gimme a dollar," related Georgie, "an' a heap of 'em ginune fo' bits an' 'lowed they would see me ag'in later. How's business with you, Hop Sure?"

The egg-shaped head of the gangling Mr. Peters roved sorrowfully around on the top of an amazingly long neck.

"Rotten, Georgie. Heah us is less'n thutty minutes till leavin' time an' not ary passenger has got on my car."

"Not one?" Georgie was incredulous.

"Nossuh. Not even a li'l piece of one. How much tips I is gwine git this trip wouldn't buy a crease fo' one pants leg. Gosh, Pullman porterin' ain't what it used to be, Georgie. Ise thinkin' of resignin' away fum the service."

"Shuh, Epic—always when money ain't flowin' into yo' pockets you gits solemncholy; an' you the tip-gittin'est man in the Bumminham station. Di'n't I see yo' name on the honor roll in the *Pullman News* las' month? An' di'n't it have a star in front of it?"

"Yeh, but I cain't cash that star, Georgie. An' besides, bofe them gemmun what wrote how good I was said in their letters somethin' like this: 'An' the wonderful part about the service rendered by Epic Peters was that he did it without askin' fo' no tip which I di'n't give him.' Bein' on the honor roll is all right, Georgie, but it don't buy a hungry man no barbecue. I reckon"—bitterly—"that does travel continue to keep up thisaway Ise either got to quit porterin' or else make up my mind to live on the sixty-six dollars a month sal'ry which I gits."

Georgie patted his friend consolingly. "Nemmin' Hop Sure. Does you not git any passengers you puffoms a good night's sleep on yo'se'f."

Georgie hustled away, traveling fast on short legs. Epic's gaze followed enviously. Both of Mr. Peters' hands were plunged into sadly empty pockets. And then his eye caught sight of a personable young gentleman descending the long stairway in the wake of a redcap. A ray of hope punctured the gloom which surrounded Epic's soul.

"Hot diggity dawg!" he soliloquized. "Tha's Mistuh Robert Furness. He's fum Bumminham, an' I suspec' mebbe he's gwine back there."

Epic eyed the young man with proprietary interest. He felt a warm friendliness toward this lone passenger. "To-morrow," reflected Mr. Peters, "is Thanksgivin', an' I an' Mistuh Furness is most prob'ly gwine be alone together with each other all day."

Mr. Furness turned level eyes in Epic's direction. It was quite evident that Hop Sure had the advantage of him, for no sign of recognition appeared in Mr. Furness' glance. It was on the tip of Epic's tongue to inquire after Mrs. Furness, but something gave him pause—some faint remembrance of rumors which had come to him via Birmingham's Eighteenth Street; rumors of discord in the Furness home on Cliff Road.

Epic inspected the purple check. "Drawin'-Room A, cap'n. Right this way. You, redcap! Tote them grips."

The redcap did as bidden, being rewarded with a fifty-cent tip. Mr. Peters eyed his passenger hungrily.

"Is you alone, Mistuh Furness?"

The man looked up in surprise. "You know me?"

"Suttinly I does. Ev'ybody in Bumminham knows Mistuh Robert Furness, suh."

The man smiled slightly. A dollar bill passed from his possession to Epic's. "I'm alone. Please make up the lower."

"Tha's the on'y thing I ain't gwine do nothin' else but." Epic set to work immediately. "Goin' all the way to Bumminham, Mistuh Furness?"

"Yes."

"Have a good trip to New Yawk?"

"No."

Epic made a clucking noise which indicated a sharing of the other's obvious misery. "An' to-morrow is Thanksgivin', ain't it? Reckon us ain't gwine have such a happy Thanksgivin', is we?"

"No."

The lower berth was ready. Epic hoped that. his passenger would experience a comfortable and happy night. Mr. Furness answered somewhat dourly that he didn't expect to.

"What time does you crave to be woke, suh?"

"Not at all. I'll get up when I wake—and eat breakfast in Washington."

"Yassuh—suttinly, Suh. I does that same thing myownse'f. Us don't depart out of Washin'ton till 'leven o'clock."

Epic closed the door and returned to the station platform. The hour for departure approached. Mr. Peters was not quite so despondent as he had been; after all, a dollar was a dollar, and where that came from there were probably others. Hop Sure gazed the length of the Pullman line, and a lilting feminine voice came to his ears.

"Epic Peters!"

He whirled and gazed upon a very young and very beautiful lady.

"Well, hush my mouf, if 'tain't Miss Edith! Where at did you come fum, Miss Edith, an' how long sence you come fum there? You gwine to Bumminlmm?"

"Yes. Goodness, Epic, you look wonderful in that uniform!"

"You is lookin' pretty good yo'se'f, Miss Edith. Golly, how time do change folks! I remember when I used to buttle at yo' house an' you was a li'l gal an'—"

There was a shadow in her eyes. "Things have changed a good bit since then, Epic."

"They suttinly ain't done nothin' else. In them days you wasn't even dreamin' of marryin' Mistuh Robert Furness, was you?"

"No." The monosyllable spoke volumes Epic did some quick thinking, then put out a cautious feeler.

"Drawin'-Room A is done made up, Miss Edith."

She handed him her berth check. "I couldn't get the drawing-room. Someone had it. I'm in Lower 12."

"H'm!"

Hop Sure was wise in his generation. He asked no questions. Miss Edith, whom he idolized, in Lower 12; her handsome young husband in the drawing-room. Thanksgiving Eve.

"Somethin' suttinly is all wrong," reflected Mr. Peters. "These heah ma'ied folks is just nachelly wastin' one entire railroad ticket."

Instinct advised Mr. Peters against mentioning to Miss Edith that the person in the drawing-room was her husband. Something told him that there were possibilities in the situation which might benefit Mr. Peters, and Epic was quite willing to be benefited. Accordingly he escorted Miss Edith to her section, arranged her luggage and nobly refused the dollar she tendered.

"Golly, Miss Edith, I cain't take no money offen you."

"Take it, Epic."

"No'm—it wouldn't seem right, me havin' buttled at yo' house so many yeahs when you was a li'l gal. Cain't take money offen you, Miss Edith."

"Here." She shoved it into his hands. "Don't be foolish."

Epic weakened. "Shuah does hate to do that, Miss Edith. Tell you what: I takes the dollar, but does you need it back, all you has got to do is ask me fo' it."

Epic again reached the station platform. Deep thought creased his forehead. "White folks suttinly is funny. Goshamighty." He strolled toward the spot where Georgie stood.

"Georgie," came the abrupt question, "what does you know 'bout ma'iage?" The shorter negro looked up in surprise. "Says which?"

"What does you know 'bout ma'iage?"

"Boy! Foolish questions what you asks. 'Splain yo'se'f, Hop Sure."

"Means this." Mr. Peters lowered his voice confidentially. "Does you believe in it?"

"In what?"

"Ma'iage."

"Golly, what diff'ence does it make if a feller b'lieves in it? It's somethin' he's got to do. But my 'pinion is that the sooner he quits wukkin' at it the luckier off he is."

"Then"—moodily—"you don't favor it so strong, does you?"

"H'm! Yes—an' no. I reckon it's jus' one of those things ev'y feller has got to try sooner or later—jus' fo' the esperience."

Obviously there was no good counsel to be derived from the pessimistic Georgie, and Epic wandered moodily back to his car. He was convinced that things were wrong. Here were two young folks, married less than three years, and traveling in the same car to the same place—apart from each other. Nice folks too. Miss Edith is the sweetest gal in Bumminham, an' Mistuh Furness seems like an awful swell feller—givin' me a dollar offhand like that. Wisht I could do somethin'."

The Piedmont Limited pulled out for Philadelphia, Baltimore, Washington and points south. Epic Peters curled up in the smoking compartment with his problem. He was convinced that something should be done and that he was the person to do it. Besides, the fact that Thanksgiving came upon the morrow brought forth all the sentimentality in Epic's soul.

The big heavy train roared through the night; came to Epic's ears the somnolent drumming of the wheels, the soothing shriek of the locomotive whistle, the restful lurch and clank of cars. Mr. Peters dozed. He waked briefly at their occasional stops, but when the train reached Washington there were yet only two passengers on his car.

In Washington Mrs. Furness rose and dressed. Epic assisted her in the task of straightening her section, and it happened that he noticed something which her suitcase contained. Ordinarily this would not have caught the porter's eye, but to-day he was in an observing mood. It was nothing more or less than a red gusseted folder, such as lawyers use for carrying legal papers, and it lay in Miss Edith's suitcase on top of all her clothes. Hop Sure found himself wondering what it was doing there; quite unaccountably the thing intrigued his interest. He noticed too, that she handled it rather gingerly, and his own eye strayed toward the door of the drawing room. Suppose Miss Edith knew? Suppose he told her? He shook his head slowly; perhaps he'd wait until they had left Washington.

"I'm going to get breakfast now, Hop Sure."

"Yassum, Miss Edith. Us goes out fum the other level at 'leven o'clock on the sharp."

"I won't get left."

She waved to him and stepped blithely down the platform, her tiny little figure all wrapped in a great fur cloak. "Dawg-gone if she don't look no bigger'n a minute. An' her travelin' all alone by herse'f with a husban' in the drawin' room. Hop Sure Peters, you has got a job to do!"

There was much straightening up inside the car, for the berths had been made down in anticipation of normal travel. Then there was Hop Sure's quest for breakfast, and after that a great deal of switching around. At 9:30 Mr. Robert Furness appeared, spick-and-span, and with an I -want-coffee look in his eyes. A half hour later he returned. He walked with a peculiarly purposeful stride down the aisle of the car and came abruptly to a halt beside Section 12. Hop Sure, inserting ice in the water cooler, followed the direction of Mr. Furness's gaze.

There was no mistaking the object of his scrutiny; it was the highly distinctive suitcase of Mrs. Robert Furness. Mr. Furness gazed at it long and thoughtfully. Then, as turned toward his drawing-room, he paused briefly to speak with Epic.

"Many passengers on the car, porter?"

"Nossuh—passengers is the most things We ain't got none of."

"Four or five?"

"On'y one, 'scusin' yo'se'f."

"One, eh? Traveling man?"

"Nossuh, Mistuh Furness. A lady."

"Ah-h-h! A young lady?"

"You said it, boss man. The beautifulest young lady I ever sot eyes on; all yaller-haired an' li'l an' lonesome on this Thanksgivin' Day. Us-all ought to be terrible thankful fa' all what we has had handed to us this past yeah."

"Pff!"—bitterly. "I'm disgusted with life."

"Shuh, Mistuh Furness, life ain't nothin' to git disgusted with. Be happy— that's my motto. 'Co'se sometimes when travel is light an' tips is lighter, I ain't so singin' bright."

Mr. Furness pressed a dollar bill upon the porter. "Reckon you can get me a cigar and keep the change?"

"I won't do nothin' else, cap'n."

Epic departed. He was gone precisely fourteen minutes. When he returned Robert Furness was in his drawing-room, puffing contentedly upon a cigar of his own.

"Boss man, how come you to send me after a cigar when you got a whole box sittin' right heah?"

"Wanted you to have one. Thanksgiving present from me."

"Well, tickle my toes! If you ain't the thoughtfulest gemmun. Ise the much-obligest cullud boy you ever seen."

Mr. Furness waved his hand with a gesture at once friendly and indicative of a desire for solitude. Hop Sure touched his cap and departed. On the platform, a few minutes before eleven o'clock, Mrs. Furness found him.

She presented a delightful picture in her tiny toque and fur cloak and with her cheeks flushed by the bracing November wind. She chatted amiably with her old friend while that person glanced out of the corner of his eye and discerned that Mrs. Furness was being observed by her husband.

"Travel's awful light, Miss Edith. Ain't got ary passenger 'ceptin' on'y you and one gemmun in the drawin'-room. He's travelin' alone."

"Is he?"

"Yassum. It do seem a terrible shame a young gemmun an' a lady has got to be travelin' alone on Thanksgivin' Day. Now, Miss Edith—"

She laughed ringingly. "I'm afraid you are trying to compromise me, Epic. No—I think I can stand the tedium. Now tell me something about yourself. How long have you been a porter?"

"Eight yeahs, Miss Edith."

"Like it?"

"Tol'able. Sometimes I think it's better'n buttling an' sometimes I think contrariwise. Y' see, us has to count awful pretickler on how much tips does we git, an' when they ain't no passengers, like to-day, f'r instance—No'm, Miss Edith—I wa'n't hintin'; no, ma'am, indeed I wa'n't, I wouldn't take no money offen you, Miss Edith, which I used to wuk fo' yo' folks."

"Just for Thanksgiving, Epic."

"Oh, well, tha's diff'ent."

Eleven o'clock. The air was tested, the A-a-a-a-ll abo-o-o-oard! shouted, and the train moved slowly out of Washington, across the Potomac, through Alexandria and so into the heart of Virginia.

The country lay bare and brown under the late autumnal sun. Hop Sure, having finished an early lunch in the dining car, returned to his Pullman and stood for a moment in the vestibule staring out at the rolling country. They were moving swiftly; past Sideburn and Fairfax and Clifton, and then pausing briefly at Manassas. Leaving there at six minutes after noon, Hop Sure closed his vestibule door and sauntered into the almost empty Pullman. His eye came instantly to rest upon Section 12, and something in the tense attitude of Miss Edith's little figure caused him to hurry forward.

Her suitcase was open, and she raised to Hop Sure's face eyes which were filled with worry.

"Epic? Where were you? I've been ringing and ringing."

"Yassum—I suttinly has."

"Has what?"

"Been right there." The mahogany face of the porter now assumed an expression of solicitude. "What you worryin' 'bout, Miss Edith?"

"Epic—something terrible has happened."

"You ain't sayin' so."

"I am. Oh-h-h, it's gone!"

"Yassum—it shuah am."

"What?"

"I dunno, Miss Edith."

"Where have you been for the last thirty minutes?"

"Gittin' my eatments."

"In this car?"

"No'm. I was in the dinin' car. Y' see, Miss Edith, it's thisaway—"

"Never mind. Epic, when I opened my suitcase this morning did you see a red folder?"

"Di'n't see nothin' else, Miss Edith."

"It has disappeared!"

Hop Sure made a clucking noise indicative of sympathy.

"I've searched the car; on the seats, under the seats. I want you to look in the berth."

The porter made a thorough inspection, turning down both lower and upper berths. "Miss Edith, that thing sho'ly is at some other place but heah."

The girl was pitifully close to tears. "This is terrible. I wouldn't have lost that thing for a thousand dollars."

"What was in it?"

"Letters."

"Shuh! Reckon a pretty lady like you, Miss Edith, c'n get lots mo' letters."

"Oh! It isn't that! I wonder if I can talk to you, Epic?"

"Havin' you talk to me is the fondest thing Ise of. I remember when I useter buttle at yo' house—"

"Epic," she declaimed tragically, "my husband and I are separated."

"Well, wiggle my thumbs!"

"We are going to get a divorce."

"Bofe of you?"

"Yes."

"Miss Edith, I ain't aimin' to be disrespective, it seems like to me that does Mistuh Robert to git divorced away fum you he ain't got his good sense."

"He—he doesn't want to get a divorce, Epic."

"But you said—"

"I'm getting a divorce from him. He's fighting it. I have just been to New York to get some letters which will make it possible for me to divorce him. And, Epic, those letters are in the lost folder."

"Well, close my eyes an' sing me to sleep!" Hop Sure's brain commenced functioning at amazing speed. "Words what you says, Miss Edith, an' ideas which they gives to me."

"I don't understand."

"N'r neither I don't, entire. S 'posin', Miss Edith, that yo' husban' was to git them letters, could you git a divorce away fum him?"

"No-o."

"An' you say he don't want you to do same?"

"Yes."

A beatific smile illuminated Hop Sure's countenance. "Miss Edith—I think I know where yo' letters is at!"

Her face brightened. "Do you mean it?"

"I never was meaner in my life."

"Epic!"

Out of the corner of his eye Hop Sure saw the drawing-room door open. He took position between the young lady and the drawing-room and his voice was low and insistent.

"Look who's comin' out of that drawin'-room, Miss Edith."

Her gasp of astonishment gave proof that she saw. Robert Furness disappeared toward the diner. Hop Sure looked down into her flushed angry face.

"You know my husband?"

"Yassum. He's him, ain't he?"

"Yes. And you think—"

"I thinks just prezac'ly that. Wait a minute, Miss Edith! Where you goin'?"

"I'm going into that drawing-room and get those letters."

"No'm. S'posin' they ain't there? S'posin'—"

"But he must have stolen them. He has sworn he won't let me divorce him. Says it's all foolishness and that those letters don't mean what they say, and of course he—"

"Now listen to me, Miss Edith. I has knowed you ever since you was knee high to a drop of rain, an' I ain't aimin' to let you git caught in no man's drawin'-room."

"But, Epic—"

Hop Sure drew himself erect. "I goes in there an' prospec's around, Miss Edith. Is that folder in there I gits it fo' you."

Her face was radiant. "Oh, Epic! Will you, really?"

"Won't do nothin' else. You jus' sit heah a minute."

Hop Sure disappeared into the drawing-room, closing the door. A great anger welled up in his heart against Mr. Robert Furness. "Committin' burglary on his own wife!" he muttered. "Stealin' her folder while she was eatin' breakfas' in Washin'ton! By goshamighty!"

But the folder was nowhere to be seen. Then, somewhat doubtfully, Hop Sure instituted a more rigid search. He slid Mr. Furness' snitcase out from under the seat, placed it on the lounge, snapped the catches and threw it open. And there, exposed to his gaze, was the missing folder. A long skinny wrist protruded from his cuff as he reached for it.

"Come to papa, li'l folder."

The drawing-room door opened. Hop Sure turned to face the startled eyes of Mr. Robert Furness. Mr. Furness saw the porter, the open suitcase—but he could not see the suddenly sinking heart of Epic Peters, eight-year service man of the Pullman Company.

Epic felt himself slipping. Here was something beyond his calculation. He made a valiant effort to pull himself together, and found himself grinning in a sickly, placating sort of way.

"'Mawnin', Mistuh Furness. 'Mawnin'."

"What are you doing with my suitcase?" The man's voice crackled through the room, cold with fury.

"Yassuh; suttinly am. Just straightened things up a li'l bit, suh."

Mr. Furness' fists were clenched. Hop Sure closed his eyes anticipatively. "One bust an' it's all over. Reckon it won't hurt so awful much. Golly, ain't this a fine way to resign fum the porterin' business!"

"Straightening up, were you? In my suitcase. Where's the conductor?"

"Conductor? Which conductor, Mistuh Furness?"

"Call him."

"Now listen to me, suh. Leave me 'splain—"

"You—"

And then someone else appeared. Hop Sure saw her as she shoved by him and confronted her husband. There was high color in her cheeks and her eyes flamed. She addressed the porter, but her eyes never left the face of the other man.

"Epic, you will keep that folder."

"Yassum."

"And as for you, Robert—"

"Yassum—as fo' him?"

Mr. Robert Furness had, at the moment, less poise than either of the others. "Edith!" he exclaimed; and then again, "Edith!"

"You will not annoy this porter," she said in an icy little voice. "He is an old family servant of ours, and was searching your suitcase at my bidding."

"I don't see what right—"

"And I don't see that this is one particle worse than your burglary of my suit-case."

"Oh. You knew?"

"I didn't know—but I know now. I sent Epic in to find it. You have done a good many things, Robert, but this rather caps the climax. I never believed that you would stoop to—to—larceny."

"I would stoop to anything, dear, if it would prevent your taking the foolish, hasty step you are contemplating."

"I'm the best judge of whether it is foolish or hasty. Epic, give me that folder."

"Heah 'tis, Miss Edith. An' if 1 c'n say somethin', miss, it soht of seems like that you an' tub Robert heah—it bein' Thanksgivin' an' you—all two bofe ought to—"

"That's enough, Epic."

"Yes, Epic." Furness' voice now that of his wife in coolness. "You may perform her robberies, but your good advice is not welcome."

"Now, Mistuh Furness, you know Miss Edith ain't nothin' but a female lady an'—"

"I know it, Epic. God knows I do."

Mrs. Furness vanished with her cherished folder and its content of damning letters. Furness stared moodily after her. Then he sighed.

"Thanksgiving?" he murmured.

"Ain't it the troof, boss man? Anyway, they has got turkey in the dinin' car."

A few minutes later Mrs. Furness went for lunch, but this time she took no chances; folder went with her. Epic stared disconsolately from a vacant section.

"Folks suttinly is peculiar—'specially is they ma'ied to each other. Seems like them two simply ought to make friends to pass the away if not fo' nothin' else."

From the drawing-room Mr. Furness beckoned to the porter.

"She said you were an old family servant."

"Ain't nothin' else, suh."

"What's your name?"

"Epic Peters, suh; but on the run they calls Hop Sure."

Mr. Furness inspected him carefully. "Something tells me, Hop Sure, that we possess a common interest.

"Yassuh—we don't do nothin' else. But just what does you mean, Mistuh Furness?"

"I mean this: I have a hunch that what we both desire more than anything in the world, Hop Sure, is to see Mrs. Furness happy."

"Well, wiggle my brain! Ain't you the mind-readin'est white gemmun in the world!"

"Mrs. Furness is making a very grave error, Sure. I'm speaking to you now confidentially—as an old family servant. She is convicting me on circumstantial evidence."

"No?"

"She is."

"Golly dam! I never did like that thing no how."

"Those letters do not mean what they appear mean. But they are sufficient to win a divorce. I stole them, Hop Sure, to make that divorce impossible. I was desperate; I have tried to talk to her her—to argue—but she won't listen to me. I wish now that I had destroyed those letters when I had my hands on them."

"Ain't it so! What I always does, Mistuh Furness, is to destroy 'em befo' they gits mailed."

Mr. Furness stared reflectively out of the window. "I haven't any undue supply of ego, Hop Sure—but I believe Miss Edith loves me. And I believe that if she cannot get a divorce from me we shall eventually become reconciled. And with those letters—Hop Sure, how far would you go to make Miss Edith happy?"

"How far—Goshamighty, Mistuh Furness, I'd go fum heah to Hoboken fo' that li'l gal! They ain't nothin' I wouldn't do fo' her. Was she to ast me to die fo'her, I'd go right out an' fall kerplunk off the train an' git runned over. Was she to ast me—"

"Very well. Steal those letters from her. Give them to me. Let me destroy them."

Epic Peters stared. His elongated body sagged slightly in the middle. "Pfoo! You suttinly is got the habit of thinkin' hahd things. Me steal that folder?"

"Yes."

"Offen her?"

"Yes."

"An' give it to you?"

"Exactly."

"Is you shuah, boss man, that you ain't forgotten somethin'?"

"Forgotten?"

"Uh-huh' You also don't want me to murder nobody, does you? Or wreck the train? Or steal some jools? Man—this heah job what you thinks up fo' me to do is plumb pestiferous."

"But you said you'd die for her. You said—"

"Golly Moses! I wa'n't cravin' fo' you to take me so se'ious."

"And you won't!"

"'Tain't 'won't,' Mistuh Furness; honest it ain't. I just cain't. My sperrit is willin', but, suh, you don't know half how weak these heah flesh is."

Mr. Robert Furness appeared considerably depressed. "Think it over, Hop Sure. You'll see things my way eventually. And if you change your mind, just bring the folder to me. I'll protect you—and I'll see, too, that it is made financially worth your while."

"Wuth while! Yassuh, thanky, Suh, I got plenty of life insurance a'ready, but I ain't cravin' to collect it."

Mr. Furness sought the diner. A few minutes later Mrs. Furness settled herself in Section 12. Hop Sure stood beside her.

"Miss Edith—you know I wouldn't git pertinent, don't you?"

"Yes, Epic."

"Well, Miss Edith—I been thinkin'; been thinkin' a heap of things; an' one of 'em is this: How come it some folks takes a whole heap of trouble to git ma'ied an' then takes ten times mo' trouble gittin' unma'ied? How come it that when a gal has got a nice husban' she goes aroun' collectin' letters—"

"Epic! No more of that!"

"But, Miss Edith—"

"You are making me angry."

Epic Peters bent over her. "All right, Miss Edith—you just got to git angry, then. I has knowed you ever since you was li'l enough to hide under a dandelion an' I reckon 'twouldn't be the fust time you got peeved at me. Now I pusson'ly b'lieve that Mistuh Furness ain't done nothin' fa' you to get a divorce away fum him fo', an' I think also that was you to go to him an' say, 'Heah I is—now what you gwine do 'bout it?' you'd shuah think mighty quick that you was glad you done it. I knows a heap 'bout Mistuh Furness an'—Now, don't you go to cryin', Miss Edith; cryin' never got nobody nowhere, an' besides I reckon you has done enti'ly too much cryin' right recent."

"But, Epic, I'm so miserable!"

"Huh! I Reckon you think I don't know what misery is? Di'n't a gal most ma'y me one time? An' wa'n't I mis'able when Mistuh Furness found me in his suitcase? An' ain't I mis'able now seein' you-all two folks travelin' all alone on Thanksgivin' Day? An' ain't—"

With a little sigh Mrs. Edith Furness motioned Hop Sure into the opposite seat. "Sit down over there and talk to me, Epic. You're, the first person I've met in months who understands!"

When Robert Furness returned from the dining car forty minutes later he met Epic Peters in the vestibule. Mr. Peters was pondering.

"Have you decided, Hop Sure?"

"Boss man, I ain't decided nothin', an' Ise uncertain 'bout that."

"If you'd get those letters—"

"Ise skeered."

"You're my last hope."

"Yeh, an' Ise got a last hope of my own, Mistuh Furness. I ain't aimin' to lose it."

Mr. Furness turned away. "It's the right thing to do, Hop Sure. You won't regret it."

He moved moodily into the car. Epic stared out at the landscape. He was busy—oh, very busy!—with his thoughts. He wanted—and he feared. He was roused from his reverie when the train paused briefly at Sweetbriar. "Sweetbriar," he reflected sentimentally; "an' Thanksgivin'. Names so pretty, an' them folks so unhappy."

Another hour passed. Mr. Robert Furness stared unseeingly through his drawing-room window.

The twilight hour set in; they flashed by tiny stations: Evington and Otter River and Clarion and Alta Vista. And then above the thrumming of the wheels and the clanking of the cars came the insistent sounding of the door buzzer. He sprang to unlock it. A tall dark figure shoved quickly in; a cloudy face turned toward his.

"Mistuh Furness—I has done it!"

"What?"

"Heah!"

Epic Peters, Pullman porter, extended to Mr. Robert Furness, husband, a red gusseted folder. Mr. Furness emitted an incoherent series of exclamations expressive of intense gratitude. With eager trembling fingers he opened the folder and extracted therefrom a sheaf of letters. He checked them over swiftly and surely.

"They're all here; all here. Hop Sure, I'm grateful. I can't tell you—"

"Boss man, don't you tell me nothin'. This heah ain't no time fo' talk. Does you gimme five minutes fo' reconsiderment, Ise gwine take them letters back again."

"Good. Open that window."

Epic opened it. The chill wind swept into the room, a miniature gale. "Tha's a col' win', Mistuh Furness—but it's hot 'longside of what I feel."

Robert Furness worked efficiently. One by one the letters were torn into tiny bits and consigned in little puffs to the state of Virginia. Epic closed the window and in the dim solitude of the drawing-room the two men faced each other.

"Hop Sure, it's done!"

"Oh, golly I Reckon I am too."

"I promised to stand by you."

"Yeh! I hope you got enough speed."

"I promised you also—"

"Nemmin' that also. I ain't cravin' money."

"Take this. You've earned it." Epic's eyes popped. "Great swimmin' gol'fish! You know how much this is?"

"It isn't half what you deserve. You've made happiness possible for me and for Miss Edith—"

"Yassuh. An' now, 'scusin' me, suh—I craves to git out of heah. Was Miss Edith to catch me talkin' to you—"

The door closed behind him. Mr. Peters stood uncertainly in the aisle of the car, his long narrow body swaying gracefully to the lurching of the train. From Section 12 Mrs. Robert Furness looked up eagerly into the dark face. He bent over her, and lowered his voice confidentially.

"Miss Edith," reported Hop Sure, "I done just what you told me. to."

"You gave him the letters?"

"Yassum. And he tore 'em all up into li'l bits an' th'owed 'em out of the window."

"Did—did he seem happy?"

"Seem? Miss Edith—that man di'n't seem nothin'. He was! An' I—Hey! where you goin' Miss Edith?"

With her hand on the door she turned.

"I am going, Epic, to ask my husband how he dared bribe you to steal those letters."

A slow grin split Epic's countenance. "You suttinly has got funny ideas, Miss Edith. If I was you I wouldn't say nothin' 'bout them letters, an' I repeat it frequent."

THE PORTER MISSING MEN

EPIC PETERS, immaculate in his blue uniform, stood beaming beside his Pullman. He was all smiles and eagerness. "Yassuh, this heah is the New Yawk car. What space, please, suh? Take yo' grips? Lawsy, boss man, tha's the one thing I ain't goin' to do nothin' else but."

The great train shed of the Birmingham Terminal Station rang with a cacophony of escaping steam, fussy switch engines, baggage trucks and chattering passengers. Through the haze of steam and smoke the elongated porter glimpsed the sunshine which streamed down over Jones Valley. He dipped inquisitive fingers into his trousers pockets and fingered the loose change he had already received.

Epic Peters felt that this was to be a profitable trip. How much better it was to be running on the Birmingham Special than on the midnight train which had been the field of his labors for so many years. Plenty of day travel here and greater likelihood of the casual tip. Daytime people wanted favors; at night they merely wished to sleep, and by morning seemed usually to have forgotten that their berths had been made up by a human being.

Seven minutes before train time Cap'n Harrison, the gray-mustached Pullman conductor, walked the length of the train with his reservation cards. He moved past Epic's car back to the observation, and so only Epic saw the two men who walked toward him from the stairway leading up from the passage connecting the station itself with the train platform.

The men were strikingly dissimilar. One was short, slender, wiry and somewhat furtive-eyed. The other was perhaps thirty pounds heavier, flat of face and feature, and he wore a black derby hat and heavy square-toed shoes. They approached Epic, walking very close together. Each man carried a suitcase. One might have judged that they were intimate friends, provided one did not observe too closely. But Mr. Peters was trained to appraise his passengers. He could size them up with uncanny accuracy. He catalogued them in terms of money. An acid-faced maiden lady usually was classified as a dime, single gentlemen of middle age rated anywhere from one to two dollars.

But these men puzzled the veteran Epic. The gangling porter could not quite place them. The smaller of the two walked with a light, catlike tread. His eyes shifted constantly, as though in search of something which he was not particularly anxious to find. The big man, on the other hand, seemed blandly indifferent to everything.

Epic leaned forward and seized their luggage. They followed him up the steps of the Pullman. They announced that they were berthed in Section 6. The porter placed one suitcase under each seat; and as he rose from his knees after the second painstaking operation, he verified a horrid suspicion which had been born the moment he first glimpsed the strangers on the platform. The men were hand-cuffed to each other!

Epic felt a cold chill run up and down his spine. Somehow he was opposed to the sight of criminal and detective, and the thought that they were traveling on his car was not at all appealing. He was determined to have nothing whatever to do with either of them. But he was too filled with his news to keep it long to himself, and he sought the very squat and black person who portered on the observation.

"Keezie, what you reckon I got on my car?"

Keezie was sad. "All the money they is on the train. Honest, Hop Sure, it's gittin' so that a thin dime looks as big to me as a hund'ed-dollar bill."

"Silliment you talks with yo' mouf. You gits all the tips in the world."

"Humph! Reckon you ain't never run on no observation car. Folks tips you fellers on the reg'lar Pullmans, then comes back in my car an' observates. I does all the waitin' on they wants an' you-all pockets the money. Seems to me—"

"Hush expostuatin' so constant, Keezie, an' give me ear. I ast you what you reckon I got on my car?"

"Well, what?"

Hop Sure lowered his voice. "A detective an' a crook!"

Keezie was impressed. "Golla!" he gasped. "Uh-huh. They is han'cuffed each one to the other."

"Honest?"

"Cross my heart an' hope to be bawn a tripe! You come back after us pulls out an' take a look in Section 6. You sees 'em sittin' awful close together. An' b'lieve me, black boy, the most thing I is gwine leave them two fellers is alone!"

The air was tested, the bell of the monster locomotive clanged a warning, the conductor gave his "A-a-a-ll abo-o-ord!" and Epic flung his portable step into the car, mounted the steps and closed his vestibule. The train quivered and moved slowly from the murk of the shed into the brilliant sunshine of a perfect May day.

Epic opened his locker, doffed blue coat and official cap and arrayed himself in the serviceable white coat prescribed by regulations. Ordinarily, he would have settled himself with professional languor to the first stages of his lengthy trip to New York, but now his interest was keyed to the highest pitch by the strange pair in Section 6.

There were, perhaps, fifteen passengers in the car, some few of whom held tickets only to Anniston or Atlanta. Through passengers would undoubtedly board the train at both those cities. Meanwhile, aside from fixing pillows for three travelers, Epic had nothing to do. But he did it with an energy which carried him past Section 6 several times.

Shortly after passing Irondale the two men rose and walked down the aisle of the car toward the smoking room. Epic stared in amazement. The handcuffs had disappeared.

The train was moving at a good forty-mile clip. Epic saw the big man enter the smoking room and the little man lounged nervously in the doorway. The porter made it his business to walk back to the vestibule. The handcuffs were certainly gone. Hop Sure edged his tall figure past the little man in the doorway and experienced a start of terror as five steely fingers closed about his arm.

"George!" snapped a voice, amazingly crisp and harsh for so small a man.

"Y-y-yassuh, boss?"

"Listen to me, George—"

"My name is Epic, boss man. They calls me Hop Sure."

The ghost of a smile flitted bleakly over the thin face of the thin man. "Very well. Now tell me this: Did you notice anything when we got on the train?"

Epic's eyes rolled. "Gosh, mistuh, you asks such funny questions! Co'se I noticed somethin'."

"What?" The word fairly crackled.

"Well," evaded Hop Sure, "I noticed that you was short an' that other gemmun was tall, an' that you-all bofe was in Section 6, an'—"

"Quit stalling! Did you notice the handcuffs?"

"Oh, lawsy! Y-y-yassuh, I sort of remember observin' somethin' of that nature."

"Well"—the words of the little man fell like icicles—"I'll just tell you this much: I'm a detective and I'm carrying that man to Danville, Virginia. If you see him make a move to get away and call me!"

"O-o-o-e-e! Mistuh Cap'n Detective, I reckon you better not trus' me too much. I ain't crazy about criminal geemmun, an'—"

"You do what I say! I can't keep him handcuffed every minute, and I've known of men jmnping from a train while it was moving."

Epic was not at all pleased. It was no part of his scheme to interfere with the law. He hastily made an excuse and departed; but when he returned to that end of the car a few minutes later the little man was in the washroom and the big man was standing near the doorway.

Hop Sure was not quite certain which of the two men he liked better. Perhaps the big one. He at least didn't heave words at one as though they were brickbats. He jerked his head toward Epic. "Hey, porter!"

Mr. Peters was certain that this was an interview he did not crave. Talking to captured criminals was most distinctly not one of his most enjoyable pastimes. "Y-y-yassuh?"

The big gentleman nodded toward the washroom. "That chap been talking to you?"

"Well, suh—"

"Come on now!" There was a twinkle in the big man's eyes. "I'm sure he has been."

"Y-y-yassuh." Certainly there was no harm in admitting the unvarnished truth.

"I thought so." The speaker seemed to find something vastly amusing in the situation. "He's a clever one, he is."

"Ain't it the troof, boss?"

"It certainly is. I suppose he told you he was a detective, carrying me back to Danville, didn't he?"

Epic was embarrassed. "Boss, honest to Gawd, di'n't ask him nothin'."

"You wouldn't have to ask him that, porter. He tried that racket once before. I merely want to warn you not to be fooled—that's all."

Mr. Peters blinked violently. "What you mean—fooled?"

The white gentleman shrugged. "Good Lord, boy, haven't you got a lick of sense? I mean don't let him kid you into thinking he's a detective."

"Huh? He said—"

"Of course he did. He probably told you to keep an eye on me too. Smart boy, Joe is. Then perhaps if you see him getting up in the middle of the night you won't think anything of it, and—"

"I never think when Ise wukkin', cap'n."

"Good enough! But it also is better that you should understand the truth." He turned away and Epic vanished. The dazed porter progressed the length of the car and stationed himself in the forward vestibule, where he might do a bit of thinking. There was a great deal to consider and very little chance to adjust his thoughts. Both men claimed to be detectives; each said the other was a crook. Mr. Peters frowned as he bent himself to the task of considering the proposition.

One thing was sure, if he was forced to choose between the pretensions of the two men, his choice would favor the big one. For one thing, that person looked more like a detective. He was broad-shouldered and confident and he didn't exhibit the nervous jumpiness which marked the little fellow. And besides—Well, what was more natural than that the little man was a captured criminal and that his first move would be to create the impression that he was the detective? The more Epic pondered on the matter, the more convinced he became that it was the big man who represented the law. No bluster there, no harsh commands; just a smiling, easy-going statement of fact. The little man, on the hand, had been rather unpleasant.

Epic was satisfied—in favor of the big man. There seemed to be no other answer. But the more thought he gave the situation the more rapt became his admiration for the clever little criminal who had made first move in the game. Quite a scheme—this creation of the impression that he was a detective. Epic voiced a fervent resolve: "There's just two things I ain't gwine do-an' bofe of 'em is mixin' up with them fellers!"

The train reached Anniston and stopped there for about ten minutes. Shortly after it rolled out of the city, a waiter came through from the diner sounding the first call for luncheon. He was stopped at Section 6 and invited to send a menu card back. Later, the meal was served to large man and small. Epic noticed particularly that they sat side by side and chatted amiably while they ate; They were not handcuffed, but after the meal had been removed and the check paid the handcuffs once again appeared.

Between Anniston and Atlanta the porter had more time to crystallize his conclusions, and there was one fact of which he became absolutely certain—he didn't like the little man. The fellow had bright, ratlike eyes which followed Epic all over the car and made him jumpy. The elongated Pullman servitor wondered what manner of crime he had committed. Bank robbery, most likely, with perhaps a dash of manslaughter. The very thought made Epic shivery and jumpy.

He wandered back to the observation car and discussed the matter with his friend Keezie. That person surveyed Epic superciliously.

"Shuh! Hop Sure, I could of tol' you fum the fust that the big feller was the detective."

"How come you to know so much?"

"I got brains, tha's all. Which of them two is nervous?"

"The li'l one."

"Which tried hardest to make you think he was the law?"

"Li'l feller."

"Which acts mos' like a crook?"

"Same one."

"Sho'ly!" Keezie rubbed the palms of his hands together. "An' there's yo' answer. Fum what you tell me, the big one don't give a good gosh-durn what you think. But the li'l one does. Them small guys is clever, an' if I was you—"

"I wish to goodness you was. Hangin' roun' with detectives an' crooks ain't the fondes' thing I is of."

"Cain't say I blames you." Keezie's eyes narrowed and he stared at his friend. "S'posin' that feller tried to escape, what would you do?"

"Me?" Epic's jaw sagged. "Did you say what would I do?"

"Uh-huh."

"Sweet sufferin' tripe! Troubles what you talk! Man, I wouldn't do nothin' an' I'd keep right on doin' it. Pullman Comp'ny don't pay me to catch folks; I gits paid fo' carryin' 'em."

"I know." Keezie was argumentative. "But you couldn't just sit down an' watch a crim'nal escape."

"The thunder I couldn't!"

"Well, I wouldn't git no law mad at me."

"No, nor I don't want no crooks mad at me neither. Livin' is the most thing I craves to keep on doin', and somethin' tells me that li'l feller is terrible bad medicine."

Epic returned to his own car. The interview with his friend had not proved at all soothing. Keezie always had such foolish thoughts and discussed them so freely! Where did he get the idea that Epic was mixed up in this? What right had he to suggest that the little man might try to escape or that in such a contingency it would be Epic's duty to stop him?

Besides, how would Epic stop the man even if he was so inclined? Gosh! The smile disappeared from the face of the genial porter. He wished that he might have been stricken ill before the start of the run. He even considered claiming illness and insisting on a substitute north of Atlanta. They were close to the Georgia metropolis now; already the train had passed Austell. Pretty soon they'd be in the Atlanta yards, cutting out one car and adding another. Then a brief stop at the Peachtree station. Epic was excruciatingly unhappy.

Many passengers left the train in Atlanta; many more boarded it. The stop consumed ten minutes, during which time there was considerable rush and bustle and excitement; but not so much excitement that Epic Peters failed to see a bit of interesting byplay.

Among those watching on the platform for the Birmingham Special were two large gentlemen. One was dressed in brown and the other in blue. Their eyes were hard and their faces were harder. Each carried a cheap paper suitcase, and they announced that they held the drawing-room.

Now gentlemen with cheap clothes, loud socks and paper suitcases do not often travel in drawing-rooms. Neither do they, when they enter the Pullman, stare through the car in the obvious effort to catch the eye of someone else. These men did. And Epic saw that they were gazing straight at Section 6.

Epic also noticed that the large man and the small man in Section 6 both stared at the newcomers, and as he settled them in the drawingroom he heard them address a few cryptic remarks to each other:

"See 'em?"

"Yeh."

"O.K.?"

"You said it!"

That was all. A thoroughly innocuous exchange of meaningless comment—provided, of course, that it was innocuous. But Mr. Peters was firmly convinced that in some way the new arrivals had boarded the train for no good purpose. He was shaking his head as he returned to the platform.

"Fust it's bad," he murmured, "an' then it gits terrible. Durned if this porterin' business ain't too much fo' me."

His curiosity, however, was overpowering; and so, shortly after the train left Atlanta, he sounded the buzzer at the drawing-room door. It was flung open by one of the evil-visaged men.

"You-all gemmun crave some pillows?"

"No!"

The door slammed in Epic's face and that colored person backed away abruptly. Things weren't what they ought to be, that was certain. Trouble was brewing and Epic entertained a profound and uncomfortable hunch that he was destined to be not very far from the middle thereof.

He settled in Section 12, which was vacant, and gave himself over to moody and disconcerting thought. Ordinarily the clackety-clack-clack of the wheels soothed him to slumber, but not this afternoon, His senses were very much alert and his nerves jumpy. His mind dwelt upon the detective and his captive, who sat in handcuffed intimacy in Section 6, and then upon the two strangers in Drawing-Room A. There was some sinister connection—Epic had not been a student of human nature for years without learning to read character at a glance.

His speculation drifted in one direction, and Epic didn't relish the direction. Instinct informed him that the two dour-faced men who had boarded the car in Atlanta were there for the express purpose of delivering the ratty little crook from the clutches of the detective. That sounded to him pretty much like action, and Pullman melodrama was one thing toward which Epic entertained a complete and lasting aversion.

His eye sought the little man and noticed that he was staring at the drawing-room. Mr. Peters wondered when the gun play would commence. So long as he admitted trouble to himself, he went the whole route and confessed that he believed it would be awful. He was awakened from his trance by the voice of the waiter from the dining car:

"First call for dinner! First call for dinner in the dining car!"

Detective and criminal ate in their section. The two men from the drawing-room went into the diner. They avoided the eyes of the men in Section 6, but they did so obtrusively. Epic shuddered.

Night was falling; the sun was dropping below the western horizon in a great red ball. Toward the east, the first gray finger of approaching night was manifest and from the foothills of the Blue Ridge Mountains a bit of chill crept into the atmosphere. At 9:30 the train paused briefly at the little town of Seneca, and half an hour later Epic discerned the pale yellow lights from the barracks of Clemson College. Already half the berths in the car had been made down and were occupied by those who sought to while away the tedium of the journey by a lengthy sleep. The Pullman conductor came through the car and paused to speak with the two men from Section 6, who had gone back to the smoking room while Epic prepared upper and lower berths.

The porter motioned to the conductor. "Cap'n," he asked, "where is them two fellers in Section 6 gwine git off at?"

"Danville, Virginia," came the response. "Why?"

"No reason," evaded Epic. "'Ceptin' on'y I never knowed befo' how far Danville was."

No need to consult his time-table. Epic knew the schedule by heart. Train due in Danville at 5:30 in the morning. Running on time and liable to remain so. A long, dreary night stretched ahead, with stops at Greenville, Spartanburg, Gaffney, Gastonia, Charlotte and half a dozen smaller North Carolina towns. It was Epic's hope that he would have sufficient courage to efface himself, yet the situation held him spellbound, as a bird is attracted to the snake which seeks to devour it.

He was' summoned to the drawing-room and ordered to make up both berths. The men went out to the vestibule for a while and returned before the job was finished. They were not nice gentlemen; Epic was positive about that. They talked out of the corners of their mouths and left their sentences half finished.

"On time?" asked one.

"Yassuh, cap'n, us sho is."

"Likely to stay so?"

"Seems prob'le. Special mas' usually don't lose no time."

"Humph!"

"Yassuh."

Epic vanished. The door shut and he heard the lock click. He jerked his head angrily. "Po' white trash!" he muttered. "What business they got in drawin'-rooms?"

The Pullman conductor appeared at the end of the car and beckoned to his porter. Epic joined the elderly captain and for several minutes they carried on a whispered conversation. Epic seemed not particularly pleased, but he finally nodded agreement with very ill grace.

When the train pulled out of Greenville at 10:25, the car was quiet. The winking lights of the bustling little city vanished and Epic pussyfooted down the aisle of the car. He glanced into Section 6. The larger of the two men was sitting in the upper berth, but he was not reading. His reading light was dark and Epic breathed his admiration. "That feller is a real detective," he decided. "Sits up yonder in the dark so's the feller underneath will think he has went to sleep. I han's him plenty on his brains."

The ratlike little fellow down below was frankly enjoying himself, or at least giving a good appearance of contented indifference. His berth was blazing and he was poring over the pages of a current magazine. The porter permitted his lip to curl scornfully. "Just let that feller try to get away an' watch the other one light on him like a cat does a mouse! Just watch! That other feller is my kind." He smacked his lips in approval. "Hot ziggity dam!" said Epic. "He's a regalar Sherlock Hones."

Spartanburg appeared. The heavy train stopped briefly; then rumbled on toward the North Carolina line. Inside the car all was quiet. The creaking of joints, the rattle of ceiling lights, the thrumming of wheels on the rails and an occasional warning blast from the locomotive whistle. Epic sat on a little stool at the end of the car, leaned his head against the wall and dozed.

At half past one in the morning the train arrived at Charlotte. Epic stood shivering on the platform for fifteen minutes before the train pulled out, then returned again to the car. He stared down the aisle. A light still burned in 6. The door of the drawing-room was shut. Epic stood uncertainly, then shook his head and retired to the smoking compartment.

After all, perhaps he was wrong; perhaps the two strangers in the drawing-room had no connection whatsoever with the strange pair in Section 6. Certainly wa'n't none of his business nohow. He thought over the situation again and again, and then the gentle swaying of the train got in its work and he dozed, not to wake again until the locomotive sounded the approach to Salisbury at 2:15.

That city was passed. So was Spencer. But between there and High Point something happened.

At about 3:30 o'clock Epic Peters found himself sitting upright in the smoking compartment. His eyes were staring and his nerves were crawling. Instinct informed him that all was not as it should be. He was shivering and large drops of cold perspiration stood out on his forehead. Common sense advised that he remain where he was. Insatiable curiosity caused his long thin legs to uncoil and to carry his loose-jointed body into the car.

His gaze quested instantly to Section 6. He knew then that something had slipped. The light burned in the lower berth, but the curtains were parted. Almost at the same instant he glanced· toward the end of the car.

He didn't see much, but it was enough to cause his heart to pound with terror. He caught a glimpse of two figures supporting a third one. He saw the door of the drawing-room close, not violently, but gently, as though the man closing it feared to rouse any of the passengers.

Epic moved slowly between the rows of silent berths. One glance into Section 6 told the story. The little man had disappeared from the lower berth! Epic knew what that meant. But still—He started to turn away, and as he did so a heavy face was projected over the edge of the upper and he found himself staring into the china-blue eyes of the larger of his two travelers. The man half closed one eye and motioned Epic to climb close to him. Mr. Peters obeyed with vast reluctance.

No sooner had his head appeared over the edge of the upper than he became absolutely certain that he had made a terrible mistake. The big man moved and Epic heard the click of steel. Then his horrified eyes lighted on a handcuff which circled the wrist of the man he called the detective. He followed the chain and saw that the other handcuff was securely locked around the steel bar which runs along the edge of the berth. Epic bobbed his head and started to descend.

"'Scuse me, boss," he said politely but firmly, "I got an idea I don't belong here."

"Stay where you are!" The voice grated harshly.

"Now, cap'n, just listen at me. I got business way off yonder—"

"Don't move!" The big eyes, steely gray now, held Epic's gaze. "Something has happened."

"Man, ain't you sayin' somethin'!"

"Two men just showed up here and stole my prisoner."

"The li'l feller?" Epic bent his head and looked into the lower. "Dawg-bite if they di'n't! What you reckon they wanted with a shrimp like him?"

"Don't try to be funny."

"Boss man, I never felt no less funnier in my whole life. I swear—"

"They came here and slugged me," continued the big man in the upper berth. "Then they took my own handcuffs and attached me to this rail. I can't move."

"Gosh! Wa'n't they careless?"

The cold eyes stared into the frightened orbs of the trembling porter. "You've got to help me."

"Nossuh!" Hop Sure felt that he was well within his rights. "Man, you sho better git you another helper, 'cause I ain't no good a-tall."

"You're going to do what I say, and when I say. I'm handcuffed to this berth." Epic descended abruptly and took three quick steps toward the end of the car. "Ise gwine—"

"Where?"

"To call the cap'n. Conductors tends to things like this. 'Tain't no porter's job."

"Come back!"

The whole conversation had been conducted in soft whispers. This command was no less quiet than the others which had preceded it, but there was a sibilant something in the words which caused Epic to turn. The face into which he stared was far from reassuring.

"You'll stay right here!"

"But, boss man, I jus' aims to git you loose."

"If you move one more step," announced the big man softly, "I'll blast a hole through your carcass!"

"Boss man, please don't git so loose with yo' threats!"

"Then do what I say. I want you; I don't want the conductor. Now listen. You are to sound the buzzer on that drawing-room door. When they open it—"

"—I die! Man, you better shoot me right now, 'cause I ain't flirtin' with them other two fellers."

"Don't try to be flip! You sound that buzzer and tell those two men I say to hurry back here with the keys."

"Keys?" Epic was puzzled. "Which keys?"

"To the handcuffs, idiot!"

"But, gosh, mistuh, how come you to espect—" Then Epic's jaw sagged in earnest and he stared in horror at the man in the upper berth. The shock was so great, so unexpected, that the words came before Epic could stop them. "Then you ain't the detective?"

"Lord, no! My buddies have got that fly cop all trussed up in the drawing-room. They're coming back here to let me loose and we'll jump this rattler at Greensboro."

"Oh, golla! Honest, you wouldn't like Greensboro so much."

"Do what I say! And remember this: One little move, one jump like you were thinking of getting away to call the conductor, and I'll let a real flood of daylight through your spare ribs."

"Y-y-y-you don't got to talk so homicide."

"I mean it! My left hand is cuffed, but my right isn't. And I've got a gun two feet long."

"Mistuh, I wouldn't git you peeved at me fo' nothin'!"

Epic tiptoed apprehensively toward the door of the drawing-room. He was distinctly unhappy. Once he turned and glimpsed the rocklike face of the criminal staring at him from the upper. Epic shuddered. "I done tol' that fool Keezie he wa'n't no detective."

Meanwhile much was happening inside the drawing-room. The two hard-faced strangers who had boarded the train in Atlanta were searching the wiry little detective for the fourth futile time. The captive was smiling cheerfully.

"Tough luck, boys, or else you're not very good searchers."

An ugly muzzle was shoved into his ribs. "Where's that handcuff key?"

"Find it."

"If you don't tell—"

"Now, listen, friends, don't you know you can't scare me with any such fire-cracker stuff? Don't you suppose I know you wouldn't dare pull that trigger? Nix! You'd like to get Wilson off this train, but you ain't willing to do murder for it. So just go ahead with your little game of hide and seek."

He was cool as a block of ice. They threatened him with dire physical suffering and he smiled that threat aside. "You wouldn't waste your time, because you know it wouldn't do you any good. If you ever tried that sort of thing—" His eyes narrowed. "Well, boys, I know a heap nicer things than getting me real peeved at you."

"Where's the key?"

"There you go again, asking me foolish questions. I told you I lost it."

"Like hell you did!"

"Maybe not. I never can just remember—"

"Blah!" The larger of the two men nodded to his companion. They shoved a gag back into the detective's mouth and tied him securely so that he could not reach the buzzer button. They flung open the door.

Epic Peters, standing just outside, jumped as though he had been shot. One powerful hand reached out and wrapped around the arm of the terrified porter. He was jerked inside the room and the door closed. A livid countenance was poked close against Epic's ashen face.

"What were you doing there?"

"Oh, lawsy, I wa'n't doin' nuthin'!"

"Don't lie!"

"Man, did I ever tell the troof, Ise doin' it now." The frightened porter saw the bound and gagged figure of the little detective. He felt ten iron fingers biting into his arm. "I—I suspect this ain't no cullud health resort," he told himself.

The men whispered to each other—then Epic remembered. "Boss mans—"

"Whatcha want?"

"The white gemmun in Section 6 sent me back to ask you-all fo' some key or other."

"Oh, he sent you for it?"

"Y-y-y-yassuh. He says he needs it pow'ful bad."

Lips were put close against his ear. "The key we want is hidden somewhere in that section. We're going out and hunt for it. You're going to help us, and you're going to keep quiet."

"Man, you sho spoke the troof that time!"

One of the men walked very close to Epic so that any wakeful passenger might not notice the gun which was pressed against the quaking ribs of Mr. Peters. But Hop Sure knew the gun was there. His heart was missing every second beat and he felt as though somebody had flung a glass of ice water into his open mouth.

There was little in the situation which appealed to Epic. But if anyone else entertained any idea that it was his duty to take a personal interest in the case, they were doomed to disappointment. During that interminable walk to Section 6, Epic Peters decided that the Pullman Company was almost minus the services of one porter whose name had appeared frequently on the honor roll. Making up berths was one thing; associating intimately with the muzzles of revolvers was distinctly something else again.

At Section 6, one of the men climbed to the upper, where he held a whispered conversation with the handcuffed criminal. The bonds which attached him to the berth were inspected. They subjected the steel rod to a minute scrutiny.

"Nothing to do," announced the handcuffed man, whom they called Wilson, "but get that key. Even if we had a file, we'd wake the whole car working. As it is—"

The gun remained forcefully in Epic's ribs. He was ordered to search the berth. "If you find that key, there's twenty dollars in it for you. If you don't—blooie!"

"Please, boss, I always did hate that blooie thing."

"Quiet! And get busy!"

There was no questioning the efficient earnestness of Epic's search. Every fold of blanket and sheet was tested; the pillowcases were tried; the pillows themselves were slit open. The mattress was treated in a like unceremonious manner. Under the supervision of the man in the upper berth, Epic and the two assistant criminals searched the upholstery. They looked over and under the seats. There wasn't a spot in or near the entire section where a flea might successfully have hidden.

The train stopped at High Point during the search, and later at Greensboro. Epic attended to his usual duties, but always at his side was the hard-boiled white man with the ugly gun. Whatever hope Mr. Peters might have entertained of fleeing into North Carolina was dispelled by this espionage.

When the train left Greensboro the men were frankly desperate. They were one hour and fifteen minutes from Danville and Epic gathered from their conversation that there would in all likelihood be one or two members of the Danville police force at the station to greet the little detective and his quarry.

Epic was thoroughly unhappy. He felt that in the next hour much was destined to happen, and that he wouldn't be very far away when it did. He did not even rebel when ordered to drag the two suitcases from under the section and place them in the lower.

First the suitcase of the detective was opened and its contents dumped on the berth. Every box, every garment, every nook and cranny was searched without avail. Then the suitcase belonging to the criminal—Wilson—was subjected to a rigid hunt in the forlorn hope that the detective might have concealed the key there. A half hour had passed before the three men admitted that they were beaten. One made his way to the drawing-room for a final conference with the little detective.

When he returned there was a whipped look on his face. "If he's got that key, he's swallowed it."

Wilson, in the upper berth, was cursing. "What am I going to do, boys?"

"How do we know?" Everything in the softest of whispers. "Haven't got a file, and if we had, it wouldn't do any good. And there's sure to be dicks at the station in Danville."

"Can't you pry this rod loose?"

"Not a chance. And if it was possible, it'd wake the train."

"And when we get to Danville—"

One of the would-be rescuers made a hopeless, helpless gesture, "Sorry, buddy, but we've done all we can. That bimbo in yonder just outsmarted us. An' it ain't gonna do you no good for us to go to stir with you, is it?"

"No-o, guess not." Wilson was very sad. "You've come across fine. Guess you'd better hop it when we slow down outside Danville. Of course, it's a helluva mess."

Epic gave vent to a sigh of relief. At least his troubles could not last much longer. In fact, he was willing to aid the two men. "Just lemme know when you-all wants to git away, white folks, an' I opens the vestibule door fo' you." They merely growled at him.

Then things happened more quickly. The engineer sounded his whistle. The train started to slow down. Two or three little signal towers flashed past. "Us is gittin' t'ords Danville, boss mens," announced Epic.

They made one last frantic attempt to extract the information from the detective. That man of ice wished them luck and divulged no information. And then, as their train slowed, the two rescuers followed Epic to the platform, watched their chance and leaped into the dull gray dawn. Epic breathed more easily as he watched them vanish into the outskirts of Danville. He hoped that they would continue running until stopped by the Mississippi River. He closed the door of the vestibule and moved back to Section 6.

"Mistuh Wilson," he inquired, "what does you to have me do now?"

"What difference does it make?" growled the detective. "Let the dick loose, I guess."

"I won't do it if you ain't willin', boss."

"I know it. You've been all right, and you can just forget where those other fellows got off, see?"

"Man, I never could remember that."

"Let him loose then. There'll be more like him getting on at Danville, and I'd rather they didn't find him all tied up."

Epic gladly did as he was bidden. The bleak little detective grinned cheerfully at Epic, stretched his cramped muscles and dispatched the porter for the train conductor.

Within five minutes it was arranged that the train was to be held at Danville long enough for Wilson and the detective to dress in order that they might accompany the Danville officers to the city jail.

From the end of the car, Epic watched the detective's approach to Section 6. He saw the little man climb up and converse with Wilson. When he descended, he was stuffing his own gun back into his pocket. Epic was delighted to know that Wilson was no longer armed.

The train snorted to a protesting halt under the shed of the Danville station. One very capable-looking man entered the Pullman and greeted the little detective. "Got him, Joe?"

"Uh-huh. Up yonder."

"No trouble?"

"Not specially."

Epic whistled. "O-o-o-e-e-e!" he told himself. "What a prevarication that gemmun is!"

The detective dressed swiftly and repacked his suitcase. Then, with unruffled calm, he mounted to the upper, produced the handcuff key and unlocked the steel wristlet which attached Wilson to the Pullman.

"Get down, you. And dress, heap quick." Wilson stared in amazement at his captor. He looked at the key. There was an expression of complete befuddlement on his face.

Once dressed, the little detective handcuffed himself to Wilson and they made ready to leave the train. It was then that he summoned Epic to his side. "You porter," he said, "you've got plenty coming to you. Here's twenty to start it off with. I'll write you about the rest."

"Oh, lawsy, cap'n, I never seen so much ginrosity."

"Don't mention it."

A smile grew once again on the face of Epic Peters, Pullman porter. He addressed Wilson, the criminal, in friendly fashion. "Mistuh Wilson," he said, "you shuah 'most got away las' night. You shuah 'most did."

"What do you mean—I 'most did?"

"Well," explained Epic happily, "you remember when you tol' me 'bout bein' locked up yonder an' I said I could fix things? Remember I started for the end of the car an' you tol' me if I didn't come back you'd blow me full of holes?"

"Yes, I remember. But what has that got to do with my escaping?"

"Oh, nothin' much," said Epic. "'Ceptin' on'y that last night this detective gemmun heah give that handcuff key to the Pullman conductor. An' the conductor di'n't want to be woke up at Danville, so he give the key to me an' I put it in my linen locker."

Wilson's face grew sickly. "You—you mean—"

"Uh-huh. I means jus' ezackly that, boss man. Up to the ve'y minute you said you was gwine shoot me, I thought you was the detective who give the key to the conductor an' I was goin' to get it for you."

The unhappy Wilson shook his head. "And I stopped you!"

"Tha's it, boss. I is only tellin' you now, 'cause I want you to understand that Epic Peters always gives service, provided his passengers let him."

THE TRAINED FLEE

EPIC PETERS, Pullman porter, was engaged in the pursuit of vanity. With enormous enthusiasm he polished a pair of overlarge shoes until they fairly glittered. Then he dusted the ultimate speck of dust from his new blue trousers. He was very particular about his linen. The shirt which he selected was of sheer soft material, spotlessly fresh from the laundry and almost free from holes. His collar was as white and high and impeccable as a signboard not yet decorated.

He donned his impressive uniform coat of blue and borrowed a can of silver polish from Sis Callie Flukers' kitchen. For fifteen minutes he devoted himself to the labor of causing each of buttons to attain mirror-like brilliance. He brushed his cap and placed it on his egg-shaped head. With great but pardonable pride he surveyed the ensemble in his mirror.

Thrown back into his eyes was the vision of a tall, somewhat angular negro of not unimpressive proportions. The face was long and narrow, set with a large, genial mouth and acquisitive eyes.

Epic carried himself with military erectness. He moved with the poise and confidence of the man who has accomplished much in the world and has ambitions to accomplish a great deal more. True, his feet were inclined to slue and perhaps to shuffle, but one could not fail to be impressed by the faint touch of professional hauteur which had been acquired during the years of railroad service, proclaimed to the world by the service stripes on Epic's arm.

Mr. Peters studied himself intently. He walked away from the mirror, then turned, posed, and advanced magniloquently toward the polished surface; his countenance transfigured by what he fondly fancied was an irresistible smile. He gestured largely with broad shoulders and tremendous hands. He made motions of a social sort, extending his arm to the touch of an imaginary lady, bowing with exquisite courtesy, smirking broadly. So impressed was Epic Peters with his own elegance that he did not see the door open, nor know that he had a visitor until the cool, admiring voice of Mr. Florian Slappey reached his ears.

"Great wigglin' tripe, Epic, whaffo' does you·cut up all them monkeyshines?"

Epic whirled. Then he grinned somewhat sheepishly as he identified the newcomer.

"Dawg my hide, if it ain't Brother Slappey hisse'f."

"Tha's the one pusson it ain't nobody else but," affirmed Florian. "On'y I never thought I was comin' into no crazy house."

Mr. Peters lounged against the bedstead. "I ain't no mo' crazy than a couple of wolfs, Florian."

"No-o? Then how come you to act so foolish?"

"Practicin'!" proclaimed Epic with engaging candor.

"Fo' what?"

"Wimmin!"

"Goodness goshness Miss Agnes, Epic, when did you git sof' in the haid 'bout feemales?"

"I ain't, Florian; crost my heart an' hope to be bawn a wiener if I am. I ain't ma'ied an' I don't crave to be. But under suttin circumstances—"

"Like which?"

Epic seated himself and nodded Florian to a chair. He welcomed this opportunity to unburden himself. "You know, Florian," he started, "that they has put on a new ve'y de luxe train 'tween Bumminham an' New Yawk?"

"Uh-huh. I has heard tell of it."

"Even so, you don't know' nothin', Brother Slappey. We is solid Pullman, with compartment cars, osservation car, lounge, club car, diner, radio, movies an' ev'y other dawg-gone thing you can imagine."

"What you mean—we?"

"Us. Myse'f an' the Pullman Comp'ny. 'Cause, Florian, I is porterin' on that train!"

"Hot ziggity dam!" exclaimed Florian with rapt enthusiasm. "I'll bet you is happy."

"It's the fondes' job I is of. Nor neither what I tol' you ain't all. There is somethin' else."

"What else?"

Epic glanced all about the room. He dropped his voice to a whisper and craned his neck. "Florian," he murmured, "runnin' on that ve'y train, us has got a lady's maid!"

"No?"

"Yeh! An' oh, sweet mamma! Boy, you ain't never in all yo' life seen such a gal. She's about the color of a mild ten-cent cigar an' she's got eyes as sof' an' gentle as an English bulldog—you know, kind of friendly like. She has class all the way th'oo, an' b'lieve you me, Epic Peters is the feller which notices such things."

"I'll say you does." Florian reflected enviously for a moment. "You has fell fo' her, eh?"

"Golly, no! I ain't never fell fo' no woman, an' don't especk to."

"But why—"

"Goshamighty, Florian, don't you use yo' haid fo' nothin' but to keep yo' ears apart? Ise plumb ashamed of yo' density."

"You said—"

"I said I was practicin' to make Miss Chlorine Garnet understan' what when it comes to men Ise the king an' fo' aces. Tha's all!"

Mr. Slappey's eyes crinkled at the corners. His lips twitched appreciatively. "I see," he observed. "You calc'late that since you has got to railroad fum Bumminham to New Yawk with a good-lookin' cullud gal you might as well let her know that you is an applicatin' papa. That it?"

"You pronounced it explicit, Brother Slappey. I got good intentions t'ords that gal, but Ise everlastin'ly dad-blamed if Epic Peters is gwine sit back an' watch some other Pullman porter stan' ace high with the fust lady's maid on the Bumminham run while he don't git to say nothin' but 'How-d'ye-do!'"

"Right you is," applauded Florian. "You got plenty of persipassity, Epic. Tell me somethin' 'bout her. Where she fum?"

"Atlanta."

"Hot dawg! They grows 'em good in that town."

"You said it." Epic grinned. "An' the funniest thing about it, Florian, is her husban'."

Mr. Slappey blinked violently. "S-s-s-says which?"

"Her husban'. That is, he ain't her husban', but he used to be."

"O-o-o-oh! Tha's diff'ent, Epic. I thought you wouldn't be so foolish in the haid as to flirt with no ma'ied gal."

"I should say not. Chlorine ain't. ma'ied, but she once was. An' tha's what makes this thing so terrible humorous. You see, Florian, her husban' is a waiter on the diner of this ve'y selfsame de luxe train we is on!"

"Oh!" Mr. Slappey seemed particularly lacking in enthusiasm. "What sort of a fellow is he, Epic?"

"Tha's the joke, Brother Slappey. He's the funniest li'l guy you ever looked at in yo' whole life. He's short an' plump an' he's got a face that looks like an apple pie which somebody made fo' las' Chris'mas an' forgot to eat."

"Is you talkin' !"

"Ain't I? Eddie Garnet don't have nothin' to say, an' he says it constant. I has looked him over, an' dawg'd if I can see how Chlorine ever come to make ma'iage with him in the fust place."

"Never can tell about wimmin," observed the astute Mr. Slappey. "They has got a habit of doin' queer things." He stood back and surveyed the gleaming porter admiringly. "You sho does shimmer like the green baryum tree, Epic."

"I reckon I does kind of present myse'f. Chlorine ought to reelize what a man I is."

"I'll say." Mr. Slappey asked a casual question. "How has you an' she been gittin' on?"

The smile vanished from Epic's countenance. His face grew unduly long and his expression serious. "Not so good, Florian—not so awful good—"

"What you mean, 'not so good'?"

"We-e-ell, it seems like she don't pay no 'tention to nothin' on'y her business on the train—lookin' after ladies an' gittin' hat bags an' performin' manicures an' all such as that."

"You mean that she ain't fell fo' you?"

"Uh-huh."

"Well, fo' cryin' out loud! How dumb that gal must be. What you reckon, Brother Peters, is the matter with Chlorine?"

The elongated Pullman porter lowered his voice. "Nuts!" he observed scathingly.

"What you mean, 'nuts'?"

"I got an awful hunch, Florian, that Chlorine is still kind of crazy 'bout her husban'."

"No?"

"Yeh. An' 'tain't nothin' but silliment. Honest, Florian, that feller is six times less than zero. He is jus' a hunk of tripe. He ain't got no face an' he has too much figger. Round like a orange, an' sour. Tha's how come I schum me a scheme."

"What kind of a scheme?"

"Nemmin' what. I tell you when it wuks. But I argufies, Florian, that the trouble with Chlorine is that she cain't see no other man fo' thinkin' of her husban'. I espostulates that once she gits woke up to what a regalar feller I is she is gwine fo'get that two-bit man on the diner."

"Humph! You don't hate yo'se'f some, does you?"

"Why should I? Besides, it ain't no conceitfulness to think Ise mo' attractiver than Eddie Garnet. Also Ise doin' Chlorine a favor."

"How come?"

"'Cause the sooner she forgits Eddie, the better off she is gwine be. He don't pay her no mind whichsoever."

"An' her a pretty gal?"

"Prettier than that. But Eddie don't see nothin' in the world on'y the tips he gits, an' not much of them. Seems like to me it would be crool to let her go on bein' crazy 'bout a guy which ain't payin' her no heed."

Florian shrugged. "Go ahead, Brother Peters. But as fa' me, I says they ain't no woman wuth gittin' into trouble about."

"Who said somethin' 'bout gettin' into trouble?"

"I did," prophesied Florian darkly. "Always when there is two mens an' a gal, there's trouble. An' when one of them fellers used to be the husban' of the gal—"

"Humph! Does that butterball ever fool aroun' me Ise gwine take him 'tween my two fingers—so—an' sqush him—so—an' then step on him—like that!"

"M'm-h'm! You is bad, ain't you!"

"I ain't bad, Florian. Not me. Ise terrible!" Mr. Peters bade his friend farewell and moved with conquering strides toward the Pullman office at the massive terminal station. From there he moved under the cavernous shed, where the cars were being assembled into a de luxe train.

The train had not yet been announced and there was, for the moment, no professional duty to distract Epic's attention. He therefore entered the train and went in search of Chlorine Garnet.

He found her in the lounge, a lonely and delectable figure in her simple gray and a dainty white apron, She was staring through the polished windowpane into the murk and steaminess of the big station. He seated himself near her.

"How-d'ye, Chlorine."

"'Mawnin', Mistuh Peters."

"Whyn't you call me Epic?"

"A'right. Epic." She was utterly indifferent. Mr. Peters leaned forward.

"Is I an' you frien's, Chlorine?"

"Uh-huh. Reckon so."

"Ain't you shuah?"

"P'raps."

Mr. Epic Peters suffered from wounded vanity. The woman simply didn't know that he existed. He meant nothing to her. But the porter was too adroit to show his irritation.

"Chlorine," he whispered, "I craves to he'p you out."

She flashed him a sharp glance—the first real interest she had ever betrayed in the gangling gentleman. Epic felt a warm glow at this indication that his scheme gave promise of working successfully.

"He'p me out of which?"

"Yo' troubles."

"Who says I got troubles?"

"Nobody says it, Chlorine, but I can see it."

"You got good eyes!"

"I'll say I has. Now listen, gal. I ain't been porterin' all these yeahs 'thout learnin' somethin' 'bout folks. They don't got to tell me ev'ythin'. An' tha's why I know all 'bout you."

No doubt of the fact that she was genuinely interested. It occurred to her that this tall, somewhat self-opinionated porter was really a very human sort of person. He was so sympathetic!

"Wh-what kind of troubles has I got, Epic?"

"Husban' troubles."

She gazed at him, round-eyed. "Understandin' feller what you is. I never seen the beat!"

"An' you never will," indorsed Epic pridefully. "Now listen, Chlorine. I uses my eyes to see with an' my brains to think thoughts. An' I has happened to observe that, divorce or no divorce, you remains crazy 'bout that waitin' husban' of yourn. Is that true?

A slow blush suffused her cheeks. "I ain't sayin' it ain't, Epic."

"Well, is it or is it ain't?"

"'Tis," she breathed.

"Hot diggity dawg! Then that makes it easy!"

"What?"

"Fo' me to he'p you win him back."

She raised blazing eyes to Epic's face and he saw that he had won. No danger that she would ever again regard him as a lay figure. Her interest had been aroused, and Mr. Peters knew that the first great move in his planned conquest of the fair Chlorine had been blessed with unqualified success.

The trouble from the first had been that in her eyes he was of no more importance than the water cooler or the fire ax. And when a man seeks to impress a woman with his general desirability he must first convince her that he is a man. That feat Epic had now accomplished. He refused to consider that, once she had acknowledged the fact that he was alive, she could continue to adore the sour, surly, pudgy husband who had discarded her, didn't want her, and refused to favor her with a single friendly glance. Epic felt very well pleased with himself, and he stage-managed things beautifully. He glanced at his wrist watch and rose hastily.

"Passengers 'bout due to git aboard, Chlorine," he said. "I got to git busy. See you after we pulls out of Bumminham."

She stared gratefully after the lean and hungry figure. Queer she'd never noticed what a marvelously friendly man Epic was. So sympathetic an' understandin', an' all such as that. Han'some, too, an' a regular star railroad feller.

For the ensuing hour there was much work for both. Passengers settling themselves for the long journey from Birmingham to New York; passengers requiring hat bags and time-tables and information and pillows; passengers desiring to know when to expect the first call for lunch and whether the diner was ahead or back, and if Epic knew whether the observation platform was crowded, and why there were so many curves on the track between Birmingham and Atlanta.

Epic performed his duties with a detached professionalism. Chlorine, new to railroading, took everything to heart. But halfway to Anniston they managed to meet in one of the Pullman vestibules and Mrs. Garnet did not hesitate to come down to brass tacks. "You was sayin', Epic, 'bout how you could git me and my husban' back together again with each other."

"I on'y said I got a scheme, Chlorine. I cain't promise it's gwine wuk, but it always does."

"Ain't you the wonderfules' man!"

"Oh, Ise pretty good." Epic regarded her gravely. "Fust of all I has got to git a li'l inflomation. Why did you an' Eddie git a divorce?"

"We got it on account of mutual consent."

"I see. But what I mean is: Who mutual consented the mos' enthusiastic?"

She hung her head. "Me."

"Why?"

"Well, it seemed like he was away fum home too much, an'—oh, Mistuh Peters, you ain't never been ma'ied, has you?"

"No, thank gosh!"

"Then you don't know. I thought I was tired of Eddie, an' after us got separated away fum each other I knowed I was wrong. Ever since then I has tried to git him to make another ma'iage with me, but he don't say nothin' but fooey! My heart is plumb broke."

"You is crazy 'bout him?"

"Awful crazy," she confessed. "In fack, that was how come I to take up railroadin'. I found out that he was gwine git a car on this train on account of his seniorishness, so I applicated fo' the position of lady's maid."

"An' things ain't wukkin' out so good?"

"They is terrible, Epic. Fierce! Ev'y time I see Eddie he disdains me."

"Po' fish!"

"He ain't no fish. Honest, he ain't. He's the sweetest, darlin'est man, an'—"

"Pff! Foolishment what you talks with yo' mouf. I reckon you has tried to flirt with him an' let him know that he is the craziest man you is about—ain't that the truth?"

"Uh-huh. Sho is."

"Gal, you acks nonsensical. Now if you craves to hear my plan—"

"I does, Epic. Cross my heart an' hope to be bawn a tapioca puddin' if I don't."

"A'right. I tells you fust somethin' 'bout men. The way fo' a gal to int'rest them in herse'f is to make 'em think that other fellers is crazy 'bout her. She's got to git lots of attentions an' then the feller which she is really int'rested in gits the idea that she must be pretty good."

"You talks so brainy!"

"Yo' job is to make Eddie jealous. Right now he's ridin' high, wide an' han'some. He knows he can grab you off any time he says the word. Tha's wrong, li'l gal—plumb wrong. You got to show him that he don' count no mo' than a bottle of ketchup when the desert is served. You got to preten' to be crazy 'bout another man."

"I—I ain't got no other man."

"Yes you has."

"Who?"

Mr. Peters placed his right hand over his heart. "Me!"

"Oh, Epic, how ginrous you is."

"'Tain't nothin'. On'y you got to 'gree to do this thing right. Whenever Eddie is aroun' us has got to ack love foolish. We got to hol' han's an' look shy an' all such as that. Ain't no use doin' nothin' halfway."

"Sho ain't. But you reckon it'll wuk?"

Epic smiled knowingly. He was regarding himself with envy. Once she entered into his scheme he'd make her forget the rotund Eddie. Reckon he knew something about Don Juaning! Humph! Swell chance Eddie would have to be remembered when he—Epic Peters—was turning loose the full power of his charm.

"It sho will!" he prophesied enthusiastically. From the Pullman came a hoarse, toneless voice:

"Fust call fo' lunch in the dinin' car! Fust call fo' lunch in the dinin' car!"

The voice was approaching the vestibule. Chlorine trembled violently. She placed a fluttering hand on Epic's arm.

"Tha's my honey boy! Tha's him pronouncin' lunch."

"You aims to start right away?"

"Yeh."

"Then gimme yo' han' an' look crazy!"

The Pullman door swung back. A short, round figure clad in official white appeared. Eddie Garnet opened his lips again to announce lunch, and his eyes fell upon a rather startling tableau.

Standing very close together he glimpsed the tall figure of Epic Peters and the very delicious form of his ex-wife. One of her hands was imprisoned between both of Epic's and words came distinctly to the horrified ears of Eddie Garnet.

Said Epic, rapturously: "Such swellegant eyes you got, Chlorine honey. I ain't never seen none such."

"Nor neither you ain't got such bad ones yo'se'f, Epic. Sof' an' gentle like a goat."

Mr. Garnet stamped his foot and as he passed into the next car Epic heard a word which he fancied had not been culled from the lunch menu of the day.

"Tripe!' exploded Eddie.

Epic grinned delightedly. "Golly Moses, Chlorine, did you see how it wukked?"

She was radiant.. "I'll say it did. Tha's the fust time I ever saw Eddie jealous."

"An' you is suttin my scheme is good!"

"Posolute."

"You is willin' to play the game right?"

"Epic," she announced gratefully, "Ise gwine play the game so right even you—let alone Eddie—ain't hahdly gwine know it ain't ginuwine."

"Sweet patootie! Now you is pitchin'."

When Eddie returned toward the diner the couple in the vestibule seemed trebly ardent. Eddie's soul seemed to shrivel in his ample bosom. He was a tense and thoughtful colored gentleman as he swayed back up the aisle to assume his duties as waiter.

Epic and Chlorine separated; the latter jubilant over her memory of Eddie's reaction to the first move in her campaign, Epic grinning to himself in unholy glee.

Mr. Peters was not lacking in personal confidence. He had bitterly resented the fact that he, as senior porter on the best train boasted by the road, should be treated by the only lady's maid with superlative indifference. Now she'd notice him all right. He had been given full and free permission to make love. At first she'd think of her husband, but Epic was certain that after a while Eddie Garnet would become of less importance and he himself would take the spotlight position.

Great stuff! Chlorine promised to do much to lighten the tedium of the regular trips between New York and Birmingham. She injected an atmosphere of romance which Epic's adventurous nature craved. Feminine contact was the one thing he had always envied his city-dwelling friends. No cullud gals on Southern Pullmans. This new lady's maid business had changed the entire complexion of affairs. It was nothing less than manna for Pullman porters.

He did not see Chlorine again until mid-afternoon. Then it was to invite her to dine with him. Her eyes flashed with enthusiasm.

"Right in the car with Eddie?"

"Uh-huh. An' when he sees us makin' cow eyes at each other he's sho gwine git jealous."

Epic was right. He was more than right. The fat little ex-husband glowered at his one-time wife and her new sweetie. He hated Epic. Mr. Peters was tall and easy and obviously absorbed in Chlorine. As for the colored lady, if she remembered that there was a man in the diner who had once been related to her by marriage, she gave no indication of that fact.

She was a natural actress and she met every affectionate glance of Epic's more than halfway. Eddie Garnet, glowering from his end of the car, plumbed the nethermost depths of despair and cursed the modernistic tendencies of railroad officials which had caused colored girls to take up railroading.

The car on which Eddie served as waiter was dropped in Charlotte. For the balance of the trip to New York, Chlorine seemed somewhat averse to playing the delightful little game which Epic had invented, and that adroit gentleman was forced to make haste slowly. However, she could not repulse his very friendly advances, and she did consent to accompany him that night to a cabaret in Harlem where they ate much and danced frequently. She was light as a feather and gay as a lark.

On the return trip to Birmingham, Epic eagerly inspected the diner which they picked up at Charlotte. Eddie was not in the crew; it was a different car. But on the next return trip it was Eddie's diner which was attached to the train in the very early hours of the morning.

By that time Epic and Chlorine were buddies. It was easy enough now to pretend affection. Chlorine had learned a great deal. Perhaps for the benefit of her unhappy ex-husband, perhaps for her own sake, she threw herself into the role of adoring lady friend with whole-souled enthusiasm. It was really refreshing to watch Eddie suffer. Just before arriving in Birmingham, Chlorine pulled Epic aside.

"How you think things is goin'?" she inquired.

"Gal," he retorted with perfect honesty, "they couldn't be better."

"You reckon Eddie is jealous?"

"Jealous! Why, that feller is so crazy with jealousy he mos' bit the table when us et together."

She closed her eyes ecstatically. "I reckon Ise showin' him that I don't think he's the on'iest man in the world."

"Uh-huh," said Epic. "I reckon you is."

Eddie's diner was part of their train leaving Birmingham. Naturally there was nothing bright or sunny about Mr. Garnet's appearance, but this day it seemed as though a thunderstorm had hit him right in the face. More than once he left the diner to ramble throught the train, and on several such trips he saw Epic and Chlorine in earnest discussion of things in general. The girl was highly elated.

"Ain't he sore?" she asked.

"He ain't nothin' else. An' why shouldn't he be; lettin' loose of a swell gal like you an' then gittin' to think that somebody else was grabbin' her off?"

"You reckon he thinks such?"

"How could he he'p it? Us acks lovin' befo' him." Mr. Peters lowered his voice. "Does you find it an awful hard job, Chlorine?"

"Nossuh. 'Tain't so hard."

"Is it easy?"

"We-e-ell, I has done things which was more difficulter."

Epic sighed. "Lucky man!"

"Who?"

"Eddie."

"How come?"

"To have you affectionating him so constant." She swept him with a low-lidded, meaningful 'glance. "Flattery what you speaks with yo' mouf."

"Tain't flattery. It's troof."

"Shuh! I should b'lieve you."

"You sho should. Ise se'ious." He touched her arm. "Why is you so crazy 'bout him, Chlorine?"

"Gal cain't he'p who she's crazy 'bout, can she?"

"I dunno. I ain't never been no gal."

"Well, was you one, you'd know."

Once again Eddie was left in Charlotte. Between that metropolis and New York, Epic and Chlorine saw very little of each other, but their one night in the big city they went once again to the Harlem cabaret where they enjoyed dining and dancing.

Epic was delighted with the success of his innocuous little scheme. It never occurred to him that he might be doing Chlorine an injustice. He was unable to see that it could be other than a favor to save her from the mistake of committing a second marriage with such a negative person as Mr. Garnet. Already the plan was bearing delicious fruit. Epic was not averse to the platonic society of colored girls. It was well indeed to be in almost daily contact with a pulchritudinous damsel who thought he was a very fine gentleman. She supplied the feminine society which he craved. She provided him with a dancing partner and a dining friend, and she flattered his vanity by professing to think that he was a wonderful chap.

The trip to Birmingham and thence hack to New York was untroubled by Eddie Garnet's presence. By the time they again reached Charlotte, where Mr. Garnet's car became once more part of the de luxe train, their friendship had ripened to a state of gooey confidence. True, there was nothing on Epic's part of deeper sentiment. He regarded Chlorine as a nice, interesting girl and a dawg-gone good companion; something she obviously could not have been had he not saved her from her own infatuation for the unworthy Eddie.

For Eddie, Epic entertained only a profound consuming contempt. Why, the man wasn't any good at all. He didn't do a thing but browse around all day looking sad. As though that was the way to hold the interest of a woman for whom he undoubtedly still cared. Chlorine, now, was different. So earnestly had she entered into the little game that it seemed to Epic she had forgotten Mr. Garnet. Certainly she was utterly indifferent to him. Epic was satisfied that so long as Chlorine continued to work on this particular train Eddie Garnet would never again become a disturbing factor.

He despised the man for his inaction. In fact, he posed before the smoking-room mirror one day when that compartment was empty, and flexed his rather powerful biceps. Some man, Mr. Peters! Knew women thoroughly, he did. Able to grab 'em off and not afraid of no gemmun friends. Not him! And specially such a worm as Eddie Garnet undoubtedly was.

Mr. Peters was, in fact, sailing beatifically through the calm which inevitably precedes a large storm. The storm broke upon him between Atlanta and Birmingham, on the very last leg of his sixth return trip with Chlorine.

That day in the diner his attentions to Chlorine had been glaring. Other porters noticed, and one of them—a small, stocky man who had for years been a real friend to Epic—took it upon himself to hold counsel with the gangling porter.

They chatted in the vestibule of Epic's car. Keezie's face was very, very serious.

"Epic," he asked, "what pretickeler kind of a fool is you?"

Mr. Peters frowned. "I di'n't know I was no kind of what you said."

"Well"—positively—"you is!"

"Now listen heah, Keezie—"

"I ain't listenin'. Ise talkin', an' fo' yo' own good."

Keezie was so serious that Epic was impressed in spite of himself. "Well," he inquired, "wha's wrong?"

"Nothin' special," responded Keezie, "cept that you is fixin' to git yo'se'f a pummanent job countin' roots."

"How come?"

"Ain't you got mo' sense, than to flirt with a ma'ied 'ooman?"

"Who is?"

"You."

"Meanin' Chlorine?"

"Uh-huh."

Epic grinned. "Shuh, Keezie, she ain't ma'ied. She on'y was once."

"M'm! I know—but it's jus' the same as ma'ied when her husban' is waitin' in the ve'y dinin' car of yo' train."

"That feller?" Epic Peters guffawed. "Honest, Keezie, I ain't never seen a guy which is less human than him. Ev'y time I set eyes on him I git historical."

"Oh, you does?"

"Uh-huh. That po' hunk of side meat."

"Pff!" Keezie was plumb disgusted. "Epic, you is a livin' example of the ol' sayin' that iggorance is foolishness."

"Who?"

"You. Now listen at me!" Keezie looped a finger in his friend's coat and dropped his voice to a portentous whisper. "I reckon you ain't never tooken the trouble to 'vestigate this feller Eddie Garnet, has you?"

"No-o. Why?"

"Because, Epic, Eddie is the baddest cullud man that ever had a job on a dinin' car or anywhere else. He's awful!"

"You is kiddin' me."

"Is I? Man, you is kiddin' yo'se'f. You don't know that feller like I do. When he gits proper mad he don't fight, he just nachelly explodes! He busts all over ev'ythin'. Reason he took up railroadin' was that he couldn't walk down the streets of Atlanta 'thout separatin' some feller fum parts of his insides. Eddie is the mos' terrible cullud boy you ever hearn tell of. He's the best friend a undertaker ever had."

And now Mr. Peters was thoroughly impressed. His head was spinning and he spoke pleadingly:

"Y-y-y-you wouldn't fool me, would you, Keezie?"

"Man, you is fool enough a'ready. I has meant to tell you 'bout this befo', but until to-day it di'n't seem like none of my business, an' besides, I wa'n't right shuah that Eddie was sore. If you wanted to flirt with a gal, that was yo' business. But when you fixes to git yo'se'f extincted, that's my business on account of I an' you bein' frien's."

"Oh, golla! You mean somethin' is gwine happen right now?"

"Uh-huh. Reckon you noticed that Eddie wa'n't happy when you an' Chlorine et lunch in the diner together, di'n't you, Epic?"

"Yeh. He di'n't seem to be celebratin' none."

"After you lef' he walked aroun' the car mutterin' an' cussin', an' when he passed by where I was sittin' I heard him tell hisse'f that you better have a casket waitin' when you got to Bumminham, 'cause you was sho gwine need it."

"No!"

"Yeh. He's awful, that feller is. An' the mos' thing he usually manslaughters about is gittin' jealous of his wife."

Epic wrung his hands. "Oh, po' mis'able feller what I is. Danger has come an' kicked me right in the pants. I done it all myownse'f—"

"I'll say you did. An' Ise tellin' you now that was I you, I'd sho hunt me a good hidin' place an' stay there until after the train stops in Bumminham. An' then I'd do anythin' in the world to keep away fum Eddie an' Chlorine both. He's plumb pizen an' he's aimin' to ack."

Epic could not doubt the accuracy or sincerity of Keezie's counsel. The other porter was a genuine friend—a sober, unimaginative, reliable chap who thought the world of Epic. He wasn't the sort to make sport of his senior, nor was he the type to become unduly alarmed.

Keezie returned to his own car and Epic stood swaying in the vestibule, staring out at the rolling Alabama countryside. He felt a distinct sinking sensation in the pit of his stomach. His knees were wabbly. Twice, when passengers walked through the vestibule, Epic's eyes started from his head with terror and he clutched the door for support.

Suppose the lethal Mr. Garnet should find him here? Suppose—Epic emitted a large, hollow groan and wiped icy perspiration from his forehead.

Most unkindest cut of all was the knowledge that he had brought this upon himself. All his life he had fought shy of women and now—when for just one single time he had discarded his scheme of things and sought the innocent pleasure of flirtation—he had stepped into a bear trap. He closed his eyes and saw a vision. It was of the roly-poly Eddie Garnet descending upon him in a cloud, happily prepared to commit homicide. Epic's lanky figure trembled violently. He was not at all enamored of the idea of demising suddenly. And most horrid thought of all was his utter indifference to Chlorine. She was a nice enough girl, but not the sort he could become genuinely interested in. Yet because of her he found himself shaking hands with the angel Gabriel!

The train was less than ninety minutes from Birmingham. Eddie was aboard. Mr. Peters gave himself over to a scrutiny of his woeful predicament. Unquestionably he must find a hiding place. Then his eye lighted and his long feet swung into action. The drawing-room in his own car was vacant. One minute later he entered that drawing-room, locked the door and sank with a sigh into the softly cushioned seat.

Epic was colossally unhappy. He did not peer too far into the future. Vaguely he reflected that he could plead illness when he reached Birmingham, and during the period of his lay-off insist on being transferred to another run. No more de-luxing for him . He was through with trains which were afflicted with colored lady's maids.

The buzzer on the drawing-room door sounded sharply. Epic sprang to his feet and stood trembling. That might be Eddie! It was Eddie! Mr. Peters cringed and refused to answer the summons. Then to his horror he heard a key fitting into the lock. He closed his eyes and his lips moved. The big head rolled around on the pivot of his thin neck.

He heard the lock click and the door swung open. Epic collapsed. It was the Pullman conductor! Cap'n Sandifer frowned at the figure of his favorite porter.

"What are you doing in here with the door locked, Epic?"

Mr. Peters gave vent to a sepulchral groan. "Ise sick, cap'n. Ise terrible sick. Mos' prob'ly Ise dyin'."

The conductor was duly solicitous. He inquired as to symptoms. "Guess you'd better stay right here, Epic. I'll get another porter to watch this car until we get into Birmingham. Just lie down and take things easy."

"Cap'n, I will. I sho will, Cap'n Sandifer."

The Pullman conductor turned away. Epic was limp. Then he heard the conductor address someone outside. He saw Cap'n Sandifer move away. And in that same horrified, awful instant Mr. Epic Peters glimpsed the arrival of a visitor. Eddie Garnet entered the drawing-room. Eddie's face was expressionless. Quietly yet ostentatiously he closed the door. He snapped the thumb lock. Then he turned a face of granite toward Mr. Peters.

"Well," he remarked bleakly, "heah we is!"

Exactly that thought was pounding in Epic's brain. Here they were indeed. Himself and his self-appointed executioner cozily imprisoned in the drawing-room of a swiftly moving train. Mr. Peters grinned pallidly and nodded.

"Uh-huh," he agreed, "we sho is." An awful silence ensued. Epic finally cracked under the strain. "Ain't we?" he questioned.

Eddie said nothing, and he said it with expression. Epic had plenty of time to study his *bête noire*. Funny how he ever fancied that Mr. Garnet was inconsequential. Fat little fellow, round and chubby—but those eyes! Oh, those eyes! Piercing like a gimlet; cold like an icicle! Mr. Peters made a gesture.

"I—I got to go—"

Eddie spoke in an icy voice. "You ain't goin' nowhere." Then, after an instant: "No time!"

"But, Brother Garnet—"

"Don't 'but' me."

"Oh, Lawsy! We gits to Bumminham pretty soon, an'—"

"We ain't gwine git to Bumminham. Maybe I is, but we ain't."

Another period of terrific wordlessness. Mr. Garnet probed into the pocket of his trousers.

"Reckon I might's well git over with," he observed.

Epic emitted a wail.

"Wait a minute, Eddie. Fo' Gaw's-sake, wait a minute."

"I has a'ready waited too many minutes."

"No you ain't. Hones'. Anyhow, it don't do no hahm to 'splain why you is sore at me."

"Hmph! Reckon I got plenty reason."

"Y-y-y-you mean Miss Chlorine?"

Eddie's countenance took on all the angry majesty of a storm at sea. He merely nodded. Epic cascaded into speech.

"They ain't nothin' 'tween I an' her, Eddie. Cross my heart an' hope to be bawn a dawg if there is. I don't hahdly know she's alive."

"No? You think I is a idjut?"

"I don't, Brother Garnet. Hones', I don't. I think you is the smartest feller in the whole world. But this time a mistake has happened to you. Hones', I never bothered no gal in my life. I don't hahdly know there's any such pusson as Chlorine. Was you to ast me what she looked like, I couldn't even say."

"I ain't gwine ask you, either."

"You think Ise crazy 'bout her."

"I think you is crazy to fool aroun' with my gal—tha's what I think."

"Aw, Eddie, listen. Lemme 'splain, please, suh."

"A'right. But it ain't gwine do you a lick of good." Mr. Epic Peters took full and passionate advantage of his opportunity. With utmost loquacity and magnificent vividity he told of his meeting with Mrs. Chlorine Garnet. He explained that Chlorine had come to him with tears in her eyes to beg his help in recapturing the fleeting affections of her one-time husband.

"An' that's ev'y last thing I an' she has been doin', Eddie. Ise tellin' the truth. Chlorine has just been tryin' to make you jealous on account she craves to commit ma'iage with you again. An' she said you wouldn't notice her. Not a-tall."

There was a happy, triumphant gleam in the eyes of Mr. Garnet. It was plain that he wished to believe, yet was deterred by his common sense. Mr. Garnet was rather acutely conscious of his own physical defects, and he thought Epic a handsome man.

"You kiddin' me, Epic?"

"I'll swear I ain't. Hope I gits struck by lightnin' this ve'y minute if Ise lyin'."

"H'm! Sun is shinin'. I wonder—" Eddie paused uncertainly and Epic was quick to press his advantage.

Anything to gain time. The train was very close to Birmingham. Twenty minutes more and he'd have a chance for safety. He became struck by a glorious idea.

"You kiddin' me, Epic?"

"I'll swear I ain't. Hope I gits struck by lightnin' this ve'y minute if Ise lyin'."

"H'm! Sun is shinin'. I wonder—" Eddie paused uncertainly and Epic was quick to press his advantage.

Anything to gain time. The train was very close to Birmingham. Twenty minutes more and he'd have a chance for safety. He became struck by a glorious idea.

"It's the truth, Eddie, an' I can prove it!"

"How?"

"By Chlorine!"

Mr. Garnet appeared to consider the proposition. After a nerve-wrecking wait he inclined his head. "I can ask her."

"Glory hallelujah! Time that gal finished describin' how foolish she is 'bout you, Brother Garnet—"

"Go git her!" ordered Eddie coldly. "An be back heah quick."

Epic leaped for the door, but Eddie must have detected a gleam in his eyes. He interposed an arm of depressing muscularity.

"Changed my mind," he announced. "You wait heah while I fetch her."

He opened the door and waddled down the aisle of the Pullman. Epic stared after him. The train had passed Irondale. It was approaching Woodlawn, a Birmingham suburb. Just a few more minutes, a very few. Mr. Peters wanted to escape. And anyway, Chlorine would straighten things up. After all, he rather fancied his role, despite the angling of his nerves over the danger through which he had just passed.

Eddie Garnet returned. With him was Chlorine Garnet, wide-eyed with wonder. Eddie closed the door of the drawing-room, stood with his back against it, and transfixed his ex-wife with a baleful stare.

"Chlorine," he said, "I craves to ask you a question."

She tossed her head. "Ain't no law says you cain't."

"A'right." Mr. Garnet selected his words with care. "This is the question: What is yo' sentiments to'rds Epic Peters?"

Chlorine stared at her husband. Then she flashed a glance at Epic. Her graceful figure grew tense and she met her husband's eyes levelly. Her words were clear and distinct.

"I is crazy about him!" she announced.

A large groan slipped from between Epic's lips and could be heard above the roar of the train. He wilted, as though from a blow. He put up a defensive hand.

"Aw, Chlorine—"

"I is crazy about him," repeated that young woman, "I think he's the grandes' man in all the world an' wuth two of such tripes as you, Eddie Garnet!"

There came a silence freighted with tragic possibilities. Eddie moved with businesslike menace toward the stricken figure of Mr. Epic Peters. That person stared through the window. The train was slowing down.

"She—she ain't tellin' the truth, Eddie. I swear she ain't."

"I guess I know!" flashed Chlorine.

Epic gave a wild glance at the sinister Mr. Garnet. That gentleman's face reminded him strangely of a tombstone.

It was a moment for drastic action. Epic did it! He gave a wild yell. His muscles uncoiled. There was a crash of glass as Mr. Peters catapulted through the window and pitched in a heap beside the railroad track. He was bruised and cut and battered, but not so completely wrecked that he was unable to rise to his feet and commence traveling in earnest.

He did not look back at the train, which was slowly moving toward the terminal station. And if he had he couldn't have seen Chlorine's astonished face as she explained to her jealous but adoring husband:

"He should of tol' me us wasn't playin' that game no mo', Eddie. Of course, I is crazy 'bout you."

Epic saw none of that. He only saw that between himself and the horizon was lots of distance. He started out to negotiate a maximum of space in a very minimum of time. Twenty minutes later he staggered into his room at Sis Callie Flukers' boarding house. He locked the door and commenced the painful and thankless task of picking bits of glass out of himself, after which he anointed his flesh with iodine and ointments.

His abysmal gloom was relieved a half hour later by the receipt of a message from Eddie Garnet that all was understood and forgiven. Mr. Peters breathed a sigh of relief, then bethought himself of his beloved job. He took pen and paper and laboriously wrote his report to the Pullman office.

SUPERINTENDENT, PULLMAN Co.
BIRMINGHAM, ALABAMA.

Dere Gentlemen: I reckon you wonder how come I wasn't on my train when it got into Birminham today. The reason is this. I had to jump out of the drawin room window to save a man from getting killed.

Yrs. respt.

EPIC PETERS

A Toot for a Toot

EPIC PETERS' instinct was at work. "I got a hunch," he murmured apprehensively, "that this ain't gwine be the swellest run I ever took." Two factors contributed to the hunch of the elongated Pullman porter. For one thing, there had been a ghastly dearth of tips from passengers boarding the midnight train at Birmingham. For another, the buzzer of his call board had been sounding incessantly since the "All aboard."

Somewhat peeved with the world in general, and his job in particular, Mr. Peters took his own sweet time about closing his vestibule as the Limited nosed out into the chilly, murky night. He poked unenthusiastically at an occasional bit of dust, arranged his car step meticulously in the vestibule corner and then lurched unhappily into the car.

Just as he suspected, the board indicated that Lower 6 required service. The training of many years came to the assistance of Epic Peters. As a sterling porter who was popular with Pullman and railroad conductors and whose name appeared frequently on the honor roll, Epic had learned to gauge the quality of those who traveled with him between the Alabama metropolis and New York.

"An' that feller in Lower 6," reflected Mr. Peters, "is the mos' kind I detest."

The person in question had waddled down the platform a half hour since in the wake of a redcap who was loaded down with many heavy bags. He was a large man with a florid complexion and an officious manner. His voice was shrill and penetrating. He wore a blue suit, gayly cut, and it was quite evident that he fancied himself considerable of a sheik.

The trousers were full, the socks fancy, the shoes of two-tone leather. His vest was piped with white braid and he sported a scarlet necktie in which reposed a huge pearl. He carried a silver-headed cane, a gaudy topcoat and wore a gray felt hat at a rakish angle. And Epic Peters saw him tip the staggering redcap a nickel.

Mr. Peters groaned.

"Tip nickels!" he grated. "I bet if he buys a ice-cream soda he wants a rebate when he returns the glass an' spoon."

The newcomer talked loudly and frequently as Epic escorted him to his berth and sought to satisfy the gentleman in the arrangement of his. bags. Once Epic dared designate the sign hanging at the end of the aisle: Quiet. The traveler glared at Mr. Peters and announced that he was paying full fare and reckoned he'd talk if he wanted to—besides, the service was rotten.

Now, as Mr. Peters reluctantly answered the summons from the fat gentleman's berth, it was to find the big head poked out between the curtains. The passenger glared at Epic and anathematized the service. It seemed that some cinders were creeping in through the screen, that there was a wrinkle in the sheet and that his spare blanket was not properly folded.

Epic bore up under the tirade with the dignity becoming a colored gentleman and philosopher. He did not even deign to inform the man that he was the hest berth maker on the Birmingham station and known throughout the Southeast as one of the finest colored men ever to receive a monthly wage from the Pullman Company. With vast and disdainful patience he performed the tasks required by the exacting traveler, and heard that gentleman say peevishly:

"Well, I hope to goodness I can get some sleep."

As Epic moved away he indorsed the wish: "Lawsy knows, I hope so too. Dawg-gone that feller. He buys one ticket an' thinks he's Mistuh Pullman Illinois hisse'f."

As Epic moved down the aisle he was conscious of certain movements in Section 8. He turned quickly—just in time to see a ratlike face and a pair of beady eyes withdrawn quickly. "That feller in Lower 8," Epic told himself, "also ain't the craziest sort I is about."

As a matter of fact, the gentleman in Lower 8 would have rasped Epic's nerves intensely had not the fat person in Lower 6 been so obtrusively obnoxious. And, had Epic known it, his instinctive antipathy for the ratlike little man in 8 was not unfounded.

The person in Lower 8 was about five feet four inches in height. He had a slender, wiry figure on which cheap clothes fitted uncertainly. His eyes were beady and he had a disturbing habit of talking out of the side of his mouth. His hands were amazing, however; strong and long-fingered and amazingly deft.

At birth the little man had been christened Aloysius Bryan by a doting and unsuspecting mother. Since that time he had, in the pursuit·of his chosen profession, used other names as convenience suggested. The police of various cities knew him as Danny the Dip, Dan Bryan, the Runt, and Dippy Dan. The name Aloysius departed with his last short trousers.

To give Aloysius full credit, it must be admitted that he was an expert pickpocket. He operated alone—and frequently. He had few friends and no confidants, and only a too great fondness for large diamonds steered him into trouble with the police. He could scissor or reef a victim with the best of them, leaving the unwitting contributor ignorant of financial loss until a considerable time after.

Birmingham had offered an excellent field for Aloysius. Pickings had been reasonably easy. But that very day a certain embarrassing situation had arisen on the First National Bank corner—something which informed Danny the Dip that he'd be wise to seek other fields for his nefarious activities. So this night found him on the Limited with a New York ticket in his pocket and a profound hope that no plain-clothes bull would impede his departure from the South.

Epic's trained eye warned him against Aloysius when that furtive gentleman sidled onto the train and slipped into his berth. Mr. Peters was not unfamiliar with gentlemen who make a living by nimble wits, fingers and conscience. Mr. Peters boasted that he could spot a train hustler as far as he could see one, and something told him from the first that this ratlike gentleman was worth observing.

Yet, as the train roared through the chilly night and sleep refused to come to Epic, that person sat in the smoking room and reflected that of the two gentlemen—the one in Lower 6 and the one in Lower 8—he'd prefer a half dozen of Aloysius to one of the former. After all, Epic was not personally concerned with undersized persons who looked and acted like crooks, but the blatant officious type brought him agony of soul and misery of spirit.

Quite early in the morning the train rolled under the shed of the Atlanta station. The Atlanta Pullman was cut out and the train made up anew for the run to New York. There Captain Sandifer, the grizzled and veteran Pullman conductor of whom Epic was extremely fond, took over the diagrams and chatted briefly with his favorite porter.

"Things going all right, Epic?"

"Not so many, cap'n. I got on my care one of them white folks that thinks he boughten the comp'ny when he paid his money fo' a ticket."

"Been riding you, eh?"

"Nossuh, not me, he ain't. But he sho ain't the fondes' kind of passenger I is of."

"I don't blame you, Epic. But, cheer up! The run won't last forever."

"Nossuh, maybe not. But it seems mos' that long."

By the time the train pulled out of Atlanta half the passengers had risen and wandered. into the diner—among them the stout gentleman and Aloysius. When they returned their sections were already arranged for the day and Epic was busy elsewhere in the car.

The stout person summoned Epic. "Porter," he snapped, "what do you mean by putting my small bag under the seat?"

"I don't mean nothin', white folks. Always puts the bags under the seats."

"Hmph! Get it out immediately."

"Yassuh, cap'n."

Epic bent over and wrestled with the bag. He rose and bowed.

"That all, mistuh?"

"No, it isn't. I want two pillows and a hat bag."

"Y-y-yassuh, boss; right away. I aims to give service, which is how come they to call me Hop Sure."

"I'm not interested in your nicknames. What I want is the pillows."

Epic was shuddering with futile rage as he went on the errand. And while he was extracting pillowcases from the linen cabinet at the end of the aisle, he saw Captain Sandifer come through the car and answer the summons of the obtrusive stout person. Epic listened in.

"Impertinent porter you have on this car," rasped the person with the white piping on his vest.

Sandifer frowned. "Epic Peters?"

"I don't know his name or anything about him. I know he is inefficient and impertinent."

The eyes of the Pullman conductor narrowed. He knew the type of man he was conversing with, and one of the great regrets of his life was that duty prohibited him from exterminating such insects.

"Epic is never impertinent," he defended frigidly.

"He was impertinent to me."

"How?"

"Do I have to give details? Isn't my word sufficient?"

Sandifer's face was dead white with anger. The man was simply insufferable.

"Perhaps," said the conductor coldly.

"I'll file a report of this with the Pullman Company," raged the person in Section 6. "It is outrageous."

"Sorry," said Sandifer as he moved away.

It was with difficulty that Epic concealed his elation as he climbed to the upper berth in search of two pillows. Bless Cap'n Sandifer's heart! There was sho nuff quality white folks. Reckon he knowed when a feller was pertinent or not. Wouldn't let no trash like this pouter pigeon put nothin' over on him! Not Cap'n Sandifer, nossuh!

The florid person seemed to enjoy his futile anger. He snatched the pillows from Epic's hand and tried to stare frostily, but Mr. Peters' genial countenance was wreathed in a smile of sheer good humor. It seemed that nothing could ruffle his calm—a fact that served to annoy the man in Lower 6 more than ever.

Humming gayly, Epic gave his attention to Section 7. The lady who had occupied the lower had left the train at a little station beyond Atlanta. The upper berth of that section had not been occupied. Mr. Peters worked swiftly and well, rather happily conscious that two pairs of eyes were focused upon him. One pair of eyes belonged to the fat person. The other was the property of Danny the Dip, né Aloysius.

Mr. Peters bent joyfully to his task. He adjusted the two mattresses in the upper berth, discarded used linen, neatly folded blankets and arranged pillows. Then he snapped the upper berth shut and commenced arranging the cushions of the lower.

He snapped the back rests into place and shoved one of the seat cushions back, and as he did so a glitter caught his eye. From the green-carpeted floor something twinkled up at him. A frown creased his mahogany forehead as he bent to pick it up.

When he straightened he was possessed of a queer excitement. He was holding in his hand a platinum ring which was set with a single gorgeous diamond.

Hop Sure's heart missed a beat. He knew that he cradled a young fortune in his palm, and his thoughts flashed ahead to the possibility of a sizable reward. It never occurred to him to do anything save report the matter to Captain Sandifer and turn in the ring to the Pullman office. Epic's honesty was unswerving. But he would have been less than human had he failed to speculate upon the value of his finding and the reward which a grateful and generous owner might bestow. His tremendous hand closed over the ring and he dropped it into the pocket of his coat. Then he turned quickly.

The stout man in Section 6 was staring straight at him. Unquestionably that gentleman had witnessed the discovery of the ring, and Epic experienced a sense of annoyance. He glanced elsewhere about the car, curious to know whether anyone else had observed the finding of the ring. No one seemed interested. Even Aloysius, alias Danny the Dip, was staring out of the window, apparently absorbed in the speeding landscape.

Epic swung back to his work. His heart sang within him, for it seemed that his early hunch that this was to be an unpleasant and unprofitable trip was only half right. Unpleasant, yes, but unprofitable—

"Hot ziggity dam!" exclaimed Mr. Peters. "Di'monds is the most thing I love to find."

Some passengers had been late in rising. Two or three had eaten breakfast in their berths and were only now showing signs of stepping into their clothes. Consequently the labor of straightening the car had dragged interminably.

When Captain Sandifer next passed through the car Epic didn't even see him. He was perched on the arm of a lower, arranging mattresses in an upper. But the fat man in Section 6 noticed that Epic did not report the finding of the diamond to the Pullman conductor, and the fact took on a sinister significance to the officious traveler.

With an armful of used linen Hop Sure made his way to the end of the car. And there, standing in the aisle, someone pressed sharply against him. He raised his head, to stare into the beady eyes of Danny the Dip.

Aloysius was trying to be affable. He spoke but of the corner of his mouth:

"Are we on time, porter?"

"Yassuh, right on the minute."

"Yeh? Nice day, ain't it?"

"Pretty nice, boss man."

Aloysius looked around. "Where's the drinking water?"

Epic designated the cooler and hastened to secure for his undersized passenger a paper drinking cup. "There you is, cap'n."

Danny the Dip thanked Hop Sure and inhaled a cupful of ice water. Then he returned to his place in Section 8 while Epic engrossed himself once more in the task of fixing his car.

Eventually the job was completed and Epic sank into an unused section for a well-earned rest. He tried to make himself comfortable, but in spite of his best efforts he fidgeted with the consciousness that the eyes of the fat man were focused upon him.

Captain Sandifer came through the car. Epic determined to turn the diamond ring over to him then and there. But before he could speak to the Pullman conductor that individual was stopped by the rasping voice of the fat person in Section 6:

"Conductor!"

Sandifer stopped in the aisle. It was obvious that the passenger was not overly popular with him.

"Well?" he asked bleakly.

"I consider it my duty to report something to you."

"What?"

"I very much question the honesty of your porter."

"Well," snapped Sandifer, "I don't!"

"You wouldn't, of course." The pursy lips of the traveler creased into a sneer. "Has he turned over to you anything which he found in the car this morning?"

Sandifer shook his head. "No. But if he found anything of value he will."

"Evidently your confidence is very great—much greater than mine. I shall write a report of this to the Pullman Company and—"

The conductor was furious. "Now, listen here!" he said curtly. "You've done a lot of insinuating and haven't backed it up with a fact. If you've got any accusations to make, make 'em. But I'm not going to be bothered with your infernal hot air any longer."

"Oh, is that so? For all I know, you're in cahoots—"

"Mister," warned Sandifer sweetly, "I value my job very highly, but not so highly that it would be safe for you to finish that sentence."

Epic wriggled with glee. That was the way to talk to uppity folks. Trust Cap'n Sandifer for that.

"Just the same," said the fat person, "when your porter made up Section 7 he found something which seemed to me to be a valuable diamond ring."

"He did, eh?"

"He certainly did."

"Was it your ring?"

"No-o-o."

"Belong to any friend of yours?"

"No, but—"

"Then it's none of your business."

Sandifer turned on his heel and strode from the car, white-faced with anger. He refused to give the fat man the satisfaction of accepting from Hop Sure at that time the ring which had been found.

Having known Epic for years, there was no question in the mind of the conductor that Mr. Peters possessed an ineluctable honesty. And he took a keen satisfaction in the look of thwarted anger which came into the fishlike eyes of the man in Section 6.

Epic himself was very happy. Cap'n Sandifer was his friend—always had been and always would be. He knew the captain for a rigid taskmaster, but one who appreciated efficient and honest effort.

The train was approaching Charlotte, and Epic noticed a bit of activity in Section 8. Aloysius was strapping his suitcase very carefully. It was evident that he was making preparations to leave the train. This occasioned mild surprise in the breast of Mr. Peters, for he happened to know that the ratlike person held a ticket for New York.

But the destination of Danny the Dip did not interest Mr. Peters for very long. He lounged in his seat and turned his thoughts into pleasant channels which had to do with the discomfiture of the fat man. Epic understood and appreciated the delicacy of feeling which had prompted the· conductor to say nothing about the ring in the presence of the protuberant gentleman in Section 6.

Plenty of time to return the diamond ring. Smiling broadly, Epic dropped his hand into his pocket to assure himself that everything was all right.

Quite suddenly, and with comprehensive completeness, the smile vanished from Epic's countenance and in its stead there came an expression of abysmal consternation. His fingers fumbled frantically and he was stricken by a chill.

"Oh, whoa is me!" he mourned as the potentialities of the situation were thrust upon him. "That ring has went!"

Gone—vanished—completely and absolutely-departed somewhere else!

It required less than a split second for Epic Peters to realize that he was in a horrid dilemma. His distaste for the fat man in Section 6 now flamed to a violent and aggressive hatred.

He had found the ring, and the fat man had seen him find it. Bulwarked behind the knowledge of his own honesty, he had taken his own time about reporting the discovery to Cap'n Sandifer, and the fat man had made a bad matter worse by suggesting to the Pullman conductor that Epic intended to steal the ring.

Now the ring was gone, and Cap'n Sandifer knew that he had found it. Sooner or later Sandifer would ask for the ring, and Epic groaned at the prospect of telling him that it had disappeared. Sandifer might believe Epic, but by the same token the conductor would make a report of the whole affair to the company officials. In addition to that, the fat man would also see to it that the matter came to the most unfortunate ears.

There would be an investigation—perhaps a trial. Epic knew that he would be dismissed from the service—kicked out of the profession to which he had devoted his life. The very least that could be proved against him was gross carelessness, and there was grave danger that he might be convicted of dishonesty.

The spirit of Mr. Epic Peters groveled. He hit bottom and continued going down. "Oh, gosh," he moaned, "Ol' man disaster has sho slapped me right in the face!"

At first Epic was unable to do anything but reflect upon the ghastly situation. Then he commenced to hunt. He hunted violently for that ring, searching every nook and cranny of the car. The fat man was regarding him sneeringly. And the beady eyes of Danny the Dip never left the wriggling figure of the distraught porter.

The ring was nowhere to be found. Epic now was in terror lest Cap'n Sandifer choose this inopportune time to demand it. To avoid such a catastrophe, Hop Sure retired to the unoccupied drawing-room. He desired solitude and lots of it. He left the door open, but managed to keep out of sight.

He commenced thinking. Never in all his eventful career had the brain of Mr. Peters functioned with such amazing speed. Logic hammered insistently. The ring was lost. It hadn't jumped out of the window, it wasn't on the floor of the car, nor was it concealed in the upholstery. Unquestionably, however, it was still in the car.

Epic's thoughts flashed to the fat man, but he immediately discarded the thought that that person had anything to do with it. Then he remembered the ratlike individual in Section 8. From the very first moment that he set eyes on Aloysius, Epic had felt an antipathy to that gentleman. He knew there was something wrong about Danny the Dip—something fearfully and radically wrong.

He cocked his head on one side so as to command a view of the car. Danny the Dip was' undoubtedly planning to get off at Charlotte. The significance of this impressed Hop Sure.

The man had a ticket to New York. Why, then, should he suddenly alter his plans and leave the train in North Carolina? Something queer—dawg-goned queer, too. Instinct informed Epic that Danny the Dip was in some manner connected with that ring. He thought Danny had witnessed the finding. He wasn't sure, but he thought so. Apparently Danny had been looking out of the window at the time, but Epic had a hunch that those beady eyes hadn't missed much.

Epic remembered something else. He recalled the queer actions of Aloysius near the water cooler. Danny the Dip had accosted him and engaged him in conversation about matters of no importance whatever. During that conversation the Dip had stood very, very close to Epic—so close, reflected the porter, that he could very easily have slipped nimble fingers into the capacious pocket of Epic's coat and extracted therefrom the diamond ring.

Epic set his feet squarely on the floor. He felt certain that he had hit upon the correct solution; facts dovetailed perfectly.

Mr. Peters was desperate. He knew that he had only a few minutes of grace. Very shortly the train would be in Charlotte and Aloysius would leave. Once away, Epic knew he'd never again set eyes on the man or the ring.

Mr. Peters was spurred to drastic action. He summoned a genial, disarming smile and plastered it on his face. Then he approached Danny the. Dip.

"Gittin' off at Charlotte, boss man?"

The ratlike eyes darted to Epic's countenance.

"Yes."

"Lemme brush you off, suh."

Epic held a whisk broom insinuatingly before the eyes of Aloysius. The wiry little man hesitated, then rose. Immediately Epic stepped toward the end of the car.

"Right this way, cap'n, so's the dust won't bother nobody."

Aloysius frowned but followed. To have reseated himself might have attracted attention.

Epic stopped at the door of the drawing-room and motioned Aloysius to enter. The professional pickpocket hesitated briefly, then stepped inside. Immediately Epic extracted a cloth from his pants pocket and knelt on the floor before the little man. He polished his shoes assiduously.

The heart of Mr. Peters was pounding. Ordinarily none too well supplied with physical courage, he was now daring everything to avert personal disaster. He rose, pocketed the dust cloth and turned.

His slim, angular body functioned smoothly. One skinny arm reached out and slammed the drawing-room door. Well-trained fingers snapped the lock. Then Hop Sure turned upon the astounded Danny an expression which had lost all of its mild good nature.

Danny the Dip stepped back defensively. His eyes narrowed to pin points and the color drained from his cheeks.

"What the—"

"Jus' a minute, white folks!" Epic's words came like drops from an icicle. "You got somethin' I want."

"Why, you—"

"No need swearin' at me, neither. I never aim to be nothin' but respec'ful, an' my rule ain't gwine be broke, but you got somethin' that Ise gwine have, no matter how you forces me to git it."

Danny was thinking swiftly. The lengthy porter showed no hint of weakness or lack of courage. Epic spoke again. Words seemed to restore his fast-ebbing bravery.

"Gimme that di'mond ring!" he commanded harshly, extending his hand.

"Wh-what diamond ring?"

"Don't try no fumadiddles with me, white folks. You know good an' well what di'mond ring you has got. An' I crave to have it."

"You're talking crazy."

"H'm, I reckon not. Mistuh, I ain't no fool—honest I ain't. Somethin' seemed wrong with you right fum the first, an' it don't look reasonable to me that no man would buy a ticket to New Yawk an' git off at Charlotte less'n he had a good reason. So if you just gimme the ring—"

"I won't give you anything."

Epic shrugged.

"A'right, mistuh. If you won't, you won't, an' I ain't gwine argufy."

Danny the Dip stepped forward. "Let me out of here."

"Not so's you could osserve it, mistuh. Heah you stays until you gimme that ring or else until the police gits you."

"Police?"

"You di'n't misunderstan' me none. I said police, an' b'lieve me, mistuh, I meant police."

"But—but, porter—"

"I don't aim to git butted, neither. If you gimme that ring I promise to let you leave the train at Charlotte an' not say nothin' to nobody. If you refuse, I han's you over to the police right at the station. An' don't think I won't tell 'em why."

"Now, listen." The voice of Aloysius had taken on a whiny, wheedling note. "A little cash—"

"Cash don't mean nothin' to me, or even less than that. It's di'mond ring fo' Hop Sure or jail fo' you. Now, which?"

Danny's lip curled. "If I had a gun—"

"Man, tha's the most thing I was scared of when I brung you in heah. You ain't never gwine know how frightened I was of that. I sho despises to git kilt."

Aloysius glanced out of the window. The train was slowing down. Already they were within the corporate limits of Charlotte. Epic interpreted the thoughts of the man and grinned cheerfully.

"Take all the time you want," be invited. "But the minute us stops at that station with you still havin' that ring, I yells fo' the police."

Aloysius knew when he was beaten. Threats, cajolery and bribery had failed.

"You promise you won't even hint to anybody?"

"Gosh—yes, I promise. All I crave is that jool."

Danny the Dip probed into his watch pocket and extracted therefrom a gleaming diamond ring. He placed it resentfully in Epic's palm.

"There!" he rasped. "And if you break your promise I'll get you if it's the last thing I do."

"Don't you worry, mistuh. I wouldn't break that promise if I wanted to."

Intoxicated with happiness, Epic sped to the platform, where he busied himself arranging suitcases for the departing passengers. He felt the need of company and lots of it. Aloysius would never dare start anything while others were watching.

The train stopped at the station in Charlotte. A half dozen passengers alighted, and foremost among them was Danny the Dip.

Epic was on the platform, and it was he who handed Danny's suitcase to that slender gentleman. The pickpocket grabbed it from the porter and strode swiftly away. Epic gazed ruefully after him.

"Well, I'll be dawg-bit! He didn't even gimme a tip."

The train pulled out. As Epic reentered his car he was conscious of the fishy, suspicious glance of the fat man in Section 6.

But that glance failed to annoy Mr. Peters now. He felt an enormous disdain for the fat person. Interfere in his affairs, eh? Reckon he'd show him something!

Epic settled into the seat recently vacated by Danny the Dip. And suddenly he felt the ghastly effects of what medical men technically term a nervous reaction.

Mr. Peters was cold and limp all over. He had battled bravely through a crisis and achieved victory, but the strain exacted its toll now, and Epic could actually feel the strength flow out of his finger ends.

His mind dwelt on terrible things. Suppose Aloysius had drawn a gun. Suppose Aloysius had attacked him. Suppose—oh, most horrid of thoughts!—suppose he had been wrong and Aloysius had not possessed the ring.

But it was all over now. The sun was shining and the little birdies were warbling their gayest tunes. Mr. Peters planned every little detail of the triumphal movement when-before the suspicious eyes of the fat man in Section 6—he would present to Captain Sandifer the gorgeous diamond ring which had caused him such agony.

He had it again, safe and sound. Brain had triumphed over dishonest cunning. Epic permitted himself to smile as he slipped his right hand into his pocket and felt for the diamond.

He blinked—he blinked again. He sat up straight in his seat, conscious of a terrible sinking sensation at the pit of his tummy.

"Great wigglin' tripe," he gasped, "that ring has gone again!"

And now Mr. Epic Peters knew that all the suffering which he had already experienced was mere rehearsal. For every ounce of misery which had been his before reaching Charlotte, there was now a ton to rack and torture him. He thought of the nimble-fingered Aloysius—' gone out of his life forever—and of the diamond ring for which he had blithely risked total extermination.

Epic uncoiled himself and searched the section in which he sat. Then he crawled the length of the car on hands and knees. A sweet-faced old lady questioned him.

"What's the matter, porter?"

Epic raised a haggard face. "Ev'ything, ma'am."

"Lost something?"

"Lady, I sho has. Seems like I has los' my least on life."

The ring did not appear. More and more certainly the conviction grew upon Epic that Aloysius had double-crossed him. He returned to the vacant section and flung himself down on the seat. Forlornly he plunged his hand into the pocket of his coat.

The index finger touched something. A hole!

Instantly an expression of eager hope crossed the troubled brow of Mr. Peters. With decisive strength he ripped the hole to several times its size. He dropped his entire hand into the cavity which existed between coat and lining.

And then something startling happened to his countenance. His jaw sagged, his eyes popped, a cold perspiration stood out on his brow.

He withdrew from his pocket a hand which trembled with an excess of excitement. Slowly he opened his fist. Sunlight, streaming in through the window, was reflected dazzlingly into the eyes of the lengthy Pullman porter.

Gleaming gloriously in his hand there lay not one diamond ring but two.

Two rings! Two diamonds! Two platinum settings!

"Great sufferin' stew meat," gasped Epic, "the ring has done twinned!"

Captain Sandifer appeared. Epic did not hesitate. He slipped one of the rings into his trousers pocket as he rose to full length.

He accosted the conductor, and before the disappointed eyes of the fat person in Section 6, Mr. Peters extended to his superior the identical diamond ring which had been discovered early that morning in Lower 7.

"Cap'n Sandifer," he announced in a bored tone, "heah's a li'l trifle I found this mawnin' while I was performin' my chores."

Sandifer accepted the ring and thanked Epic. Then he flashed a gleeful glance at the thoroughly cowed fat gentleman in Section 6. Words seemed unnecessary. But Epic Peters insisted on speaking:

"Cap'n Sandifer?"

"What is it, Hop Sure?"

"Is you willin' to do me a favor?"

"Certainly."

"Some folks is always th'owin' away aspersions. Would you mind walkin' th'oo the train an' askin' ev'ybody if they has lost a di'mond ring?"

"But I'm sure this was lost by the lady in Lower 7."

"Yassuh, boss, so'm I. But I want to feel sure there ain't nobody else in the train lost no other di'mond."

More to discomfit the man in Lower 6 than to please Epic, Captain Sandifer agreed. He canvassed the train and was back in ten minutes.

"All clear, Epic," he announced. "Nobody else on the train has lost anything."

"You got that positivel, cap'n?"

"Absolutely."

Epic trailed the Pullman conductor the length of the car. They stood together on the vestibule platform.

"Cap'n Sandifer," said Epic, "I craves to ask' you a question."

"All right, Hop Sure. What is it?"

"It's just this, cap'n. Suppose while I was porterin', a passenger on my car happened to give me—of his own free will an' discord—a swell di'mond ring—just give it to me! Would that ring belong to me, or should I turn it in to the company?"

The conductor grinned.

"If he gave it to you, Epic, it would be yours."

Mr. Peters nodded beatifically.

"Thanks, cap'n. Tha's all I yearned to know."

The Pullman conductor passed on. Epic stood motionless, busy with his thoughts. He understood everything now. He even understood why Danny the Dip had left the train at Charlotte. Danny had seen trouble brewing, and being a professional crook, was not desirous of being discovered among the passengers should police be called upon to investigate.

Mr. Peters gazed at the gorgeous stone which glittered up at him. Then his lips twisted into a smile.

"All I got to do now," he reflected happily, "is find a gal to fit this."

BEARLY POSSIBLE

EPIC PETERS temporarily had abandoned business for art. He lay stretched at full length on his bed in Sis Callie Flukers' boarding house and held his huge hands cupped against the center of his countenance.

From beneath the clasped hands came the moaning strains of an ancient opus called the "Memphis Blues." The toes of the gangling Pullman porter wiggled to the tune and his eyes sparkled ecstatically.

Mr. Peters was content. This was his off day; the room was adequately heated against the chill of early December; and he was performing upon the harmonica as never before. He injected new and weird jazz effects into his blowing and terminated the syncopated melody with a display of triple-tonguing remarkable to hear.

He lowered the instrument from his lips and gave vent to a bit of self-praise.

"Hot ziggity dam!" ejaculated Epic. "I sho is gittin' so I deals this harmonicum a fit!"

He produced a pocket handkerchief and polished the four-bit weapon earnestly. Then he placed it carefully in its pasteboard box and slipped the thing into his hip pocket. The harmonica was part and parcel of Epic's life. It was his never-failing companion in times of joy and stress; it furnished a musical outlet for his soul and an artistic expression of his pent-up emotions. It was always with him, and he was rapidly attaining recognition as the best mouth-organ player in dusky Birmingham.

He lay motionless, staring through the window at the austere sunshine of early winter. He luxuriated in this off day. His was a powerful tarrogatin' job, portering from Birmingham to New York and back again, with never an interruption save for these occasional lay-offs. Of course, there were some who eyed Mr. Peters with colossal envy, wishing that they had a job which demanded nothing but travel and plenty of it. Mr. Peters gazed upon these foolish persons with fine disdain. Reckon he knowed it wa'n't no cinch to sit up night after night answerin' buzzer calls an' impartin' answers to questions which wa'n't nothin' mo' than just plumb foolishment!

Of course, being a long-service man whose appearances on the company's roll of honor had been unusually frequent, Mr. Peters occasionally acquired a little gravy. Take this trip he was going on day after to-morrow—Epic smiled in anticipation. Reckon the pickin's would be awful good on that trip! Once before he had portered on a football special with highly satisfactory financial results.

His musings were broken into by a wail of music. He ceased thinking. From some distance came the notes of the old familiar "Turkey in the Straw." A slight frown creased the light mahogany complexion of the indolent Pullman porter. Could it be—

It was! Unmistakably and absolutely, that music could originate nowhere in the world save in the bellows of Giovanni's accordion.

The effect on Mr. Peters was magical. He leaped from the bed and slung his clothes about him. He knew what the music of Giovanni's accordion meant.

"Golly!" murmured the long porter excitedly, as he adjusted collar and tie. "I sho hope he's got that ol' bear with him!"

Three minutes later Epic departed Sis Callie's and, like a child of Hamelin, ardently pursued the piper.

A crowd of children, gathered at the corner of Eighteenth Street and Avenue F, gave Mr. Peters the information he wanted. He traversed the distance to the corner with long, eager strides and gazed upon the scene of revelry with eyes big as saucers and sparkly as diamonds.

In the middle of a circle of delighted children were three figures. One was the squat frame of Signor Giovanni Peppini, manipulator of a wheezy accordion and owner of Beppo. The second was the somewhat uncouth but muscular Emmanuel Acosti, who, having been signally unsuccessful in extorting a living from the profession of wrestling against humans, now devoted his efforts to tussling with a bear. The third in the group was Beppo—himself, in person!

It is true that in his native haunts Beppo might have been regarded as distinctly *déclassé*. He was a large bear, and very black. He was well advanced in years and vividly addicted to mange. But he was a willing, obedient servant who, instantly and without question, would perform his entire repertoire of tricks on proper signal.

Beppo knew two consecutive tricks. When his beloved Giovanni pumped the wheezy accordion and caused it to emit the strains of "Turkey in the Straw," Beppo shook himself in a rhythmic manner which his owner was pleased to call dancing. This never failed to delight the children. But the bear's big act followed the first notes of the "Memphis Blues."

At that cue, Beppo would cease shaking himself and advance upon the nonchalant Emmanuel Acosti. Emmanuel would bend forward at the waist, brace himself and come to grips with Beppo—and it was Emmanuel who was wont to complain bitterly that his job was no sinecure. He declared that Beppo was not so old as one would think and that his hug was, at times, unduly enthusiastic.

The trio had been in Birmingham for three months. Pickings had been slight but regular. But of all the contributors of cash whom Giovanni had noticed, there was no one who gave so generously or regularly as the long, tall, gangling negro, Epic Peters.

To-day, as on other vacation days, Epic trailed the bear. It was always the same performance, but each repetition brought Mr. Peters increasing delight. It seemed as though he would never tire of the grotesque, dignified dancing of Beppo, or of Beppo's fierce growls while tussling with the unhappy Emmanuel. No one ever was hurt in these wrestling matches, but Epic was in constant timorous hope that something drastic would occur.

The group moved slowly across town, stopping on deserted street corners to repeat the performance. Giovanni's music was asthmatic and the efforts of Beppo and Emmanuel somewhat lethargic, but the owner of the bear knew by experience that he was sure of one interested spectator until nightfall. Once Epic joined the procession behind the bear, he never left.

At the corner of Eighth Avenue and Seventeenth Street, North, three newcomers added themselves to the group. Epic eyed them with interest. Unmistakably, they were college boys. They gazed affectionately at Beppo and then consulted among themselves. Epic saw one blond-haired lad produce a roll of bills and do some figuring.

Mr. Peters realized what was coming. Everybody in Birmingham knew that the athletes of Hilltop University were called the Black Bears. Furthermore, it was common knowledge that this year—for the first time in the proud history of Hilltop—the football team of the Black Bears had swept unchallenged through a difficult schedule which had included most of the best Southern gridiron aggregations.

At the same time a Chicago team had been blazing a victorious trail through its section of the country, so that the experts were agreed that nothing but a game between the teams of the Illinois school and Birmingham's Black Bears could possibly settle the vital question of a national football championship.

The game had been arranged as a post-season affair. Tremors of excitement shook Hilltop. A special train had been engaged for the Northern pilgrimage and all Birmingham was in a fever.

The trio of Hilltop students approached Giovanni and announced that they wished to negotiate for the purchase of Beppo.

The owner of the bear successfully concealed his exultation. Beppo was ancient and long past his period of greatest usefulness. So Giovanni named a price which was precisely twice what he was willing to accept.

There was a great deal of argument and bargaining. Eventually the students purchased Beppo at a price which Giovanni knew would buy a new and better bear and still leave a comfortable margin of profit. The boys were introduced to the animal and Beppo appeared to respond to their advances. At any rate, he followed them docilely as they turned toward the college. Epic gazed dolefully after them.

"White boys sho is funny," he reflected. "I'll be dawg-bit if I'd crave to run aroun' with no bears."

Dusk was settling over the city as Epic directed his steps toward the colored civic center. He rambled into the aromatic atmosphere of Bud Peaglar's Barbecue Lunch Room & Billiard Parlor and ordered a lavish meal of Brunswick stew, barbecued pork, coffee and meringue pie. He was joined by the dusky fashion plate of Birmingham, Mr. Florian Slappey, who inquired solicitously after the health of Mr. Peters.

"Ise feelin' pretty tol'able, Florian. But I wuks pow'ful hard."

"Hmph! Foolishment what you talks. I reckon it's difficult fo' you to porter on that football special to-morrow, ain't it?"

"Porterin' on special trains is the favorite thing I hate to do."

"Well, I sho wisht I could see that game. How you reckon it's comin' out?"

"I dunno nothin' 'bout football, an'—"

"He dunno nothin' 'bout nothin', Florian." Both men turned to survey the newcomer, and Epic grimaced with distaste. There was not the slightest love lost between Mr. Peters and Joe Bullock.

Mr. Bullock was a squat, powerful colored person who also portered on Pullmans. He was Epic's professional junior by several years and consequently was extremely jealous of the gangling colored man.

"Epic ain't got nothin' but mouf," he declared unpleasantly.

Mr. Peters arched his eyebrows. "I reckon you think you is somethin'?" he suggested.

"I reckon I do. An' what's mo', you is some day gwine reelize same."

Joe Bullock stared hostilely. Epic merely grinned with simulated good nature.

"Tripe!" said Epic.

"Yeh? Some day, Mistuh Peters, you is goin' to git me all riled up an' then you is suddenly gwine to become ain't. An' I tell you right heah an' now that Ise also porterin' on that football special to-morrow, an' if you butt into my car or try to git any of my tips—"

"Loudness you utters, Joe Bullock. What you ain't got is no brains."

Epic turned back to his friend Florian, completely ignoring further comments from Joe. That person uttered a few uncomplimentary remarks and then ambled to the rear of the place, where he edged into an open game of Kelly pool. Joe was always ready and eager to gamble. Florian shook his head.

"You is the most unpopular man Joe Bullock is with," he remarked. "How come?"

"Jealousy," explained Epic. "He's sore 'cause I gits on the honor roll all the time an' he don't. Fum all I understan', he's lucky to hol' his job."

"Ain't you scared of him?"

Mr. Peters shook his head. "Naw, Florian. He ain't nothin' but a lot of wind. I really git amused at how much he don't like me,"

The two friends spent the evening at the Frolic Theater, and later, after indulging in ham sandwiches, walked side by side to Sis Callie's, where both boarded.

At eleven o'clock the following morning Epic presented himself at the Terminal Station office of the Pullman Company. He was not particularly happy over the prospect of the immediate future. Good tips, but plenty of work. He understood that his car had been sold out to male students. That foretold much excitement and little sleep for anybody. The young men of Hilltop were out for a good time.

"Only thing Ise grateful about," mused Mr. Peters, "is that the band ain't gwine be in my car."

The special train, eleven huge Pullmans and a diner, was on the farthest track. One hour before the train was due to depart, Epic went to his car and made a final inspection. Everything was shipshape and Mr. Peters loafed about the platform.

Joe Bullock was in uniform. Although the next car was his, the adjoining vestibules were not open, so that Mr. Bullock stood two car lengths away from his *bête noire*. Epic was pleased. The less conversation he had with Mr. Bullock, the more contented he was.

Mr. Bullock stood alone. He was suffused with unreasoning hatred for Epic. He ambitioned to do Mr. Peters a dirty trick. He stared unhappily through the steamy air—and his reverie was interrupted by two fair-haired seniors from Hilltop University, who showed him a drawing-room ticket and requested that he conduct them inside.

Once in the drawing-room, they closed the door and confronted Joe Bullock.

"Porter, you're a good scout, aren't you?"

"Yassuh, boss men, I aims to be."

"Good! How would you like five dollars for yourself?"

Joe's eyes rolled. "Money is the fondes' thing I is of."

"Then everything's jake. Now listen"—the spokesman lowered his voice—"you know our team is called the Black Bears, don't you?"

"Yassuh."

"Well, we've bought a black bear—a real one—and we want to take him to Chicago in this drawing-room." Joe stepped backward with more haste than grace. "In heah?"

"Yes."

"A black bear?"

"Right!"

"Alive?"

"You bet!"

"White folks," said Joe Bullock solemnly, "there mos' posolutely ain't nothin' stirrin'. It's against the Pullman rules, an' besides I don't crave to nurse no wile animals."

They argued, they pleaded, they attempted bribery. But avaricious as he was by nature, Mr. Bullock was not lacking in caution. He was absolutely certain that he didn't care to associate with any bears. He waved aside their argument that the bear was tame.

"No matter how tame he is, white folks, he's too wile fo' me. No bears can't ride on no Pullmans an'—an'—" An idea smote him suddenly and the ghost of a grin creased his lips. "Wait a minute—jus' a li'l minute till I gits reflective. "

They waited eagerly. "If there's any way, porter—"

Joe Bullock was smiling. "Who's got the drawin'-room in the next car back?" he asked suddenly.

"Friends of ours," answered one of the students promptly. "Why?"

"'Cause maybe," ventured Joe—"maybe I might fix things up to get the bear in that drawin'-room, provided you can swap with the fellers that has it."

"You mean that?"

"It's the one thing I don't mean nothin' else but." He eyed them speculatively. "It'll cos' you the same as you promised me an' I ain't gwine be 'sponsible."

"That's all right. Wait a few minutes." They were off in a hurry. At the steps leading up from the underground passage beneath the Terminal Station they intercepted the three students who had the drawing-room in Epic Peters' car. Explanations were made. If the drawing-rooms were shifted, the squat porter in the next car was willing to help them smuggle the mascot on board the train.

Tickets were exchanged and they returned triumphantly to Joe Bullock. Without a word to Epic, Mr. Bullock transferred the hand baggage of his passengers to Epic's drawing-room. Then he looked around.

"Where this bear is at, white folks?"

They motioned vaguely to the far side of the train.

"We hid him out there. Bunch of freshmen looking after him."

"I sho wouldn't want to be no freshman." He studied the situation. "Can the bear walk?"

"I'll say he can!"

"A'right. Then I'll stan' aroun' heah an' watch my chance. You git that bear over yonder behime them freight cars an' keep yo' eyes on me. Soon as I see the porter on this car git called away, I signals you-all an' you come with the bear. On'y, I ain't gwine have nothin' to do with puttin' that bear in the drawin'-room."

They left the train, circled it and appeared on the Twenty-seventh Street side of the Terminal Station. Then Joe commenced his vigil. Standing in the corridor, where he could spy on Epic through the window, he saw one of the students return and pass the word through the car to his fellow conspirators. The bear was to be brought aboard this Pullman and no demonstration was to be made lest the officials raise a perfectly worthy objection. The faces of the young men reflected high glee.

Twenty minutes before leaving time, Epic was summoned by the conductor. The instant he departed from his post, Joe Bullock opened the far side of the vestibule and flashed his signal. Instantly a strange cavalcade started for the cars—the two seniors and behind them a covey of freshmen in whose midst waddled the somewhat dazed Beppo. One glance at that formidable animal was snfficient for Mr. Bullock.

"Great sufferin' menageries!" he whispered. "I sho is glad I don't have to put that thing to bed."

The bear was muzzled and he followed docilely up the steps of the Pullman. They placed him in the drawing-room and, at Joe Bullock's suggestion, locked him in the lavatory.

"Better keep him there till after Epic Peters looks aroun', an' also till the cap'n takes up yo' tickets."

He accepted the bribe money from the young men and was standing by Epic's car when that elongated person returned from his confab with the conductor.

"Hello, nothin'," greeted Joe.

Epic scratched his head. "Seems like I hearn somebody makin' talk with me, but I don't see nothin' human roun' here," he observed.

"Hmph! You should worry 'bout humans!"

Delighted with himself and the certain success of his scheme, Mr. Bullock walked off. This was, indeed, the hour of his triumph over Epic Peters. Chances were Epic would stumble on the bear during the trip and be frightened out of seven years' growth. Or else the boys would tell Epic of the bear's presence and bribe him to silence. In which event Joe Bullock intended that the cap'n should learn that Epic was chaperoning a wild animal, and Mr. Peters would consequently be put in Dutch with the Pullman Company.

"He gits it in the neck comin' or goin'," chuckled Joe Bullock. "An' maybe bofe!"

And now came the rush immediately preceding departure. To the train came hordes of cheering, shouting, laughing students; small boys and tall boys; fat boys and lean ones; beautiful coeds and coeds who were not so beautiful; the gorgeously uniformed band, playing the marching song of the college; austere faculty members and their wives; friends of the college; sports writers from the three Birmingham newspapers—and Mack Varonne.

Mack Varonne was of medium size and was dressed unobtrusively. One might have mistaken him for anything but what he was. And there was no denying the fact that his success in obtaining an upper berth on this college special was little short of genius.

Mack Varonne was a hustler, which is the technical term for any gentleman who makes a living by his wits plus a nimble conscience. He was known to a great many college boys and liked by them, because his nefarious habits were not a matter of public knowledge. They knew him as a rather genial fellow who had a keen knowledge of football and a good sense of sportsmanship. What they did not know was that Mack's mental slant made him eligible for membership in the burglars' union, nor did they know that he was one of the most notorious and cleverest dice shooters in the United States.

The autumn was Varonne's happy hunting time. He haunted trains which were crowded with football pilgrims and waxed wealthy from the dice games he was able to start.

Mack didn't particularly care how he operated. He was always equipped with the works. He carried sets of hitting dice and missing dice. He was prepared for any and all emergencies. Some of his dice seven'd regularly, and these he panned off to the shooter when he was fading. Other dice found it almost impossible to seven, and he used these when he was shooting, which meant that all he had to do was to continue rolling after he obtained a point, and sooner or later that point would appear. Of course these noncubical dice were not infallible and occasionally would double-cross him, but they were constructed with such mechanical ingenuity that the odds were overwhelmingly in his favor.

Mr. Varonne knew dice. They were his reason for being. He had them with him now—all kinds and sizes, and adjusted for all tricks.

This journey promised ripe pickings. True, most of the students at Hilltop were on exceedingly modest allowance, but there were some who were known to carry heavy pocketbooks, and, besides, there weren't any on this special train who didn't have some money.

Mack Varonne planned a delightful and profitable vacation. He was sufficiently well known to the boys to make introductions unnecessary. He wouldn't be so crude as to inaugurate a dice game himself. No need for that. Mr. Varonne was familiar with his onions. He knew that nowhere in the South has a football train ever been more than two hours out of the station without someone producing a pair of dice and suggesting that he was willing to shoot two bits. Mack grinned to himself and waited. Meanwhile he rambled through the train and spoke to those whom he knew. Then he returned to his car.

The train was departing. In the vestibule stood the tremendously long-drawn-out figure of Epic Peters, the Pullman porter. Mack did not know Epic, and therefore could not understand the severe scrutiny to which he was subjected by the tall colored man.

Epic frowned. It was his boast that he could spot a train hustler a mile away. But this was not merely instinct. Mr. Peters had a remarkable ability to remember faces and events, and he recalled a certain hectic trip on the Limited when this same Mack Varonne successfully had operated a large and vicious dice game.

The porter was annoyed. He liked the jolly, boisterous college boys and didn't care how enthusiastically they won and lost one another's money. But to fall into the clutches of a professional gentleman gambler—

"White trash!" anathematized Epic. "I sho aims to keep my eye on that gemmun."

Mack Varonne attached himself to the likeliest looking crowd of youngsters. He knew football, and the boys paid great heed to his opinion of the impending contest. Mr. Varonne tactfully declared that Hilltop couldn't lose. Hadn't they an impregnable line, a pair of fleet and rangy ends, a fine punter and two elusive halfbacks? Of course Mack was popular, and so, after the tickets were taken up by the conductor, someone produced a pair of dice and invited Mack to roll 'em. He laughed and shook his head.

"That isn't my game," he lied. Then— "Besides, why shoot out here in the car? Who's got the drawing-room?"

They told him. At his suggestion two students went into the drawing-room and conferred with the holders of that space. Beppo was hustled unceremoniously into the lavatory and left there, a distinctly dazed and unhappy animal.

The dice game resumed operations in the drawing-room. The original shot of two bits increased to a dollar. One man held a hot hand and pyramided his money to twenty.

"Let it ride," he announced.

The faders covered fifteen of the amount and the shooter made a caustic comment anent poor sports. Mack Varonne pulled out a five-dollar note.

"I don't often indulge," he smiled; "but just to keep the game going—"

He lost. On the next roll of the dice he covered twenty and won.

That was the beginning. Mack did not win all at once, but as the afternoon wore on there was a perceptible flow of money in his direction. He managed his bets well and was far too wise to let winnings pile up on the floor in front of him. Whenever it seemed that his display of wealth might prove disconcerting, he shoved fifty or a hundred in his pocket and permitted it to be forgotten.

There was a temporary adjournment when the first call for dinner was sounded. One of the holders of the drawing-room went into the diner with Mack, while the other remained to chaperon the bear. Later, the professional gambler and his friend returned. The bear was so safely hidden that even Mr. Varonne did not know of his presence. The second lad went in to dinner and by the time he returned the dice game was in full swing again.

News had become bruited through the train that there was one hot crap game in operation, and consequently the real-money holders from all eleven Pullmans drifted in, fondly believing that they had a chance against Mr. Varonne.

And now the game grew warm in earnest. Epic Peters mourned just outside the door and wished there was something he could do about it. He didn't have to ask who was winning. He knew perfectly well that it wasn't football which had prompted Mack Varonne to take this excursion.

Mack was in fine fettle. Pickings were better than he could have anticipated. Five and ten dollars at a time, the surplus cash of Hilltop University wended its way into his pockets. Little by little he amassed wealth, until only a few haggard boys remained to shoot their remaining dollars.

At eleven o'clock that night there were less than half a dozen left. Two of these were the youngsters who occupied the drawing-room and they had been futilely bucking Varonne's uncanny luck with results disastrous to their own finances. Finally they threw up their hands.

"We're licked," they admitted—"and broke!"

"It's just as well," sympathized Mr. Varonne. "I'm naturally lucky to-night."

"I'll say you are! But I wish I had the money to fade you one more time."

"I'll shoot you boys once for a hundred," he offered.

"On credit?" they asked eagerly. "We-e-ll, no—not exactly. I'll shoot my upper berth and a hundred against this drawing-room for the round trip."

He did not see the quick startled glance which passed between them. He was offering good odds and they both felt—with the killing optimism of the loser who is soundly hooked—that the next shot would change their luck. They drew off into a corner and conferred. There was a great deal of whispering, but the result was inevitable. The blond boy turned.

"You're faded, Mr. Varonne. Shoot!"

Mack rattled the dice consolingly. They spun out across the floor and his fingers snapped.

"Phoebe!" he said. "I always buck a five."

The boys were hopeful. Good chance there'd be a seven before the five showed again.

Mack shot a six, then a ten, then another six. He blew on the dice and spun them out.

"Five it is!" he exulted. "Tough luck, boys. I'm right sorry." They exchanged their purple check for his yellow one. He was polite but firm. "Awful sorry," he said somewhat curtly, "but I'm dog-tired. If you boys don't mind clearing out, I'll get set for a night of real rest."

The lads were puzzled and worried. Remembering the black bear in the drawing-room lavatory, they felt almost as though they had taken money under false pretenses.

They stepped outside the drawing-room to discuss matters. If they told Mr. Varonne, they were afraid he'd eject Beppo, which act would precipitate considerable embarrassment. Perhaps the conductor might even put Beppo off the train, and that would be a disaster of cataclysmic proportions. The college was wild about Beppo. They were going to parade through the streets of Chicago with him. Everything was arranged. Beppo was to wear a cap and banner of the college colors, he was to trip the light fantastic for the benefit of Chicago fans. The two boys—taking their school spirit very seriously, indeed—dreaded the criticism to which they would lie subjected if anything happened to the beloved Beppo.

But they knew they had to warn Mack Varonne. Suppose he stepped into his own lavatory at the same instant that Beppo stepped out!

Reluctantly they turned to reënter the drawing-room when a dark figure ranged beside them and a soft, insinuating, respectful voice came to their ears:

"White folks?"

They faced the lugubrious Epic Peters, Pullman porter.

"Yes—what is it?"

"You-all fellers done los' all yo' money shootin' dice, ain't you?"

"I'll say we have!"

"An' all these other nice college boys is feenancially stringent also, ain't they?"

"Yes."

"But Mistuh Varonne—he ain't broke, is he?"

"I should say not!"

"So should I, boss men. I should of said it long ago." The blond boy frowned. "What are you driving at?"

"Gemmun," announced Epic earnestly, "that Mistuh Varonne yonder shoots crooked dice."

"What?" A pause. "You're crazy!"

"Folks, I speaks troof. You reckon I'd say somethin' like that if I wasn't good an' sure?" They looked at each other, then both smiled. "Much obliged, porter; but you're all wrong."

"Oh, lawsy ! You ain't gwine b'lieve me?"

"No. It was mighty nice of you to tell us, but we know Mr. Varonne better than you do."

Epic shook his head sadly and strode off down the aisle of the car. The two college students gazed after him with understanding and appreciation. Of course Epic was crazy. Of course he'd think an older man who won money from college boys wasn't on the level. As for them, they weren't squealers. They felt that they had lost fairly and squarely and were not inclined to raise a howl.

But it was necessary to notify Mr. Varonne of the presence of Beppo. With that end in view, they opened the drawing-room door and started to enter. A hard face scowled at them, and Mack Varonne's voice came harshly to their ears.

"Well, what do you want now?"

They were taken aback by his brusqueness. It was so much at variance with his gentle suavity of an hour since.

"Mr. Varonne, we came in—"

"I see you did. And I'll thank you to go out again. This is my drawing-room, not yours. And I prefer to be left strictly alone."

They were overcome by white anger. With quiet dignity, they bowed and withdrew, and outside the door of the drawing-room they stared at each other. "The dirty pup!" anathematized the blond. "If it wasn't that it'd look like welshing," said the other, "I'd knock his filthy block off."

"You don't suppose that the porter was right, do you?"

"No. And even if he was, we couldn't prove it. Seems like we didn't quite understand Mr. Mack Varonne, at that." The boy's eyes twinkled. "At any rate, we can let him perform his own introductions to Beppo."

Somewhat cheered by this prospect, they moved toward the smoking room, and scarcely had they gone when the buzzer sounded from Varonne's compartment. Reluctantly, Epic answered the summons. Mr. Varonne met him at the door.

"Make up the lower," he commanded, "and be snappy!"

"Yassuh," responded Epic coldly. He shuffled off indolently toward his linen closet.

When he returned the professional gambler exhibited anger.

"Listen here, boy, if you don't snap into this I'll report you to the company."

"Doin' my bestes', boss man. Now if you'll just step outside yonder while I gits busy—"

Mack Varonne walked into the vestibule, where he stood with his hands in his pockets staring out into the night. Beyond the doors the weather was bleak. The first touch of winter was in the air and a slanting rain splashed steadily and coldly against the glass doors. Even where Varonne was standing there was a decided chill in the air, and he reflected happily upon the night which lay ahead—sole occupancy of a warm, comfortable drawing-room, free from the bedlam which was certain to keep half the train awake throughout the night. That last shot of his had been clever. All the loose cash there was, plus the drawing-room.

"Soft," murmured Mack Varonne, "and very comfortable."

Meanwhile, inside the drawing-room, Epic Peters had worked with more dispatch than neatness. He didn't care whether Mack Varonne was particularly comfortable during the night. He merely tried to do his work in the quickest time and remove himself from Mr. Varonne's sleeping compartment.

The drawing-room was ready. Epic picked up the half dozen towels which he had brought from the linen locker and opened the door of the lavatory with the idea of placing them therein.

Mr. Peters' ears were assailed by a thunderous growl which contained a certain querulous note.

"Wr-r-r-r-r-f-f!" said Beppo. "Wr-r-r-o-o-o-f-f!"

The black bear did not take kindly to deluxe travel. He had found the lavatory uncomfortable and craved considerably more space for his large body. Therefore he started to shove past the goggle-eyed porter.

Epic saved him the trouble. Epic stopped being where he was with amazing abruptness. He emitted a wild howl and gave a single spasmodic leap which took him to the farthest corner of the lower berth.

Beppo stared disapprovingly at the colored man, as though blaming him for the close confinement. Epic returned the gaze with even greater distaste. Beppo growled and Epic howled, but both sounds were drowned out by the drumming of the wheels. Epic's lower jaw dangled and his chattering teeth framed a question:

"Wh-wh-where at did you come fum?"

"Wr-r-r-f-f-f!" explained Beppo.

"Oh! Whoa is me! Angel Gabr'el, blow yo' horn!"

Beppo seated himself on the floor, stretched his forepaws out along the berth and gazed up at the quivering Epic. Mr. Peters was rigid with horror. He stared at his Nemesis, and it suddenly occurred to him that perhaps his weird passenger had no particular ambition to make a meal of him.

The thought was comforting, and Epic scrutinized his visitor more closely. Then in a flash it all came back to him. This was the very mangy Beppo which had been purchased from Giovanni. Smuggled on Epic's car, he had been kept prisoner in the lavatory until this moment.

A teeny, tiny mite of Epic's fear vanished. He spoke hoarsely:

"Hey, Beppo!" The bear seemed to recognize his name. "Golly!" murmured Epic. "Tha's him, sho nuff!"

The Pullman porter did some swift thinking. He wasn't so terrified as he had been, but by the same token, he did not feel entirely at ease.

"If—if on'y Mistuh Giovanni was heah with his 'cordeen!"

And then another thought came to Epic. Gently his right hand moved back to his hip pocket. His fingers closed around his harmonica. Moving with extreme caution, he raised the mouth organ to his lips. With difficulty and courage, he blew the first few notes of "Turkey in the Straw."

The effect was instant and glorious. Happily, Beppo clambered to an upright posture and commenced to shake himself in time to the music. Transfigured with delight, Epic blew louder and harder. Beppo danced with gorgeous abandon. And finally Epic ceased his music.

"Hot ziggity dam!" ejaculated Mr. Peters. "It's Beppo sho nuff, an' he thinks I is Giovanni."

Now, by a miracle, Epic's paralyzing fear had been banished. He knew that he was Beppo's master, and instinct informed him that Beppo recognized the fact. He even made so bold as to reach out and stroke Beppo's head, a gesture which the black bear seemed to appreciate.

"Bear," announced Epic, "fum now on I an' you is buddies."

It was a glorious feeling, this sensation of control over the gigantic black bear. Epic sat down beside him and Beppo nuzzled his new master. Then Epic bethought himself of something.

"Gosh! Won't Mistuh Varonne be s'prised when he meets up with Beppo!"

The very idea started his thought processes. Epic was certain Mack Varonne hadn't been introduced to Beppo else he would have made a loud complaint against sharing his drawing-room. Mr. Peters commenced to conceive a great and glorious scheme.

Fired with unbounded courage, Epic led Beppo back into the lavatory and shut the door. Then he stood rigidly while the details of a scheme took shape. Finally he slapped a large palm against his thigh and rolled his eyes.

"Ise gwine do it! Boy, I sho is I" He opened the drawing-room door. Mack Varonne stood scowling just outside.

"What took you so long?" he growled. "I'm waiting to get in there."

"I bet you is, boss man. Yassuh, tha's the most thing I wagers."

Epic stood back so that Mr. Varonne could enter. But instead of stepping into the corridor, the elongated Pullman porter closed the drawing-room door, clicked the latch and stepped to the lavatory. He flung the door back with a noble gesture.

"C'mon in," he invited, "an' make yo'se'f at home!"

Beppo accepted the invitation. Woofing and gr-r-ring, he waddled into the limited confines of the drawing-room. Mr. Varonne flung a single terrified glance at Beppo and attempted to depart. The door was blocked by the bear, and instinct drove Mack Varonne to the identical spot where Epic had sought sanctuary. He cowered in the corner, standing on the berth. Mack was not partial to bears. As a matter of fact, he detested them.

"Bear," remarked Epic, "yonder is yo' supper."

The eyes of Mr. Varonne narrowed speculatively. He was frightened, but no fool. If this long, tall negro was not afraid of the animal, Beppo must be very tame. Mack took one step on the berth and Beppo growled. Mack withdrew hastily.

"What's the big idea, porter?"

And now Epic's eyes matched those of Mack Varonne in coldness.

"Plenty," announced Mr. Peters. "I craves to have you return to them college boys all the money you stold offen 'em with crooked dice."

For an instant there was nothing to be heard but silence, and none too much of that. Then Mack Varonne's face became contorted with fury and he expressed his opinion of Epic in no half way terms. Mr. Peters merely grinned.

"It don't make no never-minds what you think of me, boss man. I ask you, is you gwine return them boys' money?"

"I won't stand—"

"You bet you won't, Mistuh Varonne, 'cause Beppo ain't gwine leave you do such. He's a hungry bear an' the most eatments he's fond of is live dice shooters."

Varonne's courage was returning. He had no intention of being bluffed by a bear with which a colored porter seemed on intimate terms.

"In just about two minutes—" he started to threaten, when Epic did a very casual and impressive thing.

From his hip pocket Mr. Peters extracted a mouth organ. He grinned cheerfully at the bear.

"Beppo!" he ordered, "git fixed to strut yo' stuff!"

Then, with a slow, wailing cadence, Epic Peters breathed the opening bars of the "Memphis Blues." Beppo looked around. He seemed to smile. But he understood what was expected of him. He knew only two things in life. He could dance and he could wrestle, and he had been taught to wrestle with the man who was not furnishing the music.

Thereupon Beppo clambered upon the berth and crowded close against the petrified Mr. Varonne. Large paws hugged Mr. Varonne tightly and an evil face was shoved against the countenance of the dice hustler. Beppo did not hug lightly. There was, in his makeup, some instinct of the human professional wrestler who seeks to make it look good, and so far as Mack Varonne was concerned, Beppo was an artist. It looked so good to Mr. Varonne that he was convinced beyond any shadow of doubt that he was about to become divorced from his earthly existence. His shriek split the atmosphere and. He begged loudly for mercy.

Epic stopped playing and Beppo ceased to wrestle, but both man and beast remained facing each other on the rather rumpled berth.

"Fust of all," announced Epic calmly, "gimme them crooked dice you was usin' to-night."

"I wasn't using crooked dice, porter. I'll swear I wasn't."

"Gimme!"

"I tell you they was straight dice I was shooting."

"White folks, you ain't talkin' to no iggoramus. Ise seen gooder dice hustlers than you an' I know somethin' 'bout it. Somewhere you has got a pair of hitters an' a pair of missers. I crave 'em bofe."

Beads of icy perspiration stood out on Mack's forehead.

"I was shooting square to-night," he repeated desperately.

Epic did not argue. He merely sounded off again on the "Memphis Blues." Beppo swung into action with a vengeance. Mack Varonne gasped in the crushing embrace—and capitulated.

"All right," he screamed, "I'll give 'em to you!"

Triumphantly, Epic lowered the harmonica from his lips. Then, under orders from Mack Varonne, he opened that gentleman's suitcase and extracted one pair of straight dice, one pair of dice mechanically certain to pass a majority of times and one pair which was mathematically sure of missing. He also located a pair of delicate calipers and Epic used these with a deftness bespeaking long experience.

"I reckon this is mos' enough, Mistuh Varonne," he chuckled. "Fo' the rest I gits he'p."

He backed against the drawing-room door and opened it the least little bit. Within a few seconds he saw the forlorn blond student rambling down the aisle from the smoking room.He gestured to him and then whispered instructions. The blond was to get three or four of his dice game friends and come immediately to the drawing-room.

"An' be shuah," counseled Epic, "that at least all of you is big fellers."

Five minutes later five somewhat disheveled college students crowded the drawing-room and stared in amazement at the tableau. Epic gestured proudly toward man and beast.

"I an' Beppo," he murmured, "has done consid'able."

Swiftly, but with pardonable gusto, he explained what he knew about Mack Varonne and that gentleman's methods of acquiring loose cash. He told of enlisting the aid of the bear, and in conclusion he exhibited to the five pop-eyed young men the two pairs of crooked dice.

He explained the difference between hitters and missers—a slight difference in distance between parallel planes. The college boys understood readily enough. If dice are not perfect cubes, they must inevitably fall a huge proportion of times on the broader surfaces. The blond boy calipered the damning dice. The others inspected his work. Then they turned on Mack Varonne, and Epic saw something in their eyes which caused him to intercede quickly.

"Please, suh, gemmun, don't go killin' him right heah in my car. I promised him you wouldn't. "

The boys were firm in expressing their desires,and at length it was decided that if Mack Varonne returned to them every cent of money won in the night's dice game, they would compromise by pitching him off the train the first time it slowed down. Mack begged and pleaded, but they were coldly unyielding, and finally he produced great wads of money from every pocket. They apportioned this as best they could. Until that moment no one had realized how much had been lost in the little drawing-room. It really had been a killing.

The train was approaching a small and unkempt town. The speed was perceptibly less. Quietly, they escorted Mack Varonne and his suitcase to the vestibule and Epic opened the door. The bleak wind laughed at them and the rain splashed coldly into their grim faces. The silhouette of the strange town loomed miserably in the chill night.

Two of the largest boys clutched Mack Varonne by coat collar and trousers seat. With a hearty gesture, they flung him into the night. His suitcase sploshed into a puddle of water beside him.

Epic closed the vestibule door. Then the students escorted Epic back to the drawing-room and tried to make him understand what they thought of him. They explained how it happened that the bear was in his car in the first place, and told him they had been afraid Epic would report the matter, which was what Joe Bullock had suggested. They told Epic that he had saved the college money, the college honor, the college mascot and the great game. They were a happy, grateful crowd of youngsters.

The spokesman pressed into Epic's palm the sum of one hundred dollars. Mr. Peters protested pallidly—and then accepted the enormous tip. Thereupon the young men left and Epic wandered to the vestibule, where he stood staring pop-eyed at nothing at all.

Epic Peters was thinking. He was thinking of the treacherous Joe Bullock, and of how that vindictive gentleman had sought to ruin him.

And the more he thought of Mr. Bullock, the angrier Epic Peters became. He dropped one hand into his coat pocket and his slender fingers touched four celluloid cubes. He drew them forth and gazed affectionately upon them.

Magic dice! With one pair a man could shoot and win. With the other pair, a man's opponent could shoot with never a chance of success.

A thought came to Mr. Peters—a warm delicious thought. The dice seemed to swell in his hand, driving him relentlessly to his well-earned revenge. A smile creased his lips, and he started back toward the next pullman. In the aisle of his own car he passed one of the young men whose cash capital he had saved.

"Where are you going, Epic?" asked this young gentleman.

"Back into the next Pullman," grinned Mr. Peters. "I is fixin' to shoot dice with Joe Bullock."

www.ingramcontent.com/pod-product-compliance
Lightning Source LLC
Chambersburg PA
CBHW031122020726
47495CB00007B/2303